"From the boreal forests of the Yukon to Canadian Shield country in Ontario, Frayne writes with graceful, devastating power about the hold of place and family on people, and the way love runs strange and wayward and deep through both. The result is a novel with all the clean lines and stark beauty of a glacier, revealing the crevasses that tear lives apart but also, despite everything, link them together."
KATE HARRIS, author of *Lands of Lost Borders*

"The 'here' in the title is the clue: *Why I'm Here* is about place. To those in the South, Yukon is landscape. To those who live there, it's a tough, beautiful, and ultimately forgiving embrace. The challenges Frayne's characters face in this tough, beautiful and forgiving novel don't come from the land, but from their own inability to leave their pasts behind."
WAYNE GRADY, author of *The Good Father*

"I loved reading this exquisite portrait of a therapist's relationship to a teenage girl whose violent past has followed her to the Yukon, where the landscape can both wound and heal. Jill Frayne writes about the far North with the same wisdom and tenderness she brings to the lives of her unforgettable characters."
MARNI JACKSON, author of *Don't I Know You?*

"Frayne is masterful in weaving together the internal and external worlds. She builds them with equal beauty and complexity using language as clear and fresh as the northern landscapes she describes. *Why I'm Here* is vivid, powerful, and a skilled reflection on life itself. Frayne shows us our own fallibility — and pathways through it — with careful attention."
JENNIFER KINGSLEY, author of *Paddlenorth: Adventure, Resilience, and Renewal in the Arctic Wild*

WHY

I'M

HERE

——————

Why

I'm

Here

——————

Jill

Frayne

NeWest Press

NeWest Press wishes to acknowledge that the land on which we operate is Treaty 6 territory and a traditional meeting ground and home for many Indigenous Peoples, including Cree, Saulteaux, Niitsitapi (Blackfoot), Métis, and Nakota Sioux.

Library and Archives Canada Cataloguing in Publication
Title: Why I'm here : a novel / Jill Frayne.
Other titles: Why I am here
Names: Frayne, Jill, author.
Series: Nunatak first fiction series ; no. 58.
Description: Series statement: Nunatak first fiction series ; 58
Identifiers: Canadiana (print) 20210207124 | Canadiana (ebook) 20210207205 | ISBN 9781774390498 (softcover) | ISBN 9781774390504 (ebook)
Classification: LCC PS8611.R39 W59 2022 | DDC C813/.6—DC23

Editor for the Press: Leslie Vermeer
Cover and interior design: Natalie Olsen
Cover photo: Lauren Kathryn Cord / Shutterstock.com
Author photo: Jack Elliott

NeWest Press acknowledges the Canada Council for the Arts, the Alberta Foundation for the Arts, and the Edmonton Arts Council for support of our publishing program. We acknowledge the financial support of the Government of Canada through the Canada Book Fund for our publishing activities.

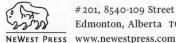

#201, 8540-109 Street
Edmonton, Alberta T6G 1E6
NeWest Press www.newestpress.com

No bison were harmed in the making of this book.
Printed and bound in Canada   22 23 24 25   5 4 3 2 1

For June and Trent,
much missed

———————

1

THE DAY OF the appointment was a scorcher in April. That part of the Territory always gets a heat wave in early spring. A hot wind whooshes over the mountains, brown melt-water rushes in the roads, and Yukoners, after a seven-month winter, walk around with their coats open, dazed as houseflies waking up in a hot room.

At four o'clock, Helen Cotillard heard the fire escape banging and rattling, an indication that her new clients had chosen to come in via the alley rather than the front door. In the late nineties, in that town, if you went to counselling it wasn't the mark of a reflective temperament the way it might be in Toronto or Montreal. In Whitehorse, seeing a therapist meant you were failing in school, or you still wet the bed.

The intake note named the stepmother as the referring agent. Helen would rather it was Gale herself who made the call. It was hard enough to engage teenagers. She was fifteen, living with her father and his wife the past two years. A transplant then. Gale had joined her father and his wife when — in the oblique phrasing of the note — "things with her mother took a bad turn."

Okay. Standard enough.

Helen hoped the father would show. The girl, Gale, may not like being presented by somebody not even related to her. Helen was on a crusade to get fathers to come to counselling — an uphill battle so far. Fathers never got their importance. Most families started by sending a scout. Nine times out of nine it was the mother, or the stand-in mother.

Judy buzzed from reception. Helen pushed off from her desk, the chair on wheels always a perk, like launching into outer space, which counselling was.

Only Gale and her stepmother were waiting. Helen smothered her disappointment and immediately recognized Sandy Veraldi, a probation officer there in town. For adults, not kids. If it were kids, she and Helen would have been on the phone every other day. As it was, Helen and Sandy had crossed paths at a dozen scintillating functions over the years. Helen noted the short dark hair rearing back from Sandy's forehead, the smoker's amber hue, her plain shirt, the flare of her hips in men's trousers.

Sandy stood up. "Gale's your client," she said shortly. "I'm just here to get things started."

Behind her, Gale sat under a helmet of bangs that reached the middle of her eyes. Helen reached past Sandy and extended her hand, a quaint custom she retained even though it baffled people. She didn't warm to strangers easily and this physical overture helped. Gale pressed the ends of Helen's fingers in the barest compliance.

Helen led the way past the work cubbies to an interview room along the back wall. Sandy bustled past her and plunked down facing the door; Gale sidled past Helen and sat across from her stepmother.

The room was furnished with straight-backed chairs in a circle around a low coffee table which, at the moment, offered several Jurassic beasts, a crocodile with a broken jaw, a doll family, two well-rubbed stuffed animals, and a box of Kleenex. The walls were painted an indefinable colour. Helen had long ago removed a print of a kitten dangling from a clothesline, with the caption, *Hang in there!*

Neither Sandy nor Gale acknowledged the presence of a husky-shepherd mix lying against the wall. The dog flapped his tail at the sight of Helen.

"That's Chief Joseph," she said. "I hope you don't mind. Five days at home alone is too long for him."

"Fine by me," said Sandy. "I have a yard full of shepherds myself."

Gale didn't comment. She balled her school blazer between her knees and prepared to stick it out.

Helen chose her usual seat facing the window and took a slow breath. *Be here now.*

She sensed Sandy winding up to take charge and turned quickly to Gale. "Thanks for coming, Gale. Sandy had just a moment on the phone with Judy. Can you fill me in on what happened at school?"

"No big deal."

"What a bummer though," Helen continued, "with the whole school there. The doctor in emerg must have had a theory. What did he say?"

Gale shook her head, as though whatever he'd said wasn't worth repeating.

Sandy put in, "He wondered about asthma. We've had her checked out and that isn't it. It's clear to me ..."

Helen raised a couple of fingers, still looking at Gale.

"Can you say what happened at the school assembly?"

Gale shrugged. "I lost my breath, and got outside. The school nurse drove me to the hospital. By then I was okay."

Sandy interjected, "Gale, it was a near blackout. It wasn't nothing."

"Is that why you're here today?"

"Yeah. To stop choking, losing my breath. No offence, but I don't see how talking to somebody can help."

"I know. It seems far-fetched doesn't it? Has it happened more than that time at school?"

"Not as bad as that."

"Sometimes these breathing shutdowns are triggered by a memory. Can you recall what you were thinking just before you lost your breath?"

"I wasn't thinking anything."

"Uh-huh. You're at Christ the King, aren't you? How do you like it?"

"It's alright."

"Ahem," Sandy interjected again. "On the honour roll last semester. Lowest mark 82 percent. I'd call that better than alright."

Helen kept her eyes on Gale. "I was thinking more socially. What would you say, Gale? What are the kids like?"

Gale's mouth turned down. "It's a pretty cliquey school. I don't bother much with anybody."

"You're here, what, two years now? Where were you before?"

"Cobalt. Down south."

Helen liked this. She was a southerner herself. "Silver-mining town, right? Broken-up roads, headframes from the mining days on every corner. I grew up in Ontario too, south of there."

Gale gave her a goody-for-you look.

"Is your mom still there? Who else is back home?"

Gale frowned. "I thought I was here because of nearly passing out at school."

"I ask because it's your family," Helen said mildly. "You probably think about them all the time. I don't know if it's relevant or not."

Gale sighed. "We have a farm. It's my stepdad's. There's me, my sister and my mom."

"What's your sister's name?"

"Bernice. We call her Buddie."

"And your name? It has an unusual spelling."

"There was a big storm when I was born."

Helen smiled. "A gale. How old is Buddie?"

"Nine. Almost."

"And the farm you live on? A working farm?"

"We raise sled dogs. There's about seventeen now, maybe more since I left."

"How do the four of you get along?"

Gale looked over at Sandy and frowned.

"Go ahead, Gale," Sandy prodded. "No point saying fine if it isn't fine."

Another sigh from Gale, not dramatizing, as far as Helen could tell, genuinely aggrieved. "They fight a lot. My mom drinks."

"What happens when she's drinking?"

Gale shook her head. "They get going."

"Get going. You mean fight?" Gale nodded. "Words or fists?"

"Both."

"What do you and your sister do when they're fighting?"

"Clear out. I take Buddie upstairs."

"Does your stepdad ever hit you or your sister?"

Gale frowned. "Neil's her father. He doesn't hit us."

"What about your mother?"

Gale snorted. "She doesn't have to."

"How do you mean?"

"You mind my mother."

Sandy drummed her fingers. Helen turned to her.

"Sandy, there're always strains taking on a kid who's half grown, eh? You've probably read the same stuff I have that says: Don't even try it if the kid is older than ten. Older than ten, they belong to the first family and will never sign on to a second. What do you think? How's it going for you?"

"We're doing pretty good," Sandy said staunchly.

"Did you ever suppose you'd have Gale full-time?"

Sandy drew herself up. Helen had the impression this was the question she'd come to answer. "Dan and I have been trying to get Gale up here since day one. I helped him get custody — which meant zero to Gale's mother. Court orders don't impress Mindy. Then it suited her to send Gale to us, and Gale started coming up every summer — our ticket, of course. That went on for … how long Gale? Years. It made me sick to send her back." She stirred herself fussily, narrowed her eyes at Helen. "I have to

14

tell you, Gale's mother is a piece of work. She's violent. She has a problem with violence. There have been I don't know how many assault charges against her. Police in the house time and again. I've seen what it's done to Gale." She looked pointedly at Gale who was gazing at the floor. "But we all had to go along. Mindy's little power trip."

She hadn't finished. Helen sat still.

"Ever hear of the reign of terror? Gale's mother is a violent drunk who has to run everything. Everybody walks on eggshells, starting with Gale's father. You should have seen him when I met him. Talk about conflict-avoidant. And he's not much better now." She straightened her back. "As for Neil, Gale's stepfather, Neil runs sled dogs and when he isn't doing that, he shears sheep. It takes a very strong man to wrangle a two-hundred-pound ram, or get a team of trail dogs to do what you want. Last time I talked to Neil, he sounded like he'd have trouble lifting a Chihuahua." She took a long breath. "Mindy breaks people."

Helen looked at Gale. She appeared to have tuned out.

"What do you think about what Sandy is saying, Gale?"

Gale didn't respond.

Sandy burst out, "Gale, for the love of Pete. This is about *Mindy.* There's no way you losing your breath isn't connected to her; what she did."

Gale came alive. She said furiously, "That was a *caper.* She pulled that shit all the time. It has nothing with to do with my ... whatever."

Sandy turned fully to Gale, blew out her breath with exasperation. "You could have *died.* You *know* how close it was. Do you think that doesn't register somewhere, doesn't have an effect on you!"

"No!" said Gale, jumping up, glaring at Sandy. "We aren't talking about this! We had a deal and now the deal's *over.*" She clutched up her blazer and flung out of the room.

A wake of silence followed her exit. Helen sighed. "Better go after her, Sandy; otherwise she'll think you're in here telling me everything and I'll never see her again."

Sandy scooped up her belongings, her expression grim. "She needs to be here. I'm telling you."

A minute later, Helen heard her bang down the fire escape.

2

THE GROUND FLOOR of Helen's office was the former home of Black's Gym, a local legend that had been going as long as anyone could remember. There was nothing fancy about it—who had that kind of money? There were just the general fitness machines, the weights and benches that are standard in gyms, with a couple of wizened coaches to set people up.

Upstairs collected dust for years until the Territory got funding for a counselling agency. Any kid under the age of eighteen with a problem could come, free of charge. The service covered the whole Territory, just under thirty thousand freezing souls, most of them living right in Whitehorse, most within walking distance.

The office occupied the entire second floor, a vast, low-ceilinged block with a warren of cubicles such as you see in magazine cartoons depicting our dehumanized work lives. Every counsellor had a cubicle with a desk, a gliding ergonomic chair, a computer, and a phone. Most of Helen's colleagues had personalized their burlap half-walls with family photographs that regularly fell to the floor because nothing adhered to the hollow baffles. Helen didn't bother tacking up photos. She brought in a table lamp from home — a skulking black panther ceramic under a red silk shade — and blocked off the overhead fluorescents with a side of cardboard from a refrigerator packing box.

Occasionally, coming out of the lunchroom, she was struck by the shabbiness of the place. How did her co-workers go about their business, greet clients, persevere through meetings as if the place had a shred of welcome? How must it be for first-timers, trudging up the stairs, disheartened, exhausted, whatever state brought them there. They pushed open the fire door and *voila,* greeted by a walled encampment the colour of parched grass, under a ceilingful of ungraded light.

Expect no comfort here.

The gym below broke the dreariness. The infrastructure between the two floors was flimsy, and through the floor, Helen regularly caught the clang of the machines, the grunts and expletives of people working out. Every time somebody dropped a barbell, the upstairs floors bounced, the ceiling panels jumped slightly askew.

Counselling was a sober business. The raucousness from the gym below perked her up.

WITH GALE AND SANDY GONE, she had the place to herself. Everyone had left for the day. She opened the doors along the back wall and planks of sunlight fell across the floors.

Chief Joseph followed her to her desk, tail rocking. "Soon we'll hit the out-of-doors, boy." She sat at her desk scribbling a note to herself in case she ever saw Gale again. *Gale Connelly, d.o.b. 03 / 02 / 1983. Mother and younger sister back in Cobalt. Sent to father in Whthrs. Hellcat mother. What happened there?* Then the day's date, *April 19, 1998,* and her prediction, *Unlikely to return.*

GALE BOLTING out of the room didn't particularly unnerve her. It happened often enough, especially first meetings, especially teenagers. Interesting kid, though. Not a talker, and not just today. Gale had a compressed, at-the-ready quality Helen had seen before. Kids who live with dangerous people.

She wouldn't be back. It looked like she could easily withstand pressure from Sandy.

Helen got on with her recording. She liked staying late. She started doing it for people who couldn't come during the day without being docked pay; then got to prefer it. The building settled down by six o'clock. There was a suppertime lull in the thumping from below and the office took on a dusty neutrality Helen liked. The effortful conversations of the day were over, the battle with discouragement that always sounded like arguing.

She loitered at her desk.

Sandy had surprised her. Helen had seen her in other contexts; she came on contentious. In general, women often showed up in counselling with an edge, towing their kids or someone else's kids. Belligerent, defensive. Helen figured women were fixers. It shamed them some way to ask for help.

But Sandy hadn't struck her like that. She could have been testy, but she wasn't. In Gale's corner, if anything.

What about the no-show father? How did he like having Gale on his hands so late in the game? How come he moved so far away when he and Gale's mother split? Helen probably wouldn't get to ask him.

She stuck her fingers in Chief's fur, rubbed the thick hairs. "Almost done, boy."

One thing for sure, if Gale came back, she'd take forever to thaw. Kids that age always did. So furious and grieving. Helen had to coax them in, sugar in an open hand.

They were her favourites.

She wondered how Gale was making out separated from her sister.

Probably lousy. Same as me.

OUT ON THE STREET, the sun was still blaring on top of the escarpment, backlighting the wind-eaten cliffs with their headdress of spruce. Daylight at this latitude stretched out so fast. After months of winter's elegiac pace, its low, glowing skies, the sun always just above or below the horizon, spring came roaring in and pinned the sun in the sky.

Helen overshot her car and walked on to the river. Chief, ever the gentleman, didn't rush ahead, not until they reached the riverbank and Helen stood still. Then he trotted off to investigate who'd been around.

The water was on the loose again. Where it curved into town, it never really froze; the current was too strong. Even in February, there'd be a rip of open water at the bend, blocks of turquoise ice shoved up, colliding along the bank, the blue unearthly in the monochrome of winter.

In front of Helen in the slanting light, the river slid past, coffee-coloured, thick and silky, bound for the Bering Sea a thousand miles away. She watched it go, matched her breath to its flow, took the balm the river always offered. From the close, claustrophobic work, trying to feel her way into another person's thinking, she could come out here to a river gliding through hundreds of miles of empty land.

She could stay as long as she liked.

HELEN'S HOUSE was in a pinewoods about twenty-five kilometres out of town. That time of year, the road in was a shambles. She eased her ten-year-old Subaru through the half-frozen mud, skirting major sinkers to park in a gap of sunlight in her yard. There was no garden. Raising a garden in those latitudes called for a greenhouse, raised beds, imported soil, forbearance of deer, voles, and whomever else. Many people went to the trouble but Helen liked her woods.

There was a shed by the house, part of the original property. When she took the place over, Helen found the inside chocka-block with gear from some bygone trapper: an upended pine sled, a clutter of iron traps and cracked leather harnesses, sled tracings hung up on twelve-inch nails. The outside walls were festooned with moose and caribou antlers, yellowed and streaked with age. Helen meant to take them down, but the shed had become some sort of hinterland, not hers to reform.

She let Chief Joseph out of the car, strode across the yard to her house, a bungalow painted midnight blue, built by her friend Juerg during his love affair with the Yukon. There were two big windows either side of the door, and a broad deck across the front that Helen meant to build a porch on. Porches made a house generous.

The inside of the house greeted her, her arrangement on the left, Juerg's on the right. Her side was a clutter of outdoor gear: skis and poles, a pair of baleen and spruce snowshoes, sundry Gore-Tex jackets and pants in faded florescent colours, moose-hide moccasins dark with years of dubbin, a stitched snow tunic, an assortment of boots and mitts, a ten-by-eight wall tent, bundled and wafting eternally a smell of canvas and burlap, and strung from the ceiling, a Kevlar sea kayak, graceful as a slipper.

Helen's gear. Who would she be without it?

This array swarmed into the kitchen on the right, Juerg's domain. There, everything was up to snuff: a gleaming black gas range, brushed steel sinks, inlaid counters — the accoutrements of a gourmand. A typical dinner in Juerg's day was Arctic char, red potatoes baked in garlic, his own salt-slaked bread. He'd toss off such fare while ranting about some lunacy in the local government. Helen sat on his sofa and laughed.

She wished he'd toughed it out.

What happened to Juerg was the old tale of the North: a European who came to the Yukon for a visit, got smitten by the land, and sank heart and soul into making a life there. Juerg built a house — not this one — his first house was log. He knew everyone, gave lavish dinners, cared extravagantly about everything.

He and Helen met at a storytelling weekend and got into an easy friendship. They weren't lovers, but were heading that way. Then one of Juerg's dearest friends, a storyteller, was murdered out of the blue by her husband and the courts nearly let him off. Some trifling sentence was meted out. The handling of it sickened Juerg. He'd been mistaken about his new home, he decided. Canadians were louts, worse than louts. He sold his newly built bungalow to the first person who offered to buy it, and went back to Switzerland, never to return.

The buyer was Helen.

That was nearly eighteen years ago. She was twenty-five at the time.

HELEN SHED HER JACKET, opened the vast refrigerator hoping she had shopped recently. Inside was a tidy, sparse array of food, some decent bok choy, a gnarl of ginger. That would do. She closed the door.

Why was Juerg on her mind today? Why the heavy mood? She laid her hands on the countertop and dropped her head. Oh, yes. It was an anniversary. Spring, when Juerg quit and went away for good, when her mother died. When Jo died.

Helen's younger sister had died out on the ice at the age of nineteen. Everybody in the Territory knew Jo died on Llewellyn Glacier on Atlin Lake with Helen standing right in front of her.

She crossed the room, touching objects on the way, concentrating on the keepsakes Juerg left.

There was his marble table, white as an ice floe, abandoned because it was too heavy to move. At the moment it was covered in Helen's tax receipts and a jigsaw puzzle she'd been fooling with.

Another of his treasures was the masonry stove, built into the back wall, a wonder of heat and efficiency. Winter mornings when Helen left for work, she tossed in a couple of sticks, and in the evening when she came home, the wall was still radiating heat. She'd back against it, let the heat penetrate her whole length, shoulder blades, spine, the backs of her legs.

Across the rear of the house were two bedrooms, one of them unchanged since Jo's time. The African baskets Helen and Jo hung from the ceiling still held Jo's mitts and toques, her balled-up base layers. Every so often Helen went in, rummaged for something of Jo's to wear.

She had weighed up the morbidity of keeping a shrine, but what was the harm? She didn't need the room for anything else.

She crossed to the front windows where Chief Joseph was trotting past her view outside, whipping his head back to catch the air. Chief Joseph did not suffer low spells in spring. Winter had broken, releasing all sorts of odours, and he was in heaven. In April the sun came back and yelled *wake up!*

Helen took her cigarette fixings and headed outside. It was too early to make dinner, too much light in the sky. Chief had moved off into the woods somewhere; she couldn't see him. She sat down on the edge of the deck and rolled a cigarette, the ritual a small pleasure. She lit up, the tobacco rich and sweet in the twilight.

In certain winds, she could hear the river. The other day, she and Chief had trudged through the little pines, juniper and kinnikinnick newly showing where the snow had gone. At the river, they found the banks still clogged with ice, small floes shrugging off, plopping into the water to be carried away. Further out, the river sped by, glass-green, the current muscular, hypnotic. They'd caught the sound of Trumpeter swans headed for Alaska. Helen had sat on the bank for an hour listening to their harsh bugling, their importunate barking, the smell of wild sage getting up her nose. The trees on the far bank stabbed up like a fistful of arrows, and behind them, the smooth domes of the mountains shone with snow.

WHEN SHE BOUGHT the property eighteen years ago, she had no great feeling for it, no thought how long she'd stay in the North. She thought she'd have an adventure and go home.

But the river on its sweep, the wind shaking the redoubtable little trees, the cant of light one season to the next had taken hold. She had absorbed these events in her body and without intending it, without ever conceding anything, she stayed on.

But she never said, I guess I'm a Yukoner.

3

AS SOON AS SHE GOT HOME, Gale went straight to her room, lifted the screen, and sat at the window smoking.

Her bedroom overlooked a chain-link enclosure where Sandy kept the German Shepherds she raised. Just like at home, she was surrounded by dogs. At least at home in Cobalt they weren't right under her nose, barking and moaning and shitting.

The meeting hadn't been too bad. Sandy hadn't dared say a word on the drive back, since she'd been the one who broke their deal. Gale agreed to see a counsellor on condition Sandy leave it to her to say how she came to live with her father, and Sandy blew it. She had been about to lay it out.

Taking off meant Gale wasn't any further along figuring

out what the matter was, but at least she'd eliminated seeing a counsellor. Talking to anyone in Whitehorse, anyone within a thousand miles of Whitehorse, was the last thing Gale would do.

It was odd though when the counsellor asked her what she was thinking just before she lost her breath. How would she know Gale was thinking anything?

She was, of course.

She'd been sitting with her science class in the school auditorium, the whole school packed in on metal chairs, Gale somewhere in the middle; nobody she knew around her, nobody bothering her. The big drapes up on stage were looped out of the way, the principal droning on about bullying or some deathless topic, Gale hardly listening. In the middle of the principal's speech, she disappeared. She just dropped out. Her mind flipped to a time years ago, something she never thought about anymore because who would want to? It came back, this little movie roaring through her mind, Colin in his basket, Gale standing in front of him. Hester and her mother were in another room. Hester was her mother's friend; "Heck," Mindy called her. Heck used to bring Colin over sometimes in a little bucket she carried him in. There was something wrong with Colin; he was born funny. Even for a baby, he was way too weak and puny, always wrapped in a lot of blankets. Gale worried about what was under the wrapping, whether Colin had all his arms and legs.

In the memory, clear as anything, she's by herself with him. She's about six. She's holding a peanut butter sandwich, looking down at Colin. She can hear Hester and her mother talking. All of a sudden Colin's face scrunches up and he goes blue and starts making these tiny choking, gagging noises, so faint she can hardly hear him. Next thing, Hester comes barrelling into the room, grabs up Colin, clamps him over her arm, and starts rummaging around in his mouth with her finger. She digs out a little wad of something, or maybe nothing, Gale can't see. And right behind Hester comes Mindy, eyes boring into Gale. *"What the HELL did you do to him?"*

In the stuffy auditorium, in the blaze of remembering, Gale lost her breath. Her lungs seized up and turned to iron. She started gasping and choking, fighting for air. She dug her fingers into her chest, trying to make space. It felt like the floor was rising up, a black sea swallowing her. She jerked out of her seat, shoved over her classmates' knees, stumbling and tripping, making for the aisle. Once clear of the row, she headed for the back of the auditorium to get outdoors, still no air coming into her lungs.

The next thing she knew she was in the school nurse's car in the roundabout on the way to the hospital, her head out the window, cold air streaming over her face.

In emerg, the doctor on call queried drugs, as if that was the only reason someone her age would show up in hospital. When her urine came back clean, he decided it must be asthma; her own doctor could follow up.

Sandy was home when Gale and the nurse got there. Sandy said, "Asthma, my foot. She's got Post-traumatic Stress Disorder." They could all rot in hell.

SITTING AT HER WINDOW, she heard the shriek of a plane taking off. It was a sound she and Buddie hardly ever heard at home and the thrill hadn't worn off. Gale spent hours at her window right there watching the tiny glitter of jets passing high overhead, their vapour trails splitting the sky. She imagined being on one of them, bound for Phoenix or Edmonton, bound for anywhere.

It was a good way to disappear; sit in the window with a cig, picture herself on a plane.

A frequent fantasy destination was Toronto. From Toronto it was a five-hour drive home to Cobalt. Gale knew the route; she'd made the trip a dozen times with Neil. She knew exactly what she'd do. Board a plane from Whitehorse to Toronto, make her way from the airport to the bus station downtown, cadge fare to North Bay, hitch the rest of the way.

The snag was what happened when she got there. Would Neil let her stay? Even if her mother wasn't around, in jail or some place, Neil might be too spooked to let Gale stay.

Flying was definitely cool.

Gale could have handled visits to Whitehorse if they were like before, just coming a couple of weeks in summer. She and Neil had a routine. Neil drove her to the airport, and at the gate he'd hand her over to a flight attendant. She'd been eight or nine at the time. She got special treatment all the way, the hostess doling out coke in a little plastic cup with an ice cube, plus a packet of about five nuts.

In Vancouver at the changeover, she'd get an escort to the gate for the smaller plane to Whitehorse. Neil wrote it all down for her in Toronto before she left. He'd buy her a boxing magazine for the trip, and when she got to Vancouver, in the time between flights, she'd look at the pictures in her magazine, the faces of the fighters stirring her up, water flying off their faces like tears.

She never minded the wait. It was the best part of the trip, the time in-between her mother and father.

Before the visits started, she hardly knew her father, except some hazy memory of when she was really young. She wasn't sure it was even him she recalled; she'd never asked him. More or less, she assumed she didn't have a dad until one day her mother informed her, "You're going to see the Chump this summer," and that was that. Gale had spent two weeks in Whitehorse ever since. Her father timed his holidays to her visits. Every day he drove her to swimming lessons at the college, even though she didn't like swimming, or even getting wet. She still hated it. In the afternoons she watched television by herself in the basement. That was the part of the visits that freaked her out, being alone in the basement. If she happened to turn the TV off — which she never did after the first time — the house was silent. At home, with her mother slamming around and Buddie having a fit, it was never quiet. Gale always knew what was going on and where everybody was. At her father's though, it was like something *had* happened and it was already too late. Or worse than that was the feeling nothing was real; Gale herself wasn't real. She could be an inch-high baby doll living in Buddie's dollhouse, with inch-high plastic parents paralyzed somewhere upstairs.

After two years, she still didn't feel real. What was she doing thousands of miles from home? How did it happen? All she knew was, one evening after it got bad with her mother, Neil started up the ladder to her and Buddie's loft. He got halfway up and stopped, just his head and shoulders showing, no hat for once, a halo pressed into his forehead from the band. He said, "With you coming into the teenage years and all, Gale, maybe it'd be better if you went to your dad's. What do you think?"

Pure Neil. He always put things like a question, hoping Gale would help him out. Why didn't he just say, "You're gone, because your mother says you're gone." He'd already called her father, the plan was made. Gale had no say at any point.

Neil wasn't even a relation of hers. What did he have to do with it?

Gale stared out the window. A neighbour two doors down was whacking away with a hoe around some shrubs, getting set for spring. His house was exactly like her father's. All the houses in their cul-de-sac were identical. Except they had a chain-link fence and zero grass.

In a way, she didn't blame Neil. Neil was just outmatched. When he and her mother went at it, Gale always rooted for him, prayed he could make her stop. He'd be like a beaten bear, backing up and backing up, finally throwing out a punch, a frantic paw. Blood would pop out of her mother's nose and her eyes would gleam.

Neil was busted, that's all. And now she was.

Why her? Why did it have to be Gale shipped off to the land of the husky? Why not her mother, who took off all the time anyway, either jail time or just gone because she felt like it. Why couldn't Mindy disappear on one of her outings and leave Gale where she was? That would be a way better plan.

Now she was getting these fits, which Sandy claimed were from living with Mindy, which would make Gale a head case, right? And that just couldn't be. No way had Mindy gotten to her.

Gale smoked and chewed on her cuticles, flicking ashes down onto the dogs. She inspected her fingers, black nail polish chipping off, cuticles raw. She pushed her hand under her thigh out of sight.

After Neil talked to her that night, Buddie crawled into bed with her. As a rule, Gale didn't allow this because Buddie peed the bed, but she made an exception that night. She and Buddie had never been apart in her life except when one or the other of them went for an overnight to Neil's parents'. And even then, if it was Gale who was away, she sweated how Buddie was doing at home without her.

Summers were no problem. Buddie stayed full-time at her grandparents while Gale visited her dad in Whitehorse, so that was okay. But now Gale was living up here all the time and Buddie was alone with her mother. It made her sick, actually.

The night Neil made his big announcement, Buddie crawled into bed with her and scrunched her fingers into Gale's collarbone. "Go, okay," she whispered, breath minty. "And when I'm big, come back and get me." Gale's stomach took a lurch thinking about it.

"Gale, down here to set the table, please," Sandy hollered from below.

Gale lowered the screen and ground her cigarette out on the sill. She wrapped the butt in a piece of foil, popped a Tic Tac into her mouth, and used a baby wipe on her fingers. Covering her tracks out of habit, she glanced around the room, yanked the bedspread over the tossed sheets, pausing to appreciate the spread. It was a quilted number in the same dark green ivy pattern as the curtains. She had to chuckle. Buddie would sure get a kick out of that bedroom.

4

GALE'S INTENTION was never to see Helen again. She had done her bit, gotten Sandy off her back; that should be the end of it. But the "attacks" — whatever — were worse. She never got any warning. There was never time to clear out of wherever she was. That was the thing she hated most. She might get hit by one when people were around, like happened in the school auditorium. She'd rather fight for air with no one gawking at her, thinking she was having a fit.

So far, she always came around pretty fast, but what if one time she didn't? What if she just kept gasping until all her brain cells winked out?

There had been another one last week. Gale was slogging up

Two Mile Hill on her bike, giving it her all in low gear. Halfway up she'd gotten walloped by some memory she didn't even recognize. She'd barely had time to get off the road onto the shoulder before her lungs seized up, dry heaves coming out of her like a fish gasping on a dock. A woman in a minivan swerved over and ran back to help.

"Are you alright? I have a satellite phone. Can I call for help?"

Gale flapped her hands trying to tell the woman to get away, but she couldn't get the words out. Even after the spasm passed and she could breathe, the woman wouldn't leave. She stayed crouched beside Gale, white as a sheet.

"Where do you live? I can take you home. We'll just pop your bike in the van there and I'll take you home."

"No. Please. I just need a minute."

What was going on? Was someone slipping her drugs? Was she having acid flashbacks — without the LSD? Where would the morons at her school get LSD? And it wasn't epilepsy. She wasn't thrashing on the ground swallowing her tongue.

Whatever it was, it had to STOP.

The latest one had come on in her sleep. *Really* bad this time. It knocked her fully awake, bolt upright in bed, fighting for air. Her lungs wouldn't budge. It was like somebody had a pillow over her face, suffocating her. She had panicked; she'd clawed the air, eyes full of tears.

Then a big square of light shot in from the hall. The door whammed back against the jamb and Sandy bounded into the room in her flannel pajamas, landing on the bed so hard Gale bounced. Sandy started kneading Gale's back. "Easy, Gale, easy."

After a few more throat-ripping gasps, Gale's lungs began to let go. She felt a reed of air come in, like a cramp easing off. She flinched slightly away from Sandy, dropped her head. How many more of these could she do?

"Alright, Gale, alright. We're going to fix this."

A DAY LATER, Helen went out to reception to greet her next clients, who happened to be thirteen-year-old twins vying for who could starve herself down to eighty-five pounds faster.

Sandy Veraldi was waiting for her, her wool coat covered in rain.

"I need five minutes. I already spoke to these girls. They're fine waiting."

In Helen's interview room, Sandy plopped down and wiped her face with a voluminous handkerchief she took from her bag.

"I want you to see Gale again," she told Helen. "I know she didn't talk to you the other day. Gale doesn't talk to people. I couldn't do anything about it because that was the deal. Gale told me if I spoke for her, she'd walk out. So I left it to her, but there are things you need to know." She took a breath. "It's not just these episodes with her breathing. Gale is too alone. Two years here and she's made no friends. She's never on the phone except when Buddie calls. Weekends she takes off on her bike and is gone all day. I know she's up on the mountain trails and the snow isn't even off. Anything could happen. She doesn't tell us a thing." Sandy took her glasses off and wiped them dry, replaced them. "She was into some stuff at home. Neil told us. She has an interest in boxing. So does her mother, but from what Neil said, this wasn't boxing. It was bare hands. Gale was in some kind of fight club. Two kids face off while the others watch, like cock fights." She regarded Helen, outraged. "Gale could find that kind of scene here. You know she could."

Helen took a breath. Sandy said, "I'm not allowed to tell you why she was sent to us," and charged right on. "You need to get that out of her. The story is she overdosed on pills and landed in hospital getting her stomach pumped. Neil said it was close. The thing is, that isn't Gale. Pills are her mother's thing, not Gale's. If Gale were to harm herself, she'd more likely run her bike off a cliff. You get the difference?" She waited for Helen to nod and said grimly, "If it's true she overdosed, she was goaded."

"Who would goad her?"

Sandy snorted. "Four guesses." She mashed her handkerchief back into her bag and yanked the drawstring. "You need to talk to Gale about her mother."

RELUCTANTLY, Gale headed over to Helen's office. She tried the fire escape in back, but the door up top was locked, obliging her to go around to the front. If anyone she knew spotted her, she'd say she was taking out a membership at the gym. She yanked open the glass door, noting that it was a big day at Black's. The smell of body odour wafted all the way into the foyer. She plodded upstairs to reception and picked a chair. There was a kid racing a toy ambulance up and down the chair legs, wailing like a siren. The woman with him, presumably his mother, looked up from her magazine and started counting very slowly. "One — two — two and a half, I'm warning you, Brendan. Two and three-quarters." The kid stopped and his mother returned to her magazine. Then gradually, very quietly, the wailing started up again.

HELEN MANAGED to wedge Gale into a twenty-minute time slot. They sat together in her tasteless interview room, Gale looking no less impregnable on this occasion, fortressed behind her hair, limbs rigid in her school blouse and kilt. She had a packed look to her, Helen thought, like a pipsqueak samurai.

"Can we talk about home?" Helen ventured.

"Can we talk about me practically suffocating."

"Let me do my job, okay, Gale. Maybe the two are related."

When Gale was silent, Helen took it as consent. "You mentioned the fights at home. You said your mom and Neil get going, and I asked whether she hits you and you said something I'm still pondering. You said, 'She doesn't have to.' Do you recall that?"

Gale shrugged.

"Now I'm noticing those two little scars up on your cheekbone and I wonder what happened there."

"Not her," Gale said.

Helen let a silence run. Eventually Gale seemed to undergo a shift. She let her shoulders drop, spoke evenly and low. "My mother isn't like other people. She doesn't yell or hit like you see people do. She never raises her voice. But wherever she is, everything stops. Everybody just stops and waits, like something's coming."

Helen made a guess. "Except you one time."

"Yes."

"What happened with your mom before you came up here?"

The silence in the room took on weight. Gale didn't look at Helen. "I lost it one time. I just lost it and stood up to her, which I normally wouldn't do. I guess she wanted to teach me a lesson … and it got out of hand. That's all I can think of. We were by ourselves at home. I ended up taking a bunch of pills. I don't

know whose idea it was. It might have been both of our ideas."
Gale broke off. "Anyway, she didn't stop me. It was Buddie who
called 911."

Helen sat still. "Your sister."

"Yes."

"Do you think she would have gone all the way? You must
have asked yourself."

"I can't see her backing down."

5

IN THE NINETEEN HUNDREDS, Cobalt, Ontario saw a booty in silver worth millions taken out of the bitter ground. A sign next to the railway station by the lake still recalls town life at its peak. *Toronto? Isn't that where you catch the train to Cobalt?* Cobalt had all the snazz of boomtowns everywhere. It had the only other trolley line in the country besides Toronto, its own opera house, write-ups in the *New York Times*, even a visit from the Prince of Wales. There's a photograph in the silver museum of the prince passing in an open car, looking bored. By the time he got there, it was already over. Like a circus come to town, the owners set up their tents on the tortured rock, packed in the crowds, and when the ore was gone, moved on.

Now the place was busted. Most of the businesses were closed. Residents had to go up to New Liskeard to get groceries, schooling for their kids. But fifteen hundred sons and daughters and grandchildren of miners still pitched themselves around the rusted-out headframes, bent streets, and waste rock. Downtown, a clean wide road twisted and yanked along the escarpment. Flat-faced buildings lined the sidewalks. The bedrock under the town was honeycombed with drifts and shafts. Every so often somebody's driveway caved in. Last year a bridge collapsed.

COBALT WAS NEIL'S TOWN. He was Cobalt, bread and buttered. His grandfather was a hardrock miner, a Swede on his way to the Klondike fields in 1903 who got sidetracked. He worked underground in the dripping tunnels, skillful with a drill, careful not to let it overheat or snap off buried in the rock. His son Carl, Neil's father, was a miner too, though the high-grade was long gone by Carl's time, the money moved north to Kirkland Lake and Timmins. Carl worked the dregs, leasing mining rights from absent owners, making no living at all. He lost a thumb under an ore chute, but that was nothing. His father had died of silicosis at the age of forty-seven.

Neil never knew his grandfather, but he was raised on mining stories. He knew every mine and everybody who'd worked in one. He listened to the old men talk, and it was as though the sweetest thing in world had come their way, a brush with a beautiful woman who'd danced them around, poisoned their lungs, broken their backs, and left them flat. They didn't care. Just to have known her. Just to have been there.

Neil grew up in the emptied-out air the boom left behind, everybody in town dreaming and musing how to get it back, nobody seeing it was long gone. All Neil saw was blasted rock and broken roads, rotting headframes. He turned away from it, steered away from his father's cough and cronies. He watched for his chance and bought a barren farm on Giroux Lake south of town, taught himself to shear sheep. He told people he'd rather break his back in sunlight over a live thing than wear out in the dark in a mineshaft. He'd be gone all shearing season on sheep farms in Quebec. For company at home, he acquired two yellow-eyed huskies shipped from the Northwest Territories. Later on, he got three more, built kennels in the yard, and began to stock a side of beef at a time in the freezer. At an auction he picked up a used sleigh and traces, and when freeze-up came, he harnessed his dogs and ran them on the lake. Any time he could, he bought another dog. He liked them. He got so he could read his animals, gauge their temperaments, tell who the leaders were, which ones would run best together. He'd laugh and tell people it was like running a kindergarten that never let out.

He didn't marry. Women liked him, and from time to time he'd bring someone home, but he didn't stick with anyone. He was restless and solitary. In his sleep he'd groan and thrash himself awake, and he didn't like it if there was a woman there to see.

When he ran into Mindy, he had been in his log house above the lake for eight years. He'd built a barn and horse corral and put in two hundred Scotch pine. He had eleven dogs. He was thirty-six years old.

HE'D SEEN HER AROUND. She wasn't from Cobalt or he'd know her. She worked at the liquor store; he wasn't sure how long, a few months. She wore a green cardigan over her uniform against the air conditioning and had a baleful look, which distinguished her from Cobalt women. Women in his acquaintance considered surliness bad manners.

They didn't meet until midsummer. He was at the Fraser on a hot night having a beer after baseball practice. Mid-evening, he excused himself and went out to get some air. As he walked past a tavern at the other end of town, his attention was caught by scuffling in the cinder parking lot behind the tavern. He went down the drive to have a look, and in the yellow light from the open rear door, he recognized Mindy and a man from New Liskeard, a road worker who liked to drink in Cobalt. Mindy and this Brad fellow were in a fist fight. She was crouched low, holding herself like a boxer, fists up in front of her face, panting and bouncing on her toes. Brad was out of the light, but Neil could make him out, twice her size, swaying drunk. Nobody else was around. Brad got a hand up, open, to cuff her. Mindy grabbed his wrist, arched back and jabbed a foot high up into his chest. Neil heard the wind go out of him like a tire blowout. Mindy let go of his wrist, Brad staggered backwards until he hit the grille of Gary Thibodeau's pickup and sat down. He stayed there, trying to breathe, huge, rasping sucks of air lifting his chest. Mindy hopped around, fists up, exhaling through her nose like a horse. It was all over.

Neil was impressed. No woman he knew would willingly get into a brawl. Fighting was viewed as a desperate business a woman would get the worst of. This girl was sticking around, hoping for another go, looked like.

Neil stepped into the light where she could see him. She glanced at him, backed away, still bouncing on her toes. He showed his hands, the way he did with a dog he was trying to quiet.

"Excuse me," he said. "I see you've got things under control here, but I was wondering what you're doing later." He grinned to show he knew he was being corny.

Mindy slowed down, bent over and coughed, drew some long breaths. When she straightened up she said, "Depends whether you're another asshole or not." She didn't smile.

"I know a place in Haileybury," he said. "Not an asshole crowd."

Mindy looked him over, glanced at the man on the ground, looked away.

"Alright."

His truck was back at the Fraser. They walked the short distance, the road empty, the night air thick as a blanket. His truck was an old Chevy V8 he'd eased along for ten years, hard on gas, but in these used-up towns, it had to be a truck. Mindy climbed in beside him, ignored the seat belt. They turned north out of town. She didn't speak during the drive and Neil was loosened up enough not to worry about it. When they got to the bar and settled themselves, she barely glanced around.

"Looks like that guy you were tussling with didn't know how to behave himself," he said for openers.

"He was getting to be a nuisance."

She sat back in her chair, brooding. Maybe she was bored, but Neil didn't take it that way.

The Beverly was an old place on the lake, out of vogue, and quiet on a weeknight. It had air conditioning and he noticed her shudder. She bent her fingers around her beer glass. The knuckles on that hand were scuffed raw. She saw him looking and turned the knuckles against the chill of the glass. "Forget it," she said.

They sipped their beer. She made no effort to size him up. He was accustomed to women moving in on him, setting the pace, but he didn't mind her reserve.

"What do you make of Cobalt?"

She smiled a turned-down smile. "Funny town. The party's over but nobody knows enough to go home. Must have been quite the blowout in its time."

He liked this. It was what he thought. "What have you been doing with yourself, before here?"

"Odd jobs. Timmins the last couple of years. Heavy equipment capital of the world." She ran her fingers over her mouth. Neil got the feeling she was still back in the parking lot, waiting for Brad to get up. "A real dump," she said. "I came up to Kirkland Lake with somebody years ago and stuck around. Good a place as any."

She went back to brooding. He let the silence float. There was a Willie Nelson tape on, one of his favourites.

"What do you like to do?" he said. "What turns you on?"

She jerked her chin. "What's that supposed to mean?"

He leaned back. "It doesn't mean anything. I'm trying to get to know you. It's a normal question, isn't it? In the course of things."

For the first time she seemed to notice him. Her eyes flickered. "I like to fight."

"You mean kung fu stuff, like tonight?"

"That wasn't kung fu. I box. I enjoy boxing." She mused a minute, deciding whether to elaborate. "In one of the foster homes, I knew a kid who belonged to a club. I used to tag along to practices and finally they let me put gloves on. I got a guy to train me." She sipped her beer, shrugged. "I've gone some rounds, done a couple of tournaments. That's what turns me on, if you want to know. The only thing, actually." She lifted her glass, tilted it at him. "That and drinking."

When the place closed, Neil drove her home. She sat against the door and watched the headlights' streaming halo of light. By the time they got to town, the thread was too thin to mention seeing her again. She opened the door and dropped out of the seat. "See you around."

For a week or so he thought it over. He liked the way she stood off from him, how she talked, not tough so much as raw, unappeasable. He pursued her and she dated him, indifferent, closed off usually, but once in a while a look, some heat. She saw him after work for a couple of beers, or took a lift to the gym in New Liskeard. She had quite a drinking arm, as good as his, though he had a hundred pounds on her. She didn't invite him to her place. He knew she had a child, a three-year-old his friend Brenda babysat when Mindy was at work.

When he finally had sex with her it was August. The town was in the throes of a heat wave, a thick, dirty wind from Ohio hazing the air, the backs of the leaves white against the wind. They met outside the hotel in the square. It was her day off and she wore a dress, the first time he'd seen her in one, pale blue, with old-fashioned hooks and eyes closing the back. The skirt fell smooth over her hips in a way that caught him. He suggested they drive over to Haileybury for a swim. When they were just north of town, she stuck her arm out. "Can we go in there?"

Ste-Thérèse Cemetery was on a hillside on their left, muzzy and fogged in the heat. He turned at the side road, took the gravel-top up, and parked at the crest. The place was deserted. Skinny poplars, hissing in the wind, surrounded a clearing of rough, poor grass that dropped off down a hill. A huge wooden cross and a row of cedar in perfect spade shapes marked the ridge. A few of the graves at the entrance had gooseneck stands with thin metal chimes pinging and spinning in the wind.

Mindy cranked the door handle and got out. "I want to stay here awhile, okay," she said. "I like these places."

She started to walk among the headstones, the wind gluing her skirt to her thin legs. Neil hadn't been up there in years. He walked the rows, looking at the graves. The names were French: Fortin, Ouellette, Sauvé, the children of miners born in Cobalt or foreign born, arriving after the boom. His grandparents were buried here. He found their markers side by side, the worn bricks flat in the ground. *Father. Mother.* His mother's family was buried over in Latchford. Timber people.

Mindy walked towards the crest. She took her sandals off, left them, started down the hill where the ground was rougher, the grass gone to wild strawberry and vetch. The graves there were older, lichen-scabbed, broken. The names were Russian, Italian, Irish, silver miners and miners' wives. The dates told the story: infant deaths, young women dying in labour. *Genevieve Arcand 1918 – 1937.* Mindy moved among the stones. *Nicole Sauvé. Deux ans. Notre Petite.* The leaves shushed and rocked, the wind streamed up the ragged hill. Mindy stopped at a cracked headstone at the edge of the trees. *Ever Remembered, Ever Loved.* Neil approached her and she turned around. Her face was waxy, her eyes glittering. She said, "I'd rather die when I'm two years old and have my mother bury me, than her leave me and I'm still walking around."

He took her shoulders and brought her to him. She slid her mouth over his, pushed her tongue into his mouth. She dug her fingers into his back, pulled him onto his knees by his belt. He tried to slow her but she wouldn't have it. She undid his buckle, yanked his shirt out of his pants, sat back on her heels shaking, knocked his hands away when he tried to stroke her. She pushed him onto his back in the harsh grass, climbed astride him, reached under her skirt to move aside her underwear, took him and started working herself down on him. She was dry and tight. She shoved down, moved her hands to his shoulder joints, pinned him, her face livid and taut, a slice of hair making a Z across her cheek. He gripped her buttocks under her skirt, tried to ease her. She loosened and started to rock on him, her face grim, her hands still digging into his shoulders. He took hold of her thighs, lifted her away from him. His erection was dead anyway. "Mindy, for Christ's sake."

She opened her eyes, focused on his face. She got her feet under her and sprang up. Her eyes filmed over.

"Fuck you."

She yanked away, walked hard up the hill, her skirt whipping in front of her, her white legs flexing. He stayed where he was. The ground bit into his buttocks. He lifted his hips, pulled his jeans up, lay on his back looking at the spongy sky. On the return he picked up her sandals. When he got back to the truck, she was gone.

6

DURING A BREAK, Helen took a stroll out to the Robert Service Campground at the edge of town. This was a favourite walk of Chief Joseph's, but he hadn't come to work that day. He was accompanying Helen's neighbour while Conor did his forestry rounds. Conor and Helen were an item briefly, and their breakup didn't include Chief.

In summer, Robert Service filled up with backpackers from anywhere in Canada, Europe, or the States. They came to climb in Kluane, have near-encounters with grizzlies, roll around with one another in grubby sleeping bags. This was a day in May, too soon for the hubbub. The big lakes still had a skin of ice on them, waiting for one more good wind. While she walked along, Helen thought of spring at home, the apple trees in her parents' orchard weighed down with blossoms, the two magnolia trees in front like exotic visitors from a different hemisphere.

Summer in Yukon was never lush. The lakes were too cold to be any use for swimming, even in August. There were not the broad-leafed forests that ribboned the south, the emerald maples, their leaves sliding and rocking in the sweating summer air, the hot shrill of cicadas, the ruffle of small waves on sand beaches. Yukon was sere, a silver cast to the land at any season. Sky and rock, no earth.

The campground hadn't opened yet and Helen didn't see anyone. She found a grassy spot along the river and spread her jacket on the ground. A family of mergansers filed past, a mother and one, two, three—fourteen offspring. Helen kept so still they paddled right by her, like a gang of punks with their slicked-back crests.

She was inclined to believe what Gale had told her, either because of the girl's dry telling, or because, over the years, Helen had met some lethal mothers. Either way, Helen believed her. That was a lot of harm for a kid to absorb and no way to resolve it. It made sense she'd been sent away, a line had been crossed, but to land so far from home? Didn't that just freeze Gale in time? It was plain she hadn't latched on in Whitehorse, not to anyone. Kids stranded like that were time bombs. Young and outraged, and especially with a sister at home she needed to protect, Gale might do anything.

A tide of feeling welled in Helen's throat, a worn-out ache like homesickness.

Think of something else.

Think about coming north that first time, fresh out of school, long before their lives tore to pieces.

She'd been older than Gale that first time, twenty-one. Old enough to come out alone in a car. Three years with her face in a book at university, she needed to get away from her cracking brain and certain pratfalls. She was looking for somewhere she could drive to, somewhere far, where she could stretch out.

Pondering a map of Canada, her gaze was drawn to a big wedge of territory tucked up in the corner of the country. Yukon looked like a rocking chair set on a tilt, an appealing shape, and far enough from home. She spotted a skinny slit between the mountains, a ribbon named Atlin Lake with no habitation on it but one tiny dot.

She would drive there.

Her parents deliberated over Helen making a drive of four thousand miles alone. She'd gotten her driver's licence only the summer before, and in the mid-seventies the Alaska Highway was barely scratched in the dirt — no road for novices. But Helen had already been three years away from home, putting herself to bed and getting to classes on her own. How much say did her parents have?

They didn't worry long. Helen was their oldest, the careful one. She'd be fine on a summer adventure.

What did they know? Helen was *not* careful or fine. She was getting far from home because of the wreck she'd made of her final year at school. The whole exercise, the good school, the English degree, had all been a giant fake that only taking a huge powder could mend.

Sitting by the river, letting her mind go back, she was rueful. She'd never told her parents the truth, even when it was all long over.

Graduation day made her sweat with shame. There were her

parents, making the trip to Montreal in a heat wave to sit in a former hockey stadium with thousands of other parents. Helen was appalled to have them there, her mother leaking breast milk, her father barely staying awake due to an all-nighter at the hospital just before the drive, Jo in a brand new spring dress, squirming on her chair. Where were her brothers? A nanny must have been hired.

After the endless parade of graduates, the family had adjourned to a swank lunch at the hotel, Helen's latest boyfriend in tow. The whole thing a total fake.

She'd gotten pregnant that winter, crazy in love with a rough boyfriend who was already an alcoholic, as well as a stranger to condoms. The minute she found out she was pregnant, the love affair iced over. The colour on the test stick cancelled the boyfriend's existence. He phoned and phoned and finally called her a bitch and gave up. She never told him why she'd broken it off. She had no idea what became of him.

The days of clinics hadn't yet come. A girl needing an abortion had to know someone. Somehow or other, Helen *did* know a girl in residence her same year. On a freezing Saturday morning, she took a bus over to an address on the east side of town, a working-class, francophone neighbourhood she'd never been to. She didn't have any French friends. Anglos, especially from McGill, were exempt from the real life of Montreal. It was a brown brick house in a row with others. The man she'd come to see was a policeman making money on the side doing abortions. How she knew that she couldn't remember. It wasn't likely he had told her.

There didn't seem to be anyone else in the house. Helen didn't hear a sound. By then, her awareness had tunnelled. She couldn't even say what he looked like. A man of size, that was all. Maybe she never looked at his face. He took her into a room, a large, square room with counters and a sink and stove along the wall, and a table in the centre of the room. *Oh, a kitchen table abortion,* she remembered thinking. He explained he would insert some tubing and packing into her uterus that would cause contractions later on. He offered to reduce the fee if Helen would blow him when it was over. She couldn't recall whether the procedure was painful or not. She focused on a high corner, slick enamel paint on bowed walls. When he said she could get up, she paid the full fee and went home. She didn't feel anything. Not relief, nothing at all. That night in the residence she went into spasms, eventually hemorrhaging some thick, dark matter, a little unperson.

We get a coating of shock during bad times; Helen had seen it time and again, but it had worn off by graduation day. Her hands shook all the time. Sitting with her parents and her little sister and her impeccable new boyfriend in the Ritz-Carlton dining room was sheer torture, her parents' pride in her unbearable. If she had told them, they wouldn't have blamed her. There was no God in her family she had offended. It was the *way* it had happened that shamed her, sordid and blunt and her so unfeeling. When she moved back home from Montreal, she bought a used car, a white Honda, lightweight enough that she figured if she drove it into a ditch, she could always put her shoulder into it and shove it back onto the road. Once she'd spotted her destination, she loaded it with camping gear and road maps, patted her brothers on their diapered rear ends, and set out for the Yukon. Her sister Jo, age eleven, stood in the driveway scowling.

With twenty-twenty hindsight, Helen concluded she should have stayed home. Everything, everything would have played differently. She would have gotten to know her brothers, who were born just after she left for Montreal. As it was, she had never lived with them and maybe never would. She drove north and got hooked and stayed on, and now the boys were almost twenty-two.

And if she hadn't driven off, she might have found her way to her mother. Luze died two years after Jo's accident, of a cancer that had spread everywhere before anyone caught it. Luze thought it was grief making her so tired. Helen remembered her saying, whatever killed her, it wouldn't be cancer; she wasn't the type. Luze had had all kinds of unfounded and headlong theories, unmodified by medical training.

Time had softened Helen's memories, of course it had, but the years when she was growing up, she'd been dismayed by her mother's temperament, her vehemence about everything. Helen had shied away, nonplussed. Luze was in medical school when Helen was born. What chance had there been to resolve this, to acclimatize to one another? Helen had no early memories of being on her mother's skin, or being carried, or being in her parents' bed. Her memories were of being read to slumped against a babysitter, while her parents worked seventy-hour weeks in medical residency.

She would say her first experience of a primary relationship was Jo. There was no other way to account for glomming onto her baby sister with such ardour. Her whole life at home was Jo until she was eighteen and went away to school.

Then she took up with the North, and on one of Jo's visits to see her, Jo had been killed.

Two years after that her mother was gone.

Helen would never make up the time.

Think of something else.

7

BY NOW it was the long light, the sun stalled in the sky, evening an affair that went on for hours. Gale had a head cold. She didn't want to keep the appointment but felt too wasted to call; it was easier just to walk over.

In the interview room, she sat slumped in a fog of congestion, her face waxy, the edges of her nose bright red. Helen had an old music stand set up between them with some sort of diagram on it. During a cancellation that afternoon, she'd drawn a map of Gale's family — what she knew so far. Circles represented women, squares were men; the lines connecting them were the relationships. Helen turned the stand so Gale could see. Gale glanced at it and put up her guard. Her family consisted of one person: Buddie.

The generation above Gale's mother was blank.

"Gale, can you tell me about your mother's family?"

Gale drew back. It was hard to imagine her mother had ever been a kid, had had parents at one time, and been vulnerable.

"She doesn't have a family. Her mother died or took off, I'm not sure. She never talks about it." Gale chewed her cuticles awhile. "She grew up in those places where there's just staff, where you go when you're too bad for a regular family." Gale didn't know where.

"How did she and your dad meet?"

She shrugged. "High school, I guess. Probably Dad was just the first volunteer. The first pothead to come along." She was trying to be funny. She had no idea. "My mother calls him the Chump. You're going to see the Chump this summer."

"Describe her, will you? Besides the day you've told me about. The day of the pills."

Gale sighed. It was weird to think there was someone on the planet who didn't know anything about her mother. "Small," she said finally. "Smaller than me. She never eats, just smokes and drinks. I get the smoking from her."

"What does she drink?"

"Beer mostly. Whatever's there. Weed, pills — any kind of pill." Gale's voice had the flatness of old anger. "I think she's in jail now for drugs. Plus assaulting a cop." Gale held up two fingers. "Two cops."

"How do you know she's in jail?"

"Buddie phones me sometimes when she's not around. My dad and Sandy let her call collect."

"Uh-huh. That's good. When you were home, how did you handle your mom?"

Gale shook her head. How *did* she handle her? How could anybody? "Just stayed out of her way."

Something in her tone caught Helen. The girl was too alone.

"Any common ground there at all, Gale? Anything between you that isn't hard?"

"No," Gale said sharply. "I've got more sense. I've had more sense since I was three."

"Name one thing, Gale."

"Why should I?" And then, "Okay, boxing. She works out and I do too."

"In Cobalt?"

"No. Cobalt doesn't even have its own school anymore. She works out alone. Neil fixed up a bag for her in the barn and I'd go out there when she's not around. Wail away." Gale half-smiled, missing home.

"And the fights she had with Neil? They must have scared you. You said she's small."

Gale scowled. "Not to worry. She doesn't need protecting."

"No?"

"No way."

"What happens in the fights?"

Gale turned her head. The question summoned noise, furniture crashing over, Neil's grunts, her mother's silence. Remembering made Gale want to bolt out of the room. She took a few breaths, twiddled her fingers on the arms of the chair, hung on.

"Okay, they're fighting," Helen persisted. "What do you and Buddie do?"

"We clear out. I take Buddie outside. Upstairs at least."

"So you guys aren't part of the hitting?"

Gale shook her head.

Helen waited a minute. "Gale, I need to ask about other dangers, apart from being hit. Did your mother or Neil ever bother you or your sister?"

"Bother?"

"Sexually, Gale."

Gale was vexed. "No."

"No one at all."

"No."

"And sex you consent to? It's a big deal for kids your age. Where are you on that?"

"I'm nowhere on that," Gale said hotly. "Take a look around. Who would I be screwing, and when?" Colour came up in her face. "The whole thing turns me off, if you want to know. I don't want anybody knowing me that way, especially around here. I don't even take gym. Undressing in front of that crew?"

Helen nodded. "So you're hibernating right now?"

"Whatever."

Gale gnawed on her cuticles. Helen let the silence run. "I'd like to hear about the farm," she said.

Home washed over Gale like it did a hundred times a day. "It's old," she said at last. "It has a barn and a lake. Neil had horses when we first went to live there, but not anymore. Now he's got sled dogs. Someone up here breeds them, a guy in Yellowknife, and sends them down to us. I go along with Neil to Toronto to pick 'em up." She warmed to this; it was a good memory. "Sometimes the dogs get freaked from the plane and Neil needs help." Gale straightened in her chair. The yard at Neil's was covered with dog pens; every dog pegged to their own house. "When they get excited, they jump up and down, bark like they're insane," she said, grinning. "Sometimes they jump so high on their ropes, they land on top of their houses and just keep on jumping, barking like crazy."

Helen leaned back. Gale's chatter was off the point, but it was good to see her come alive. Neil made his living shearing sheep, and in the winter when there was no work, he took people dogsledding around the property. Visitors could sign up for the day, with a lunch, or if they wanted, camp overnight in the snow. Gale never handled the dogs, she told Helen. They were too strong for her. If she got too close, doling out meat or filling their water pans, and one of them jumped up on her, or even just leaned weight on her, down she went. "They're like Neil," Gale said. "Just really strong all the time."

Mindy used to work with Neil. She was no bigger than the dogs, not nearly as strong, but she wasn't afraid of them. Neil trained her on the sleighs and she was very tough with the dogs. She'd yank them around, plow right in to break up a fight. Gale's face was serious. "One time, when she couldn't get a dog to behave, she punched him in the face. I didn't see it, but Neil did. He never struck the dogs — he didn't have to — and he wouldn't let her." Then Mindy got tired of working with him. She didn't care for the customers. She'd get ticked off with them, even though all they had to do was sit in the sleigh or maybe stand on the brake. She'd get mad and spoil things. "After a while Neil stopped taking her," Gale said. "He went back to hiring our neighbour's kid, Matt."

This was the longest Gale had ever spoken. "How did that work out?" Helen said.

Gale shrugged. "Matt was okay. Not as good with the dogs as my mother. He'd never wade in and break up a fight. But he was better on the people side."

Gale flopped back in her chair. During the pause, Helen studied the diagram on the stand between them. She nodded her head at the father side. "Why did your dad come up here?"

Gale had never thought about it. "A fresh start maybe? Isn't that what everybody's doing here?"

Helen laughed. "Is that what you think? How about you?"

"I never asked to come," Gale said sourly. "It sucks here. There's nothing to do. The kids are all jerks or stoners." She put a Kleenex to her nose, blew, balled the tissue in her lap. "As soon as school's done, I'm gone."

"Gone where?"

"Home. Cobalt."

Helen knew this. All kids want to go home.

"I get it, Gale. Buddie's there and you need to know she's alright." Gale gave her a look, acknowledging.

Helen shifted in her chair. She had to stick with what brought Gale to her in the first place. "You came here with a problem, right. Shall we get to that?"

Gale nodded.

"Tell me everything you can about these bouts when you can't breathe — when you started to have them, what they're like, what you're thinking just before one comes on."

Gale was more ready to answer — at least in part. "I don't remember the first one. I never had them at home. There was the time in the assembly at school, that might have been the first. Then there was one in class, and one the other day pushing my bike up a hill. Plus, the other night when I was asleep. That was a bad one."

"And just before any one of them? What's going through your mind?"

Gale didn't care to say. She didn't understand these flashes herself and they scared her. Were they memories? Were they *her* memories?

"Can you recall what you were thinking just before?"

She shook her head.

Helen watched her. "Strong emotion, fear for example, can shut down breathing."

Gale said dryly, "I'm not scared sitting in science class. Or when I'm asleep in bed."

"Not if science class is where your mind is. But minds roam around. We can be one place and our thoughts are miles away, like when we dream and everything seems so real, right. We're *there*. What's happening can feel real enough to get our hearts pounding, or wake us up, or even constrict breathing."

Gale made no comment.

Helen sighed. "Gale, I've done this work a long time. I found out we do what we have to in order to survive. Some terrible thing that happens, we tend to bury it, forget it, because we have to keep going. Whatever's incomprehensible or overwhelming, we wall off. The brain is smart that way — protective. The emotions that come with the memory get walled off too. It's called memory repression. Do you know what I'm talking about?"

Gale shrugged.

Helen kept her eyes on her. "Later on when things are better, when we're older, or we're in a safe place, it sometimes happens we let out what we've buried. The memory comes back, or the feelings at the time, or both."

"Why would we do that?"

"I don't know if we have a choice. It seems to be the way it works. Some people have to settle the past to move on, to imagine a future at all."

"And you want me to remember what went on at home?"

"You're already remembering, aren't you?"

A furious tapping started on the window, rain forming pearls on the glass. The thump of the machines downstairs jostled the floor. Helen stood and lit the standing lamp she'd brought in to make working late homier. She and Gale sat in the lamplight, Gale glassy-eyed, recalling the memory she had in the school auditorium, Colin in his carrier, choking.

"I'm not trying to sell you anything," Helen resumed. "I'm telling you what it looks like. You're having panic attacks when there's no danger. I keep thinking you must be returning emotionally to the state you were in all the time as a child."

Gale's eyes flickered. "You're talking about flashbacks."

"I am."

Gale was interested. "Is that what you think these are?"

"I do."

"How do you stop them?"

"You can't stop the memories. They're coming out, like a barrier that's worn through. But there are ways to help."

"Like what?"

Helen felt herself relax. She had Gale's attention at last. "Use your imagination. Imagination beats fear. Emotions are just works of the mind anyway. You can override them." Her voice was slow, wanting Gale to take this in. "You could experiment sometime. When your breathing shuts down, get your imagination going. Bring up a scene that's more powerful than the memory that's tormenting you, something that has more wattage, if you know what I mean." She paused. "It won't be easy. You'll be fighting for air and a mental trick will seem way underpowered. But it's that or find a doctor to put you on sedatives and go around in a fog."

Gale grinned. "What's wrong with that?"

Helen had a hunch, but she was afraid to push. Instead she said, "It's Darth Vader stuff, Gale. Oppose something dark with something that has a lot of light."

Gale was ironic. "So when I can't breathe, have a happy thought?"

"Pretty much. Do you have any good memories?"

She frowned.

"A time when you were safe."

Gale didn't answer. Helen hadn't really expected her to. Practice told her it was time to close. "Is there anything else bothering you besides the panic attacks?"

Gale sniffed. "I can't sleep, if that's what you mean. I have to have the TV on. Sandy gets on my case, but mostly she doesn't know."

"What happens if you turn the TV off?"

"I can't hack it. At home, with stuff getting smashed and Buddie yelling and the dogs freaking out, at least I knew everybody was alive. Here, it's like a grave." Gale squirmed in her chair, balled Kleenexes rolling off her lap, and went back to chewing her cuticles.

The room was so quiet Helen could hear the battery moving the hands of her watch. It pained her to look at Gale's raw fingers. She said, "Gale, do you believe people can change? Do you think people can exert themselves and change what's going on? Or ... you know ... is it all just coming down the pike and there's nothing we can do?"

It was a pointless question. Gale considered whether to answer. Finally she said, "The only change around our house was when the cops showed up and sent Neil to his folks for a cool-down and my mother went to bed for a week. Then Buddie and I were on our own. That was a change." She frowned into space. Helen kept quiet. "You know what's pathetic? I used to think I could change her. I thought if I was very good, she'd be … like other mothers. She'd be nice. Happy. I thought it was up to me." She glanced at Helen.

Helen said gently, "And you tried really hard."

"Yeah. I was Superkid. I did everything. After their all-nighters, their fights, I cleaned up. I cleaned the whole house. I did the chores, looked after Buddie, made the lunches, heated up cans of soup. I had to stand on a chair for that one. Whatever happened, whatever went missing or went down, I took the blame." Gale arched her back, stretched, slumped back into her chair. "And you know what? She didn't change. She'll never change."

"If your mother doesn't change, what then?"

Outside, drawers were banging, people were calling goodnight to one another. Gale played with her kilt pin. Helen sighed. "Well, you're here. You made the walk over from school today. You must at least be entertaining the possibility something can change."

ON THE WAY HOME, without her thinking about it or trying at all, a memory came to Gale.

She's sitting on her grandfather's lap. He is in his favourite bristly brown armchair in a corner of the room. Everything in the room is brown, one shade or another. There's a worn rug with a pattern of gold in the brown, a sofa with a knitted blanket over it, a brown coffee table with curved legs. The television sits on a bureau that has brass handles on the drawers. There's a stand on one side of her grandfather's chair with a dark glass ashtray held in it by a ring. When Gale's grandmother washes the ashtray and holds it up to the light, Gale sees that it isn't black but amber, like the swamp water at the bottom of the property. Sometimes her grandmother lets Gale carry it back to the stand. Gale likes the heavy feel of it and uses two hands. Today she has on a white T-shirt with Niagara Falls stencilled on the front and red jeans with a stretch waistband. She wears slip-on runners without socks. Her grandma has fixed her hair in pigtails with red plastic baubles on the ends. She climbs up on her grandfather's lap to examine his missing thumb. It's like a plum. It has no bone. He's told her he lost it mining. She imagines the thumb lying in a tunnel waiting to be found. She sits high on the mound of his stomach, turned sideways into him, her face against his shirt collar. The fabric is worn thin, warm from his neck. She feels snug on her grandfather's stomach, not slipping at all. He's talking to someone in the room. His voice sounds funny. She can hear it in two places, in his throat and out in the room. He holds her while he talks and she feels sleepy.

8

THE TAKHINI HOT SPRINGS is one of the great boons of life in
Whitehorse. Over eons and eons, volcanically heated water ekes
its way up from deep in the earth, frothing out into a crater sixteen kilometres from Helen's house. In the fifties the Territory
built a bathing pool on top of it, now badly in need of sprucing
up, the walls crying out for a new coat of paint, but the water is
as miraculous as ever.

The Hot Springs functions as a village square. At any time
of the year, there are mothers standing waist-deep in the pools
chatting together, babies on their hips, teenagers cannonballing
into the deep end, old people in sagging bathing suits comman-
deering the hot jets. In autumn, yellow poplar leaves sail over

the fence and drift onto the surface. In winter, falling snow sifts down past the night lights, vanishing in the steam.

The first time Helen visited was years ago, before she bought Juerg's house. She drove up from the place she was renting at the time in Atlin and spent the late afternoon lolling in the hot end, stupefied by the honey light glancing off the water. Eventually it got too late to drive home. In those days, she kept a tent at the ready in her car, and she pitched it on the property. In the morning, she woke to a high, creaking sound echoing in the mountains, an eerie keening like a clothesline in need of oil. She hadn't a clue what it was; there was no one around to ask. She listened for half an hour, mesmerized. Finally someone hurried past her tent, heading upland, camera gear slung over his chest.

"Elk," he grinned.

THAT AFTERNOON when Helen arrived at the Springs after work, Rita and her two boys were already there. She recognized Rita's vintage station wagon by its unmistakable sag and the storage box mounted year-round on the roof. No point taking it off between ski seasons, Rita claimed.

Rita was Helen's colleague at work. She and Helen were the ones who took all comers. Everyone else in the office had a specialty: babies, autism, developmental complexities of one kind or another. Rita and Helen were the most office-bound, the most flexible, with the biggest caseloads. They were forever debating how many sessions they could do in a day and still function. For Helen it was five.

Rita left the office at five sharp every day, and went home to a jumble of hockey equipment blocking the door. Helen went home to her dog, everything just as she'd left it. But the work they did joined them. They'd eased into a partnership, like cops paired in the same patrol car, facing the same hazards.

Rita spotted Helen when she pushed through the plastic curtain that led into the pool. She issued instructions to her sons and plowed over, shoulders rolling. She and Helen propped themselves along the wall.

Rita had corkscrew hair, haphazardly dyed black. At present there was a three-inch band of iron grey at the roots. "I heard yelling when I left today," she said. "Were you seeing Hesses?"

"Yup. Same as ever, all three start hollering the minute we sit down. Especially Carla. Did I tell you, one time I even left the room to get them to stop? Nothing fazes them."

Rita had her eyes on her sons, colliding at the end of the pool. She cupped her hands around her mouth. "Philip! No tackling." She glanced at Helen. "You'd never know he's the same boy I brought to work today, sick as a dog."

Rita's husband was self-employed and perfectly capable of staying home if one of the boys fell sick, but he was never called upon. Rita's boys were the sun and the moon. She doted on them with a keenness that baffled Helen. Rita had four sisters, all dispersed to places where they could make a living, and a tiny mother in her nineties at home in Newfoundland, still roaring around on a snowmobile defying cancer. Maybe the surfeit of girls in Rita's family had put a premium on sons.

Helen absorbed the heat of the pool, trying to take in its soporific effects. She was not jovial today. One of her teens was on a run from her foster family. Eve had landed in foster care in Faro, hours north of Whitehorse, after she did what kids were coached to do: she told someone her father was molesting her.

She hated the placement she'd found herself in. Of course she did, she didn't know anyone. It had never occurred to the authorities to relocate her *father*, not Eve. There was only the one road out of Faro, and that road had about six cars a day on it. If Eve was hitching, odds were she'd be stranded that night.

"Did you see that Brit movie about doing social work?" Helen said. "It had a catchy title: *Sammy and Rosie Get Laid.*"

Rita shook her head.

"One of the characters referred to social work as 'the feeble cure.'" Helen adjusted the sunglasses she'd worn into the pool, letting the description sink in. "I suppose you know Karen Barker's been at Children's Aid seventeen years? *Seventeen.* She and I were on the phone the other day. I asked her how many times she thought she'd actually been useful — you know, really made a difference in a kid's life. Know what she said?" Rita looked wary. "Once or twice," Helen stated. "She was pretty sure, once or twice."

"What's going on, Helen?"

"Remember Ron Power, that kid this winter? I counted it up. Ron and I went to court seven times to deal with his charges. Every time, we were remanded, one reason or another, never because of Ron. I wrote eloquently to the judge on his behalf, his probation officer wrote eloquently. Ron made a Herculean effort to stay out of trouble. I told you about this. We finally got his case heard and the judge acquitted him. Ron went back to the street, and I found out the police busted him that very night. He had nowhere to go and they busted him on sight."

Rita looked at her. "Do we have to do this now, Helen? It's nice here. We could give it a rest."

"Why do we muck around asking everybody how they're doing?" Helen said, raising her voice. "We know how they're doing. Why don't we just hand out money?"

Rita sighed. "We see poor people, Helen. They have money problems. That doesn't mean we're useless."

Rita wasn't speculative. She didn't worry about whether her job was solving a fundamental problem. Her view was, if some good came out of a conversation she had with someone in one of their wretched interview rooms, fine.

"Every spring you go through this," Rita said.

"Oh please."

They looked down the pool. Rita changed the subject. "How's it going with what's-her-name?"

"Gale." Helen shrugged. "She's okay — what there is so far. She's got that post-traumatic flatness. I don't know the whole story, but the mother sounds nuts. There's a little sister at home." Helen smoothed the surface of the water as if trying to quiet it. "You've seen her. Hair cut like a crash helmet. That white face. She isn't into anything here. She doesn't even date."

A foam ball plopped in the water in front of Rita. She lobbed it back to the child who lost it. "Who's around for her now?"

"Her dad. The stepmother says he's a potato."

Rita gave Helen a shrewd look. "You haven't met him?"

"Not yet."

Rita scratched her arm. Her fingers were white and pleated like gills. "So how long have you been seeing Gale on her own?" she said. "Leaving out her dad and what's-her-name."

Helen flushed. "What if I am? Who's she got here? She didn't know her father until she was eight. Her mother's a lunatic. Why shouldn't I try to get in there?"

Rita rounded on her. "Because it's not your job. Remember therapy school? You build from who's there, from the people the kid has, no matter how subpar you think they are. You can't stand in, Helen."

Rita could be a real spoiler. She thought Helen was at a disadvantage doing therapy because of what happened to Jo, that she was prone to hoarding certain girls who showed up in her office, auditioning them for the role of little sister. Whereas in Helen's view, she was on top of it. No question. "Don't worry about it," Helen mumbled. "Gale's not a customer. She's still on my Unlikely to Return list. Half the time she doesn't show up."

Rita's boys appeared: two pairs of prune feet at eye level. Philip, trunks dripping, put his hands up in prayer. "Please, please, Mom, oh pretty please can we get the Frisbee out of the car?"

Rita pointed out they hadn't had supper yet. Quesadillas in the cafeteria was a better idea. She hauled herself out of the pool, gestured an invitation to Helen, but Helen shook her head. She was going to take a drive up the Klondike Highway, see if she could spot her runaway.

9

GALE WAS IN THE KITCHEN shaking out cereal for breakfast.
The door to her mother's room was closed tight, something new
since Mindy got back. Neil always left the door open overnight.
But he was already gone on some early morning errand. Gale
heard his truck cough and start up an hour ago. She just wanted
to get breakfast into her and Buddie, and get down the road to
the school bus. Ever since Mindy came home, she'd been like a
storm brewing. She'd been gone all winter; in jail Gale assumed,
though Neil would have said. More likely she just took off.

It was funny how, when her mother was gone, nobody
remarked on it, no one commented, as if any mention would
jinx it, and Mindy would be back next day.

The house felt uneasy with Neil absent.

Her mother had been away too long, that's what it was. Gale had lost the habit of her, had gotten past the state of watching out. And she didn't want to start up again. Neil and Buddie seemed like always, right back walking on eggshells. It was Gale who wasn't on the programme. She'd really dug having her mother gone. She'd gotten to do more things. She was older now and Neil let her work right alongside him; she'd even run the chainsaw.

MINDY HOLLERED through the door, "You won't be going to school today, Gale."

Obviously she was sick as a dog. Gale set the box on the counter and looked at a line of canned goods on the shelf in front of her. It was a June morning, a Wednesday. Like always, her mother wanted to keep her home because she was hungover and Neil wasn't around. Usually Gale didn't mind. Keeping up her grades was easy, and for sure nothing at school was a big draw. It was fine with her to stay home, tend the dogs, look after things while her mother slept. Except today was one day she didn't want to miss. Today was track and field, her favourite thing about school. If she even said the words, "track and field," her mother would suss out she wanted to go and stomp it.

Gale cleared out her voice. "Gotta go, Mom. Stuff at school."

There was silence, then Mindy said in a tone that meant the discussion, such as it was, was over, "Forget it, Gale."

Gale put juice and milk on the table, went to the ladder of the loft. "Down here now, Buds. Right now." Her head felt light.

Buddie steered into the kitchen wearing the green corduroy jumpsuit she wore every day without exception, while other eight-year-olds switched off pink and purple. Gale had tried to get her to change her outfit, but Mindy said, "Leave her. Not your problem."

Gale and Buddie ate in silence, Buddie as aware as Gale who was in the house and who wasn't. Gale put a sandwich in Buddie's backpack, took her jacket off the hook, propelled her down the drive to the bus. They waited together for the bus and when it came, Buddie got on without looking back.

By noon Gale had the chores done, the meat divvied out to the dogs, water in their bowls. She remembered then, Neil was in Quebec shearing until that night. She came into the house and started a pot of coffee, rattled around making a sandwich. The bedroom door opened, Mindy emerged, wobbly, in a grey sweatshirt with off-kilter numerals printed on the front. Ninety-nine. Her hair was stuck to her scalp, her face puffed out. She passed Gale, dropped into a chair at the table, reached for her cigarette makings. She shook tobacco into a trough of paper. Without looking up, she said, "Quite full of yourself since I went away, aren't you." Gale's stomach turned watery. "Track and field today, isn't it. And you were all set to strut your stuff." Mindy lit up and huffed smoke. "Fetch me my sweater from the bedroom. It's like a Frigidaire in here."

Through the screen door, sunlight fell along the floor to Mindy's bare feet under the table. They looked too delicate to hold her up. Gale went into her mother's room. It was dark and fusty, a sour smell coming from the bed. She brought the sweater and draped it around the back of her mother's chair.

"And I'll have some of that coffee."

Gale's head was so light she was dizzy, as if she'd sucked helium from a balloon. She found she could not lift the coffee pot and turned instead to the door, very keen all of a sudden to get out of the house. Her mother was up like a cat and caught her by the hair, yanked on it until Gale stood still.

"Getting pretty big for your boots now, huh," Mindy said. "Bet you think you're queen of the hop." Mindy's radar for one shred of confidence in another person was uncanny. Her breath stank.

Gale went limp, as she always did, but blood was surging into her arms and legs. She felt sparky, so light-headed she could faint. She ducked and turned out of her mother's grasp, headed for the door again. Mindy sprang in front of her, not touching her this time. "Tell you what. There's only one queen around here and it sure as Jesus isn't you."

Gale was extremely tired of hearing this. The surging in her limbs was making her shake. Outlandishly she said, "Why don't you kill me then?" It sounded corny even to her.

Her mother's eyes filmed. She backed up, appraising, then she shrugged. "There's pills in the medicine chest. Be my guest."

She was bluffing, Gale assumed. At the same time this felt like a true moment with her mother, a dare lying in wait all along. She went into the bathroom, found the row of pill bottles in the chest, snapped off the childproof lids and spilled out some pills, washed them down with water. She avoided looking in the mirror. She could not be the one who folded. She went back to the kitchen. Her mother was leaning against the sink, arms folded. "How many did you take?"

Gale showed her the bottles in her hand. "A few of each."

Her mother glanced at the labels. "That won't do it."

Gale saw she had pushed it too far. There was no one to stop Mindy now. She returned to the bathroom and washed down a handful more. Then she went to bed.

AFTER THAT, she had only a few snapshots in her memory: puking her guts out into a stainless steel basin, sitting on a gurney in a corridor, bare legs hanging over the edge, Mindy and Neil's voices somewhere. A doctor told her she might have liver damage. They thought she tried to kill herself. She didn't mention about her mother being home.

The reason Gale didn't die was because Buddie called 911. Eight years old and her sister had the snap to call 911. She came home from school and found Gale passed out and her mother sitting in the living room.

Buddie said Mindy was just sitting there. She wasn't even drinking.

10

HELEN SAT ON HER DECK examining a fleece jacket she'd left out overnight by mistake. There was a sizeable gouge in the back. Some squirrel foraging for nest material must have gotten at it. *Shit.*

The jacket was her favourite, teal green with purple trim. Jo had presented it to her on one of her visits. "Forget wool, Helly," she'd said proudly. "Fleece never dies."

That would have been the spring Jo was sixteen. One of her last trips. Helen lay back on the deck, her legs off the edge, the ruined jacket rolled under her head. Chief Joseph was in freeze-stance in the woods investigating a partridge. Helen could hear him holding his breath.

Whitehorse airport was minuscule when Jo was sixteen, the airfield a single asphalt strip running along the escarpment above town. Passengers deboarded onto the tarmac, fought the elements into the terminal. There was no customs gate, domestic flights only to Whitehorse, one carousel.

That year, Helen spotted Jo's plane from the highway, a pink dot floating over the mountains like an escaped balloon. Inside the terminal she stood with the other greeters, an easy group of parents collecting kids home for March break, underdressed locals meeting a buddy coming off shift from a job down south, a couple of jumpy girls, eyes rimmed in kohl, waiting for their boyfriends. Jo burst through the doors, bounding past stragglers in her scarlet parka and electric ponytail. Helen hugged her through wads of feathers, breathed her in. *My girl.*

Jo belonged to Helen. Helen was ten when Jo was born, too big an age gap for them to be siblings. Except for breast-feeding, a ten-year-old can look after an infant. Their mother's medical practice was in full sail by then, and Luze Mery left Jo to Helen. The twins didn't come until later, when Helen was twenty, away at school. Luze claimed spreading her babies out was a stroke of genius. One every decade meant the most recent offspring could raise the next one. Which suited Helen; at last she had someone of her own. She'd dash home every day from school and elbow the nanny aside. *No! She doesn't like those tights. She wants the green ones!*

WHEN THEY HAD collected her gear off the carousel, Jo shoved the cart through the doors and sniffed the air. "Still winter," she pronounced. "It was so hot in Vancouver, I thought we were done for."

Helen lifted the hatch on the car and Jo dumped in her duffle and skis, spun away to return the cart. Halfway back she yelled, "Helly, let me drive. You haven't seen me yet." Helen braced herself for one of Jo's commanding arrivals. Jo got into the driver's seat, hunched over the wheel, eased the car through its gears onto the highway. "Did I write you about passing my test?"

"Tell me again," Helen said. They were moving down the Alaska Highway at a crawl.

"It was incredible. You know Dad, I had to learn on a standard shift, so we took Mom's Forester, and of course the day of the test was the storm of the century, cars skating all over the road. Unbelievable. The inspector said if we hadn't had all-wheel, she would have cancelled my test."

Jo checked the rear-view, groped for the signal, and turned onto the Klondike Highway. "I don't know how I passed. I was scared out of my mind. Zero visibility. I couldn't take it above twenty-five the entire time. We *crawled*. I thought she'd fail me for sure. But she said I drove to conditions." Jo took her eyes off the road to beam at Helen. "Next news: Renee's dog was killed right in front of her by a pit bull terrier. Renee was screaming the whole time, trying to pull the pit bull off. Her mom saw it all. Afterwards her hair started falling out. Not all of it."

"Good grief. Here's our road, sweetheart."

"I know. Plus, Rafi has started violin lessons. Luze goes with him. She loves it. That Suzuki method where your parent learns with you, and you stand facing each other."

Jo had called their mother Luze ever since she could talk. She put it down to having had a full-time nanny since she was four weeks old. Plus Helen.

"Rafi is *six*," Helen said. "He's taken up the violin?"

78

"Luze wants to have someone in the family who isn't trying to fix everybody."

"You aren't."

"Oh yes, I am. Nick takes a lot of work." She turned a worldly eye on Helen.

"Your boyfriend? What needs fixing about Nick?"

"He's so *bleak*."

"Pessimists have a point," Helen said.

AT HOME she turned on the gas under a saucepan of milk while Jo settled into her room, greeting the clothes she'd left behind last year. "Oh *there's* my yellow vest."

They spread a map over the table and sat down to it, blowing on their cocoa. This part was pure ritual. All winter, while the sun barely cleared the mountaintops, Helen waited for March break when Jo came hurtling off the plane. First thing, they cozied up in Helen's house, bent over their maps, and made a plan.

It was always Jo who came, the family ambassador. Nobody else in the family had ever seen Helen's house. When Helen called home, her father said wittily, "Come home, all is forgiven." It didn't occur to her parents to visit Helen up there beyond the pale, or to bring her brothers up to see her life. It was Jo who came.

Helen went home every Christmas, when there was no sun in Yukon and the sky dropped low over the steaming lakes. That was her chance. It was Jo who coloured in the time between, interpreted family life. An inexhaustible subject for the two of them was their parents. In the fascinated, lifelong way siblings do, they speculated how these temperamentally opposite people could have been attracted to each other.

Their mother, Luze Mery, was the daughter of a Chilean diplomat, raised in a privileged family where intelligence in daughters was thought to be best applied hosting parties. With typical obstinacy, Luze immigrated to Canada to enrol in medical school. In Toronto she filled a vacancy in the boarding house where Helen's father lived with a half-dozen other med students. But she'd overlooked that she needed landed status to enrol in medical school. As a solution, her housemate Georges Cotillard calmly volunteered to marry her. Their mother relished pointing out she and Georges weren't going together at the time, didn't even *like* each other. Georges was just being practical.

By all accounts, the marriage that started as a legal convenience turned into a barnburner. Georges and Luze had a hold on each other's attention nothing could interrupt. It started with arguments at boarding house dinners or on the streetcar going to classes, and gradually progressed to Georges' bedroom on the second floor. Eventually they moved out so they could knock over the furniture in private. Their father's composure infuriated Luze, but his stamina in debate had her captivated.

Helen was wary of their mother in a way Jo did not share. There was a heedlessness in Luze that Helen never got used to. Aroused, her mother might do anything. Once, when she was tiny, Helen had been in the room during an argument between her parents, at the height of which her mother had thrown a knife at her father, catching him on the elbow he had raised to protect his face. Georges still bore the scar, a perfect sickle, and whenever she saw it, Helen flinched. It never occurred to her mother to rein in her temper. She thought Canada was stodgy and her husband a perfect ambassador. The less restraint around the family table, the better.

None of this fazed Jo. She wasn't bothered by volatility in others — she was volatile herself. She and Helen used to say their parents had produced near-replicas of themselves in the two of them. Helen was solitary and slow to rouse like their father; Jo flamboyant and charismatic like Luze Mery.

In the Cotillard family, the showboats were both gone now. Only the introverts left.

HELEN AND JO'S backcountry adventures began years ago, building kwin'zahs in the backyard. When Helen was in high school racking up outdoor courses, she brought everything home. Every knack had to be tried out on Jo. While other teenagers were lighting a match to their childhoods, Helen was introducing camp craft to her seven-year-old sister.

The way to build a kwin'zah was, take a super-light Alpine shovel and heap up a giant mound of snow, a huge muffin as high as Helen. Let it set a few hours, then excavate a tunnel. Helen hollowed out the inside, Jo was outside on all fours, scooping away the snow Helen shoved out to her. They kept it up until they had a hollow inside big enough to crawl into, a silent dome of blue snow, a foot thick.

In the house Helen made a Thermos of sugary tea while Jo packed a Ziploc with cookies, then they wormed into their fort and served tea in enamel cups, cross-legged on the ground.

They next built a kwin'zah with enough floor space to lie down and dragged in their sleep mats and feather bags. At bedtime, they scooted out into the yard, parkas over their pajamas and crawled into their cave. They lay cocooned together, fanning their flashlights over the dome above them, listening for a single sound. Helen switched out her flashlight for effect.

"What happens if the roof collapses," Jo whispered.

"It won't. Snow sets pretty strong."

"But what if it does, and we can't breathe, like an avalanche?"

"It'd be a really small avalanche. We'd just sit up."

"But say it snowed and our house fell in on us while we were asleep?"

"Should we go inside so you can sleep in your bed?"

"No."

When Helen moved to Whitehorse and Jo began to come in March, it wasn't long before Jo wanted to build snow forts in the mountains. Helen put a Space Booster on the roof of the car and they'd spend a night or two on a nearby frozen lake. They chose the edge of lakes so they'd have a water supply and easy running for their toboggans. The challenge of camping in the cold, venturing further and further off-trail, deeper into their own resources thrilled them. Not Helen more than Jo, as Helen had reminded herself a thousand times. With all her heart Jo chose to be there.

The year Jo brought the fleece to Helen was the year they advanced to the White Pass, using the old Klondike railroad bed to run their toboggans into the valley. The Pass was harrowing. In summer it was a desolate place of tortured rock, every growing thing stripped away by ferocious winds tunnelling up the valley. Just the dauntless little spruce, like stick soldiers, managed to take hold. In winter though, the lakes and bluffs were buried under polished snow, the landscape pillowy and glistening, a rolling satin cape a traveller could move over.

That year the weather was perfect, the wind flat calm, the land breathless. Helen and Jo hauled their toboggans into the valley, built their kwin'zah beside a frozen lake, stabbed through black ice to reach water. Ptarmigan whistled in the willows, invisible except for their blueberry eyes and the perfect chevron on each wing as they scrambled away. Jo spotted caribou tracks. "Here we are in the famous White Pass," she marvelled. "So close to the road I can almost see it, but there isn't a soul."

The year they went into the White Pass was the year Jo could do everything. She knew how to take a compass bearing, read a topo map, plot routes. She could test for slides, for weak ice at the mouth of creeks. A mere three days from home, from school assignments and central heating, Jo was fully acclimatized to winter. She had the hang of cold, the way there's no end to it, the way every move has to answer to it.

Jo had stood in a dazzling valley with her goggles pushed up on her forehead, studying the map, wiping a runny nose with the back of her mitt, cheeks flaming, and Helen saw how at home she was. It struck her that her sister had edged into what Helen used to do alone, that Jo now shared any task. To butt against Helen of course, like any little sister, but that wasn't the biggest part. Jo relished being there for its own sake, for the challenge of living in the cold, for the joy of congress with a formidable foe. At sixteen, she was a snow walker, a full companion.

Helen had three more winters before she lost her.

11

IT WAS A SATURDAY when no sane person could stay indoors;
a lull in winter, a brief pause in a long season, when frost welled
out of the ground and moisture in the air glittered in the sun.
Helen stuffed a windbreaker into her backpack, added some rice
crackers and cheese, a Thermos of green tea, a litre of water.
She washed the breakfast dishes, tamped down the stove, and
loaded her skis and pack into the back of the car. Chief Joseph
had been standing adroitly at the door from the second Helen
took her backpack off the hook. They were headed down to Atlin,
two and a half hours away.

That time of year the lakes were still gripped in ice, their
surfaces tensing and thumping, the mountains floating above.

As often as she could, Helen went down to ski in the space between ice and sky and to visit Gwen, her oldest friend. Atlin was the smooth pebble she kept in her pocket.

By the time she reached Jakes Corner, the sun had a hazy ring around it, harbinger of change. The string of sparkling days they'd been relishing was about to end.

Helen left the Alaska Highway and turned south, lowered the back window five inches so Chief could get his nose out. Now the drive got tricky, the road a thin gravel shelf cut into the mountains above the lake, a twisting ribbon, hair-raising in any season.

Helen never tired of driving it.

At the border with British Columbia, she glanced right to catch sight of the survey line, a pure gap running through the trees down to the lake, and across to Mount Minto squatting on the far shore, a monolith of ice and stone. Sighting Minto was a ritual of the drive. For her, everything about Atlin Lake had the quality of touchstone. Half an hour later, she made the last turn into town, pulled into Gwen's driveway, let Chief out, and walked into the house.

HELEN MET GWEN the first time she came north. She was camped on Pine Creek, doing dishes in her campsite one morning when a tiny, white-haired woman tramped by and asked amicably if any bear cubs had visited her, as if nothing could be more delightful. Gwen explained she was there to greet Antoinette, who had climbed Monarch Mountain the evening before carrying only a garbage bag for overnight gear. Antoinette was an anthropologist from New Zealand, Gwen explained, studying safe communities, Atlin being one. Gwen expected Antoinette to descend that morning. When they said goodbye, Gwen apologized for not being free to invite her on a boat trip that afternoon since there wasn't space. She and Helen had been friends ever since.

Gwen's house was immense. When she served as postmistress, she had converted downstairs into a post office, with living quarters upstairs. Since her retirement, the post office had moved. The ground floor was now full of her neighbours' storage items, along with Christmas decorations for the church, a ping-pong table used to collate the town newsletter, and a couple of freezers full to the brim with casseroles in an advanced state of freezer burn and moose chuck for the dogs.

When Helen trotted upstairs, light was pouring in the bank of windows that faced the lake, seed trays stacked against them, minuscule emerald shoots craning out of their dirt towards the sunlight. Gwen stood at the stove with her back to Helen making a special doggy stew for Bongo, her oldest, who was recovering from a stroke. Bongo greeted Helen manfully, eyes dim, bandy legs shuddering, tail flapping. The tail is the last thing to go, Gwen said.

Over her shoulder she told Helen, "I'm going over to Krist Johnsen's after this. You can come."

When the dogs were seen to and had had a thorough greeting from Chief, Helen and Gwen walked down to the hotel. The town tipped into the lake, telephone lines dipping on their poles, inclining to the shore, rusted machinery from the gold rush reclining in the yards, much of the town unchanged in a hundred years. The town jewel, a coal steamer called *The Tarahne*, sat in dry dock, snowy as a wedding cake, fresh paint laid over her rotting sides. Across the lake, lording it over the town, shone three-crowned Atlin Mountain.

The sight still affected Helen. When she passed the Atlin Unincorporated sign so many years ago and rounded the last bend, the mountain had smacked her in the face. She'd caught her breath and she still did. Atlin Mountain was visible from anywhere in town, like a bearing point, the arbiter of town life.

KRIST JOHNSEN was one of the people Gwen was keeping an eye on. He would be ninety-five that month. Krist nearly burned his house down a couple of winters ago, so now he stayed in the hotel from October to May. The Atlin Inn was still hanging in from the glory days and took good care of him, bringing him the tinned soup and saltines he preferred.

When they called on him, he was making his bed, smoothing the heavy floral quilt in a small plain room that smelled unoccupied. He came around the bed and shook hands shyly with Helen. His hands were smooth and dry. She saw he didn't remember her, though she had met him two years before when Wayne Burgess gave them a ride in his plane to Easter dinner. He'd grown fainter, since then. He had no eyelashes, almost no hair on his pale skull. His tall body looked light as paper.

Krist was the last old miner in Atlin. He'd arrived in 1925 from Norway, a young coal miner ready to try his hand at gold. Most of the mining in Atlin was placer, the gold washed down from the mountains and culled from creek beds, but there were a few underground mines, and Engineer, on the back of Atlin Mountain, was one of them. Krist was there during the boom, living with a hundred other men in a bunkhouse dug into the mountain. One time he got a tubercular gland in his neck. He wouldn't go to the hospital, preferring to get the medic in town to cut it out. It didn't heal, and a woman he knew advised him what he needed was some good sea air. A cruise, she suggested. So he booked passage from Vancouver and sailed to Panama, and when he came back his neck was all healed up. He didn't go back to the mines though. He had some savings and used them to build a café and installed showers and the services of a washer woman for the miners' use, which turned out very well. The miners came into town, dropped off their dirty clothes at the laundromat, showered, donned fresh clothes, visited the sporting house, topped it all off with a meal in the café.

Gwen bragged how strong he was. In his prime Krist could walk on his hands from the wharf up the road to the fire hall. If you knew the pitch of Atlin, that was some feat.

CHIVALROUSLY, he took the lead in conversation. "Some valuables here I want you to lock away for me," he told Gwen conspiratorially. From a bedside drawer he drew out an old velvet jewellery box and opened it for her inspection. It contained a couple of Masonic pins and metal tie clips. Gwen took the box solemnly. "It's safe with me, Krist."

Helen asked to hear about the old mining days.

Krist smiled and raised his long arms over his head. Helen saw that the lines on his palms were all rubbed away. "We worked like this," he said, arms still raised, lifting his eyes to the ceiling. "The tunnels always wet. Always water trickling down." He dropped his arms and folded his big hands over his rib cage like wings. "The water so cold."

"Are you the last miner from Engineer left in Atlin?"

"Oh yes. The mine is closed a long time now." His eyes crinkled and lit. "But there's still plenty of gold."

IN THE EVENING, Helen and Chief cut over the lake and went along to Gerri's cabin on the shore road. The edges of the lake were starting to candle, heat snatching at the ice. It was like walking on a galaxy, the surface a deep blue filigree. Three ravens made heavy, careless jumps on the ice in front of First Island. The sun was setting behind Atlin Mountain, buried in a creamy gold cloud. They walked up the shore into Gerri's yard, and Helen took the key from a tin by the back door where Gerri had left it for her.

Winter was fairly vanquished from the yard, the brown grass around the house flooded, tools and bicycles leaning on a forlorn tilt under the eaves, a three-foot rampart of rotted snow making a wide ring around the front.

The cabin always reminded Helen of a boat, with its low ceilings and big windows facing the lake, breasting the weather. Gerri got it years ago when prices were still cheap, but she rarely used it. She was up in Whitehorse now in a new love affair.

Helen put a fire in the wood stove, melted a kettle of snow for tea, squatted on the front step to catch the last of the sunset. Chief made a brisk investigation of the yard and lay down by Helen with a huff. One of his favourite sidekicks lived a few doors down the road, but he saw he'd have to wait.

The snow on the mountains was the colour of lilacs. Helen warmed her fingers on her tea mug, slowly opened and closed her eyes to see the sky over and over.

This place was kind to strays. Most kind.

She felt what she always felt, something inconsolable. She set it against Krist Johnsen's contentment, the mildness in him, and in Gwen. When Gwen was on the phone with Helen, she always said, We were wondering when you're coming. We. Gwen meant the dogs. She didn't see herself as living alone. Not like Helen who always felt alone, in spite of the Chief.

Gwen's life had not been easy, no easier than Helen's. Helen asked once about her husband's defection, thinking what a blow it must have been. But Gwen answered it was just what happened. Harold's first wife had died in a fire with their three children. He was frantic to replace them but, as it turned out, Gwen was past childbearing. He left her to marry someone younger, signing over the house to her, at least. Of course Gwen needed to find work. So she became the postmistress and worked that job for thirty-five years. She planted a garden, made meals for friends, read everything, and loved a good laugh. It was her grace — and Krist's — their equanimity about their straits that struck Helen. She and Gwen had walked and talked together for so many years, Gwen the closest person she had to an intimate, Gwen's interests so wide and ranging, her views always firm, but held lightly, open to revision. Not like her, who must always be fervent.

Even with Gwen though, there came a time after an hour or an afternoon, when Helen's restlessness set in and she wanted her own company, her anxiety for it grew. She'd take her leave and as soon as she was alone, she would rather be back. She'd want Gwen's obliging presence again.

It was her way, Helen realized, to sustain this oscillation, a tension she could hardly remember being without, even when Jo was alive. She yearned for comfort, sought it out in wild land, certain people, and then, barely absorbing, threw it off.

Since that first drive north so long ago, she had cleaved to loneliness rather than refuse it. She didn't know why.

Gwen would say it was just what happened.

12

DAN CONNELLY was on his way out to wash the truck when Helen phoned. Their conversation lasted a minute and a half, after which Dan headed to the kitchen, opened a can of Five Alive, and wandered into the alcove where the piano stood. He paced between the piano and the wall, a room without windows, painted algae green. As if these fits of Gale's weren't distressing enough, now she had a counsellor who wanted to see him. On the phone he'd tried to get out of it, at least have Sandy come along, but the counsellor said, "Just the two of you this time, Dan. You and Gale are the first family." This was a frightening thought. Anything that took him back to the time with Gale's mother brought on a cold sweat.

He ran his fingers along the piano, lifted the dusty lid and settled it gently, pressed a few keys carefully so that they didn't sound. It wasn't the finest baby grand money could buy, but fine enough for a place like Whitehorse. It had belonged to his mother, left to him in her will. When the estate was settled, he'd been surprised Sandy let him have it shipped. It occupied what ought to be the dining room, but Sandy didn't mind. She said a piano gave a house tone.

He pictured his mother's hands, the way she sat on the bench, her back straight, her expression intent and peaceful. It had so pleased her, Dan labouring through his levels. They'd sit side by side, Dan adding one-hand chords when his feet still stuck straight out from the bench, then later, when he grew more adept, doing the melody to her accompaniment. Then it annoyed his father and they stopped playing together.

When his mother died, Dan went over to his father's house to claim the piano. He'd barely seen his father since the funeral and was stunned by the change in him. He found him sitting in his accustomed chair in the den, the old rancorous expression on his face, but not the same man. With the loss of flesh and muscle, the ferocity had gone out of him, as if muscle had been where he stored his venom. The collar stood out from his neck, his leg bones showed through his trousers like rails. Dan could hardly stop himself putting his hands on the old man, the instinct to cover him. They sat in his father's domain, and Dan told him he was going away to Whitehorse and wanted to take the piano.

"The hell you will," his father said. "Everything in this house belongs to me."

When his father died and Dan had the piano in his keeping

at last, he found he didn't care to play it. He had no talent for it after all and no interest now that his mother was gone.

He set the lid back down.

What could he possibly say to the counsellor? Gale had been wandering around in his house for two years, and he didn't have the faintest idea what she was thinking. And he didn't want to know. Gale could get a look on her face sometimes that brought the hair up on his neck. She was a bigger girl than Mindy, different from her, but her face could go so cold sometimes, flat in the eyes, exactly like her mother.

When he told Sandy only he and Gale were invited to the meeting, Sandy just nodded. "She'll want you to get more involved with Gale."

He didn't want to get more involved with Gale. He'd wipe that whole time in his life off the board if he could. It was Sandy who had insisted, first on the summer visits and then, when Neil phoned, that Gale come for good.

Sandy had her reasons, he knew that. Sandy had a daughter, older than Gale, who took off the minute she turned sixteen. That was years ago. Edie would be—what?—in her twenties now. Sometimes he wondered if he had dreamt Edie, Sandy was so silent about her. When he and Sandy met, Sandy was living with her mother, trying to raise the girl. The father had been a one-night stand when Sandy was very young. The way Sandy put it, very quickly he was as gone as a man can get. Her letters to him came back "not at this address." Sandy had to leave Edie in her mother's care while she went to work, and that was the trouble. The old woman contradicted everything Sandy did. The girl ran to her grandmother for everything. Sandy would get home from work expecting to take over, and her mother would send her to the kitchen to scrape the carrots for dinner.

Sandy hoped moving in with Dan would add heft to her side, but it didn't change anything.

The way Dan saw it, Gale was her second chance.

THE DAY OF THE APPOINTMENT, all three alarm clocks in the Connelly household went off at once. Sandy staggered out of bed, brushed her teeth, and headed downstairs. By then she'd given up trying to rouse Gale or persuade her to eat breakfast. She left Gale to it and went to see about the dogs, setting out their food and water. Dan grudgingly made himself instant oatmeal, carried it to the breakfast nook, banged his head for the hundredth time on the hanging lamp. Gale appeared just in time to pour coffee into her Thermos cup for the drive to school.

Dan had never known anybody Gale's age to drink coffee black. Or drink coffee at all. In his day, kids stuck to pop or alcohol. Pop *with* alcohol. He wondered whether Gale had been around any drinking at school, given that her mother, at the same age, was already an expert. It wasn't a subject he would approach.

That day they made the drive in silence. Gale's wet hair gradually puffed out in the truck's heater, the local CBC radio station droned the world news, followed by local announcements: a May Day piñata bash hosted by Marsh Lake Public School, a reward for a lost dog answering to the name Texaco.

"We got that meeting with the counsellor tonight," Dan reminded her outside the school. Gale slid off the seat and threw the door shut. "See you."

ON THE DRIVE to town, Helen eyed the seeping cliffs and sighed. Spring Equinox, halfway between the light and the dark. A call to wake up or give up.

The light was returning, but there would be weeks and weeks of a liminal season that was not spring. A skin of grey ice like old silk still covered the lakes. One more good wind would blow it off.

It had taken some doing to convince Gale to invite her father. Gale wanted no part of it. "See him yourself if you're so keen," she said. "I won't be there."

But Helen had stopped stalling. If Gale was going to take root in Whitehorse, she had to be tied to someone. The obvious choice was her father.

What did Helen hope to gain by meeting him?

She wanted him to say something that was news to Gale, something that disturbed her point of view, compelled her, however subtly, to think her father might have something to offer. A change in her perception could put them on a different course. For that to happen, Gale had to be in the room.

"Okay, Gale, what about this," she finally tried. "Come with your dad, sit in, but don't talk if you don't want to. I won't call on you. Just hear what he has to say."

Whether Helen could make something happen was another matter. Today might be her only shot. Dan and Sandy hadn't signed on to counselling the way Gale had. They'd implied that whatever was ailing Gale was Gale's business. Dan might not come a second time.

On the phone she'd phrased it as needing his help. It was what she did with fathers, as if she were asking for roadside assistance.

And her strategy could backfire. Dan might have nothing to say.

AT FIVE O'CLOCK when Dan and Gale arrived, the office was closing up. Judy had her coat on when she summoned Helen.

Helen's first reaction was surprise. Dan Connelly was young. She'd forgotten he was a teenager when Gale was born. Salt and pepper hair, Gale's eyes black as outer space, shoulders humped forward as if he had a cramp. Helen had pictured him emptied-out. This man looked pent up, harried.

They made their way to the interview room, Gale hesitating while her father sat, and then taking the chair next to him. She gave Helen a warning look.

"Gale, I'm going to spend our time talking with your dad," Helen said. "You can be a fly on the wall if you want."

"Cool."

She turned to Dan. "Nice girl you have."

Dan gave her a sharp look to make sure she wasn't being sarcastic. They went on to debate the differences between Ontario, where they both grew up, and Yukon: the clear air, the rarity of thunderstorms, the ease of finding a parking spot. Gale frowned. Helen had never been so chatty. Eventually Helen settled down and asked how Gale came to live with him. Dan told the story she'd already heard from Gale and Sandy.

"What kept you going?" she asked. "A lot of fathers give up a long fight. The trail gets cold."

"Sandy helped," Dan said. "She wanted the visits to be regular. Then when Neil called . . ." He stole a glance at Gale. How much had she told Helen about this? What should he say? But Gale was chewing her fingers, looking into space. Dan went on, "When Gale was thirteen, Sandy brought it up, having Gale come to live with us."

Helen frowned. That wasn't what she'd heard. What about

the cry for help from the stepfather? She looked at Gale, expecting her to interject, but Gale only blinked.

"But even before you and Sandy got together, if I've got it right, you wanted to get custody."

"Yeah." Dan coughed. "When Mindy and I split up, I thought Gale better come with me."

"Why was that?"

Dan flexed his neck, pushed his fingers through his hair. "Gale's mother's pretty wild."

"Were you worried Gale wouldn't be alright with her?" Helen prompted.

Dan shifted in his chair, pushed out his chest as though it were paining him. Distress started coming off him like a smell. Helen thought, *my god, he's never gotten over her.* Dan said irritably, "Yeah, I was worried. Gale's mother drinks and she's had assault charges."

This wasn't news. Helen was looking for a new angle. "It must have been different in the beginning though, when you were first together. What about before all the trouble?"

Dan was nonplussed. What could he say?

"I'm asking for Gale, Dan," Helen said. "All children want to believe their parents once loved each other."

This was too bald for Dan. He stared at Helen as if she were out of her mind.

"What did your parents think?" Helen said.

Dan looked away out the window at the spring evening, the sun still hours from setting. When he told his parents he was quitting school to live with Mindy, his mother went to bed for two days with a migraine. His father told him he was a fool. His father said not to bother coming around the house "with that item," as he referred to Mindy. "She's going to make you good and sorry, that one," he'd said.

"We were just screwballs," he told Helen. "I don't remember what my folks thought."

"Was Mindy pregnant when you left school?"

Dan snorted. "Not even."

"You mean, how dumb can a guy get?"

"You could say."

"Did you keep in touch with your family in those days? Did you call your folks when Gale was born?"

Dan raked his hair again. "Not right away."

"Have they ever seen Gale?"

Dan's mother seemed to shrink in size every time she was in the same room as Mindy. It was pitiful to see. "My mother drove over a few times," Dan said. "Brought things for Gale, baby stuff." He took a deep breath. "She was just trying to help."

"How did you like being a dad?"

He rose to this. Colour flooded his face. "I didn't have the first clue," he said. "Mindy didn't have a clue either. I came home from work one time, Gale in her crib, worn out crying looked like, Mindy not even in the house. I believe that's illegal. Gale's diaper was soaked, this raw rash on her. Nothing in the house for it." He glared at Helen. "I didn't even have a frigging car. We took the *bus* to the drugstore."

Helen nodded. "And then?"

Dan blinked, annoyed. "What d'you mean? Her mother got worse. She stayed away a lot. She was drinking. She said being at home bored her. Gale bored her. I bored her. I'm not talking about this anymore."

Gale had been sitting with her hands under her thighs

staring into space. Now she looked at her father, who was trembling. She threw Helen a how-could-you glare. "It's cool, Dad."

Helen watched them. So this was how they were knit. The hellcat had her brand on both of them, deep in. And their misery linked them, if she could find a way to use it. "Well, you're the ones that got away," she said. "Do you talk about her?"

Dan looked up, distracted. "Gale and I? No, why would we?" Then he changed his mind, shook his head. "Well, sure we do. Anything Gale wants to know, she can ask."

"Uh-huh. That's good. She probably needs to talk sometimes."

"Yeah. Well, she can come to me."

Not likely. If Helen were Gale, she wouldn't dare jostle this stricken man. Too bad. The ban they had on upsetting each other shut down everything else as well, cut them off from each other.

They were nearly out of time. What had she gotten for Gale? Helen chose her words. "What do you think Gale needs from you now?"

Dan was baffled. "What do you mean? Someplace safe to grow up in, same as any kid."

"Do you ever worry she'll want to go back to Ontario? Or her mother will send for her?"

"No," he said sharply. "She'd a smart kid. She wouldn't go back. And Mindy won't send for her. She doesn't work like that."

"How do you mean?"

"I told you. She keeps her grudges."

"So you figure you'll have Gale until she grows up?"

"Long as she wants," he said.

Helen slipped a look at Gale. She was sitting perfectly still, unreadable. "It's a big change coming up here," she said. "How do you think she'd doing?"

Dan sighed. She was here, wasn't she, seeing a counsellor? How fine could she be? Out loud he said, "I think she's okay. When she first came she was like ... an orphan, a little grey girl. Dressed bad, hardly said a word. Now she talks. She watches the boxing on TV ... helps out Sandy. She's a good student ..." He tried a laugh. "Better than her old man." After a pause he said, "I don't know if she's made any friends; we're kind of out of the way, but there's plenty of time for that." He was groping. "She and Sandy have their moments. Sandy's not the easiest. She likes things a certain way." He glanced at Gale again. As a last-ditch effort he said, "Gale's doing her best."

Helen longed to ask Gale's perception, but she'd left it too late. She couldn't bring Gale in this far along. "You two need to do stuff on your own without Sandy," she said, knowing a prescription was pointless. "Sandy isn't her mother, Dan. She's only got the one. You'll have to cover, like you did years ago. It still has to be you."

"I know. I know that." Dan sat miserably, then groped for his jacket, mumbled something to Gale, and left the room, leaving the door ajar.

Gale was livid. "Brilliant," she said. "You made him feel like crap."

She got up and strode out, leaving Helen in an empty room. *Damn.*

She blew it. She rigged it all wrong. They needed to talk and Helen hadn't let them. She'd *advised* them to talk. How would they do that, these two people who could barely look at each other? How would Gale take root, even the frailest root, if she and her father had no clue how to talk to each other?

Helen should have helped them, right while she had them in the room with her.

Advising them didn't cut it. Advice wasn't useful to people. Saying "Do this when you get home" did not help. People usually knew what they should be doing instead of what they were doing. They came to therapy because they couldn't get to it. The therapist (Helen) had to make it happen. She had to *cause* it. While Helen had Gale and her father in the room, she had to cause them to start talking to each other.

She had known ten minutes into the interview what needed to happen. She should have turned to Gale and said, "Gale, I've changed my mind. I want you to join this conversation." Then she should have asked Gale how she liked it in Whitehorse. Gale would have said it sucks, and Helen could have prompted Dan to ask his daughter to elaborate. Gale and her father might have ventured into an exchange, and if they survived that, other exchanges might follow.

Little by little, Gale might gain an ally, something to hold onto in this foreign land.

Helen banged her head on the back of her chair. There was nothing wrong with this guy. He was a good enough dad. At eighteen he took his baby on the bus to buy rash ointment. Without much coaching from Helen, Dan could help anchor Gale. What were the chances they'd risk it once they were back in their regular lives, out of the disturbing, unbalancing atmosphere of the therapy room?

Helen stared at the floor. Did she think he was fragile? Had she joined the protection racket Gale was chairperson of? Her intention had been to catch a gem for Gale, but instead she'd ensured Gale and her father stayed isolated from each other. Why had she done that?

13

THE PLACE TO CATCH the news and gossip in Atlin was the Pine Tree Café. Businesses came and went in town, but so far, the Pine Tree was the exception to Atlin's abysmal luck. One summer there'd be four locales to eat a meal, the forays into solvency always enterprising; the next year, there'd be one. Last year, Gary Cargill set up a burger stand on shore, a frame of bright blue plastic around a prep table and gas burners. He served barbecued patties and hot dogs on spongy buns, but he couldn't defeat the wind coming off the lake. Even with the wraparound tarp, he spent so much money on gas he had to quit. Once again, the town was down to the Pine Tree as its sole eatery.

A posse of men gathered every morning, coffee drinkers and sifters of town news. They had their regular table in the window looking out at the gas pumps, though the rules were loose. A woman sometimes joined them. In a town of a hundred, nobody was barred.

Helen was in town for the weekend, staying with Gwen. Wayne Merry happened to be giving his famous talk on his 1954 ascent of El Capitan. She'd heard it before, but Wayne was a wonderful storyteller and he was all a mountaineer should be: trim, serious, understated. Gwen slept late so Helen slipped out of the house to take breakfast at the Pine Tree. Chief Joseph had spent the night outdoors with Bongo and Nikki, but he rose when Helen appeared and trotted over with her.

Atlin Lake had an early morning wreath of fog mid-point on its flanks. The lake was still frozen but streaked black, the water barely penned beneath the ice. Helen thought she'd heard a snowmobile out there last night. The rider must be insane.

The fellows were already at the Pine Tree in force, sitting back in their chairs with sober expressions. Chief parked himself outside. Helen found a chair indoors, close by.

Something had happened.

"Search and Rescue went down this morning," Archie said. "All I heard is they got caught up there, couldn't get off before dark. Wind must've come up. They'll be in bad shape this morning."

"What the hell were they doing on the glacier anyway?" Steve McCarthy said. "It's May, for the love of Mary."

"Showing off. That new RCMP fellow we got. He cornered Dennis into taking him down. Dennis thought they'd be okay. And they were, by the sounds of it. Lake ice held. It was when they got up on the glacier."

A man Helen didn't recognize said, "Must have been a helluva night. The old man went with them. A night on the ice would go hard for him."

Helen didn't wait to hear which old man went with them. She left her glass of ice water on the table and walked out. Shirley hadn't even taken her order.

It was Llewellyn they were talking about.

Llewellyn Glacier was a wedge of ice stretched between the mountains at the foot of Atlin Lake, a prairie of half-submerged peaks called nunataks that you could see from town on a clear day. The glacier had an otherworldly, impregnable look, though it was accessible enough. You could take a boat in summer if the waves weren't too rough, get into one of the creeks running off the lake and work your way to the glacier edge. You'd find a rising, dirty blue wall with a vast plain of rotting ice beyond, navigable and dangerous. In winter the odd adventurer visited by snowmobile, manoeuvred up onto the great pan. Some had even crossed it.

Getting close to the glacier was a draw for Helen and Jo; they'd dared themselves for years. Even more beckoning were the wild mountains around Sloko Lake, to the east of the glacier. They'd pored over the topo map, counting the height lines surrounding Sloko, so thick they looked like one black smudge. Three thousand feet at least. If they camped in one of the protected bays close to the glacier, they could snowshoe over the portage into Sloko Lake. They'd have to bushwhack it; the old Tlingit trail would be long gone. Hardly anyone came that far down the lake anymore, certainly not in winter. Maybe the odd trapper, or a couple of Rangers used to distance, riding big Skandics. That was part of the draw for Helen and Jo: it'd be an expedition people didn't make anymore. Find the old trail into Sloko Lake and, if time and cold allowed, take a run to the glacier as well.

JO WAS NINETEEN the year they got their chance. The day she got off the plane, Helen told her the ice on Atlin Lake was two feet thick and nobody had run into slush anywhere. Jo looked up, winked at her, all bold, "It's what we dream of, eh, a run on good ice. Let's go, Helly. This won't come around again for another ten years."

Helen thought, why not. Regardless of the condition of the ice for travel, Jo would be tied down in university next year. Who knew when their next shot would be?

Sloko was forty kilometres down the lake. They'd have to up their supplies, ask Bob, a man of all trades in town, to lend them his Super Wide Track for the extra load. They'd carry another gallon of gas, chainsaw, the walled tent, and stove. No kwin'zah this time; they'd need wood heat.

The morning they left the temperature was −35°C.

BOB RAN THE SKANDIC off his trailer at the rendezvous, and Helen took a photo of Jo out on the ice bundled like the Michelin Man, her arm extended to indicate the toppling load on the sled.

"You girls have a good time," Bob said, giving them his big smile with the gap. "See you back here on the 16th. Use the satellite phone if you have to."

Bob's Skandic handled nothing like Helen's little Bravo; it had a mind of its own, but when they left the shore behind, Helen got a rush like leaping into mid-air. The distances out on the lake were long and pure, silver-blue to the edge of sight. Silver sky, silver mountains, the surface of the ice ridged like frozen waves. Clyde — as Bob called his big Ski-Doo — bucked along, Helen keeping the speed down. In spite of good running that year, there was no trail. No one had been down ahead of them. Helen ducked her head to check on Jo scrunched behind her, not a slit of exposed skin showing.

Jo wore the new Christmas snowmobile suit their parents had given her, racing red, an unheard of colour. Snowmobilers wore black or stayed home. Helen caught Bob eyeing Jo's getup in amusement when they met up.

Jo had the visor down on her DOT-approved helmet, and around her neck she'd wrapped a strip of sheared beaver she'd cut off an old coat of Luze's, her own touch. Moosehide mitts, expedition-rated boots good to −70°C. She could hardly move.

They stopped for lunch at Janus Point, the halfway mark, sinking to their thighs in deep snow. They liberated their snowshoes from the load and plowed to shore out of the wind. The brilliance of the sun was death to the eyes without protection, but — strange for March — it held no heat. They ate their thick sandwiches, slabs of cheese and salami, cucumber slices which had already frozen, washed down with hot, sweet tea.

As they approached the south end of the lake, the islands rose sheer in an amphitheatre of mountains, the shore too densely treed to permit camping. Helen kept Clyde idling along, watching for an opening, conscious of time. They finally found a bay with a flatter shore, space in the trees to pitch the tent. Helen checked her watch. Three o'clock. Four hours of daylight left; they'd have to hurry. She pulled her snowshoes off the sled, freed the chainsaw from Clyde's carrier, clumped off to cut tent poles. This would be the time guzzler, finding sixteen straight feet of dead tree. Jo took the Swede saw and prowled the shore for driftwood stakes. While she worked, Helen's eyes strayed to Mount Adams, a monstrous fang at the end of the bay, its shadow creeping towards them over the ice.

The tower of bundles that had been on the sleigh slowly inflated into shelter. Helen and Jo raised the tent, hoisting two scissored poles under the ridge pole, and stretched the guy lines tight. Helen fiddled with the chimney while Jo worked inside, excavating snow to build a sleep bench, piling it with their mats and feather bags. As a final touch she spread spruce boughs to scent the floor.

The lake turned the colour of copper, the sun dropped behind the mountains, and the cold took itself down another notch. Cold came up off the snow like breath while Helen worked assembling the stove. There was nothing in her mind but speed.

As dusk came on, Jo crouched on the shore struggling to light the camp stove. Her lighter had frozen. She unzipped and tucked it into her armpit. Helen interrupted her stove assembly to saw a few lengths of firewood, enough to get them through the night.

In the last light, Jo split the logs that Helen had cut, the pine popping open in the great cold.

All this time, they hadn't spoken twenty words to each other. They'd worked out long ago, the direr the straits, the fewer words needed. In stern cold they got on with it. To dither, to wonder whether they should have come, was a waste of energy. They kept a lookout on each other though, tuned to signs of fatigue or cold. On that trip, Helen registered how steady Jo was, not a murmur of complaint.

Jo got the gas lit under the camp stove, squandering some of their precious drinking water for the pasta. No time to dig a hole in the ice that night. In heavy dusk, her eyelashes freezing, Jo held her breath and watched the chimney of the tent.

Inside, Helen donned her headlamp, laid kindling in the little stove, put a match to it.

First a wisp of smoke drifted from the pipe. Another wisp, this one thicker.

"YES," Jo screamed.

Before turning in that night, they stood out on the lake, barely able to make out the mountains, black on black, a trillion stars dashing the sky. Behind them in the trees, the tent glowed from the candle lanterns inside, a hollow of warmth and light in bottomless dark.

IN THE MORNING, Helen wormed into her parka while she was still tucked in her bag, straddled Jo climbing off the sleep bench, pulled on her moccasins. The thermometer on her pack outside measured −36°C. A wind chill like that shifted priorities. They would concentrate on staying alive, not on getting to Sloko Lake. Helen walked to shore, a pearl sky in the rising sun, ice fog furring the mountains, a ravishing, lethal morning without a sound. The crust drummed hollow under her snowshoes.

It took all morning to dig a hole in the ice for water and to lay in a good supply of wood. By noon, the sun had disappeared into a milky overcast. It was not as cold, but the absence of sun took a different toll. The landscape turned forsaken, comfortless. The bleakness weighed on Jo. She piped, "Is it too late to try for Sloko?"

Helen looked at her watch. "Let's see how far we get."

HELEN HAD ASKED HERSELF a thousand times, what if they hadn't gone to Sloko? What if they had taken the break in the cold to go home instead? Why stay in that formidable place?

But they always stayed. They were young. They didn't think unduly about risks. They only had two weeks together. Every adventure had to be a go.

CLYDE TOOK THEM down into the farthest toe of the lake, the afternoon drained of colour. The snowmobile floated through deep snow, black cliffs rearing beside them, drifts of fog filming the rock. When they reached where the portage should be, Helen made an arc and parked Clyde along his own track, pointing back to camp.

Jo was solemn. Without the sun, they were castaways. She nodded at Helen's colossal fur hat. "I'm glad you wore that thing. It cheers me up."

Jo had been with her when Helen bought the hat at the Rama reserve back home. It was the size of a breadbox. Helen had come across it years later, mashed into a back shelf. Wearing it was beyond her, but she hadn't been able to give it away. It made a good pot cover in high wind.

SHE AND JO debated skis or snowshoes and took their skis.

They located the trail — a coup — and followed it by compass bearing. Obviously no one had done any trimming with a chainsaw in years. Eventually the windfall got so dense it was impossible to make headway. They passed trail mix back and forth. Jo was in her snow pants, her hairline soaked with sweat. She'd shed her parka back down the trail, leaving it hanging on a tree.

"We must be about here somewhere," Helen said, pointing at the map. She glanced up at a square of sky. "It'll be dark by the time we get to Sloko, even if we're on the trail."

"In other words turn around," Jo said. "Have you noticed we *never* get to where we're headed?"

"And yet we're out here. How many other people do you see?"

THE SECOND DAY was too cold to ride the snowmobile. Nothing budged, not a raven, not a creature. There was only the silence great cold imposes. Helen and Jo kept to their routines, hung the sleeping bags to air, split wood, plodded to the ice hole. Their tracks around camp had hardened enough they didn't need snowshoes. Jo laboriously warmed her ski boots by the stove and made a dash to the end of the bay. Helen took her picture, a tiny red dot against a mountain rising like a mirage, with its own cloud cap. They skied stiff and slow in the back bays, hunkered in a clump of pines that caught the sun. Helen passed the field glasses to Jo. She waved them off. "Everything's too sharp. It hurts my eyes."

And once again, the day softened in the afternoon. The sun moved over Clyde, shedding infinitesimal heat on his engine. Chances were, he would start. They might have packed up then and gone. They'd be home by nightfall.

"Too late to try the portage to Sloko," Jo said. "Let's ride to the glacier, Helly. Just an hour. We've got time."

CLYDE TOOK THEM to Llewellyn, the afternoon well on, all their gear back at camp except the satellite phone, water, an extra vest each. They parked Clyde where the river narrowed and went on by skis, easing between rock boulders to reach the broad plain below the glacier. Llewellyn rose above them, a turquoise wall studded with gravel. They sidestepped up onto its surface and began skiing over a prairie of snow into the sinking sun. There was wind. After ten minutes, a drift offered a rise of shelter and they stopped, took off their skis, and crouched to rest.

"Not bad," Helen said. "Hop up on Llewellyn at thirty below."

Jo grinned at her, dug out her camera, and stood up. She took a step back for the photo, another step, and vanished into a crevasse invisible under the snow. She didn't lose her balance, she didn't cry out, she was just gone. Helen stared at the space where Jo had been standing. It was like magic, like a practical joke. Her sister was laughing and backing up; she made one yip of surprise and *gone*. Helen crawled forward, not believing. She found the break in the snow, a slight depression, crystalline blue, and below that, black. She lay on her stomach and called and called. When there was no answer and still no answer, she moved away from the edge. She spread out the map, shaking, gulping air. She took a bearing, called the RCMP on the satellite phone, and went back to where Jo disappeared. There was no sound.

Shock is a kindness. Helen lay on her stomach talking to Jo, and when she got very cold, she sat on her pack and sang to her, old songs, songs you'd sing to a child. Jo was likely dead or dying all the while. Helen wished for a fire while she waited, but there was no wood. She and Jo were there and a beautiful evening came sliding over the ice. There was always wind on the glacier and great cold, and there had been supreme cold for days, but that night the wind dropped.

It was full dark when three headlamps bobbed over the ice, Search and Rescue, coming for Helen. It had taken them a long time because the snowmobiles had trouble getting up the river. They'd come by a different route than Helen and Jo, where the ice was gloss, utterly without friction. They had to hike in on crampons. It was Bob who came, on a borrowed snowmobile since Helen had his. He brought two other men. They had ice-climbing gear to pull Jo up, but in the end it was too dangerous. They manoeuvred Helen out to the sleds. She was hypothermic and could not speak. Bob forced hot tea into her from his Thermos and hefted her onto the seat in front of him, encircled her for the long ride back.

It was the American Army that got Jo out, flying over from Juneau by helicopter the next day. She was a long way down. Her neck had broken in the fall.

14

Gale was sitting on the floor of the apartment where she lived with her mother, in a two-storey wooden building that was once a garage. The business sign was still there, too faded to read. The windows on ground level were fogged with dirt. A flight of steep stairs attached to the side of the building led up to a deck with a buckled tin floor and a barbecue against the rail, a metal ball like a spaceship on a tripod. Gale and her mother used the stairs to come in and out, but didn't bother with the deck. In summer it was a frying pan; in winter, knee-high in snow, just their tracks going to and fro. The kitchen had a linoleum floor and high, veneered cupboards along the wall. A low partition topped by a murky fish tank joined it to the living room. Two bedrooms beyond, the living room overlooked the street.

Gale didn't remember the details of her bedroom. She remembered her mother's because that's where her mother usually was. There was a maroon towel pinned over the window. The bed was piled with couch pillows and magazines: AutoTraders, crosswords, boxing tabloids. Mindy's clothes were heaped on an office desk against the wall. A lava lamp sat on a nightstand beside the bed, slow bubbles jogging up and down in a viscous green fluid.

Gale was on the floor in the living room beside the Christmas tree. There were presents under the tree wrapped in blue tissue with little stars. Gale had on flannel pajamas with pink strawberries and red buttons. She was opening her presents. She got a baby doll with rigid arms and legs and a hole in her mouth for a bottle. The bottle had real liquid in it, but nothing came out.

It was hot in the apartment, the heat turned way up. Gale's mother was in bare feet and cut-offs. She never wore shoes indoors, even in winter. Her legs were thin and white with pale veins showing under the skin. She had on a grey sleeveless T-shirt, her breasts loose on her ribs. She wore her hair in a ponytail that showed a tattoo on the back of her neck, a blue sea horse. Her face was colourless and small, her dark brown eyes protruded, the lids stretched over them. Sometimes her eyes looked grey, as if she had a second set of lids, thin as gauze, under the first. She was smoking and walking around the bare wood floor.

Neil was on the sofa. From where Gale sat she could see his knees in jeans, and his chest and arms beyond his knees, one arm laid along the back of the sofa. Neil was thin like her mother but much bigger. He looked like he could spring out of the sofa any minute. Gale was nervous about opening her presents in front of him. He was looking at her. Was the doll from him? He had combed black hair, pale green eyes, and a sharp brown face. His hands were big, the fingers knobby, with hairs sprouting up on the backs. Gale kept her eyes on his hands when he moved them.

He said, "Go ahead, tadpole. Open the next one."

Gale looked at her mother and saw she was in a bad mood.

HELEN WAS ENCOURAGING GALE to remember, to call up times when she was a kid. The point — a stretch for Gale — was to lay hold of these memories, rework them in her mind so they didn't ambush her anymore. She went into the exercise with the utmost reluctance, but once she let them, old scenes came to her smooth as anything. It was like finding a trove of forgotten snapshots on a high shelf.

"What was Christmas like?" Helen asked.

Gale had her eyes open. She didn't need to close them; she could see the scene at Christmas. The weirdest part was recognizing that the kid on the floor was *her,* about four years old.

Helen could tell by Gale's abstracted look that she was attending to something. "Any news from the front?" she asked.

Gale shrugged off the picture in her mind. "She hates Christmas. She thinks it's a con. The tree came from Neil. He was always the one who made Christmas for us. Mom just threw her presents in the garbage, never even looked at them, just stayed in her room drinking."

"Is that what you were remembering just now, your mother in her room?"

Gale didn't answer. She wasn't happy about this new facility she had. She was going along with Helen because, right then, she couldn't think of what else to do. She didn't feel like blowing Helen off — she could see Helen was trying — and she'd had a point about the choking for air episodes. Gale had actually thought of her grandfather one time, about being on his knee in the scratchy armchair. She'd stuck the memory right in the middle of her mind when she was starting to lose her breath, and it worked.

Gale hadn't made up her mind about Helen. She didn't remind Gale of any counsellors she'd come across before; for instance at the shelter Mindy had taken her and Buddie to a couple of times.

Those had been real low points.

They hadn't needed to go. Generally, after a fist fight, Neil would just hang out in the barn a few days or go to his folks, but occasionally Mindy would drag her and Buddie to a shelter. For sport, it seemed like — or free daycare.

Mindy thought the women in the shelter were stupid. Any woman who let herself get hit had it coming, to her way of thinking. The three of them kept apart from the other women and kids, even from the counsellors, who acted kind of fake, Gale thought, as if everything was going to be fine.

Helen wasn't like that. Helen almost never smiled. She had a chip in her front tooth Gale had spotted once or twice.

"CAN WE TRY SOMETHING, GALE?" Helen said. Gale looked over. "Try playing the scene again, only this time change the way it goes — the way we do with the breathing. Put something else there."

Gale frowned. "Now?"

"Yeah. Just let it roll, like you were doing just now, but make revisions. Maybe someone comes to the door. Maybe Neil makes your mom laugh. It can be whatever you like, just introduce a change. But do it with intention, Gale. Mean it."

Gale closed her eyes. She recalled the scene, but it looked the same, her mother pacing, Gale on the floor, Neil's knees at eye level.

"Are you in the apartment? What's going on?"

"Nothing."

"Keep watching. Go closer in. Does Gale have her doll?"

Gale shrugged yes.

"What's she doing with her doll?"

"Nothing. Just looking at her." Gale surveyed the child on the floor with disgust. She looked so helpless sitting there. A real wimp.

Helen prompted, "Her mom is in a bad mood, walking around. Neil is on the couch. You don't know him very well. Watch the little girl, Gale. What can you do for her?"

Gale shifted in her chair impatiently, opened her eyes. "I can't do anything for her. This is stupid."

"That's okay," Helen said quickly, anxious Gale not get discouraged. Gale hadn't come back for three weeks after Helen blew the interview with her dad. "We know how it ends. You survived. You grew up." Helen waited before going on. "What did you think of yourself at four?"

"Skanky," Gale said.

"What?"

"Me — her — whatever. She smells. She's stupid."

"Gale, she's a kid. Little kids aren't stupid, they just don't know anything. Adults are the ones who know. It's up to them to explain, to take care of things ... to run a bath when their kid needs it, all that stuff. Your mother was supposed to make a nice Christmas for you. It wasn't your job; it was hers."

Gale didn't answer. Helen was so serious about everything. She didn't seem to get it about Mindy. All this memory stuff was a waste of time.

Helen was studying her. "Who mothered you, Gale?" Gale

stared at her. "You know, did mothering things. Played with you, hugged you."

Gale's mind was a blank. She backed up from the question. Obviously Helen didn't mean Mindy. Gale never knew what Helen meant. Then it came to her. Helen meant Gale's gran, Neil's mother. Thinking of Lois, Gale had a memory of the bathroom in her grandmother's house. She had a bird's-eye view looking over the rim of the tub, years ago. Beside the tub was the stool Lois used when Gale was having a bath, piled with fresh pajamas, a clean towel neatly folded. Her grandmother would poke her head around the door and crack a joke about not recognizing Gale so sparkly.

"That would be my gran," Gale said.

"Uh-huh. What things did your gran do?"

Gale shrugged. "Just her. The way she is. She lets me talk. She looks at me."

Helen leaned forward. "Gale, it doesn't matter who mothers you, as long as somebody does. It doesn't have to be your own mother. Whoever loves you, it goes into you and it's yours."

Gale's eyes brimmed. She was still back there, in the bath at her gran's. She closed her eyes to make it stop. She was so homesick she could die.

15

GALE BALANCED on her bike at the top of Two Mile Hill, waiting for the light. She shimmied the front wheel back and forth, keeping her feet on the pedals. The red light lasted forty seconds. Her record was thirty without setting a foot down.

Her bike was outstanding. For once, her dad and Sandy had gotten it right, a GT with a suspension seat post, Shimano gears, rain tread. It was her birthday present, with apologies for a gift useless in February but, of course, winter had never stopped Gale. Bike riding was her area of expertise. She and Buddie were cyclists par excellence. With nothing but hills back home, every Cobalt kid was breathtaking on a bike.

She remembered their favourite run. It started at the top

of Prospect Avenue, went into a wicked right turn onto Cobalt, then pitched straight down to where Grandview made a natural escape ramp. Hugging that inside turn at speed onto Cobalt Street was the trick.

Neither she nor Buddie ever had sensational bikes. Every hill, whatever crate they had at the time, they had to get off and shove. No sweat on the downhills, of course. Gale recalled a nice, low number she and Neil found at the dump. She could get a leg out, really lean. Buddie had a proper helmet, filched from the lost and found. Gale wore an old football helmet of Neil's that wobbled on her head.

Any weekend errand Neil had, she and Buddie hopped a lift, pulled their bikes off the back of the truck when they got to town. All the roads were frost-heaved wrecks, which made it interesting. She and Buddie weren't the only kids into bikes, of course. They saw other kids out riding, but they never hooked up with them. Other kids came from another planet. Nobody's life was like her and Buddie's and that meant they were clueless. Gale and Buddie kept to themselves.

While Neil did his errands, they raced their bikes, running against their own best time. At the top of Prospect, they counted off for each other. *One contraption, two contraption.* Neither of them knew what a contraption was, but the beat was right. They went by the honour system. When you had your bike stopped and both feet on the ground, that's when you yelled up the hill to stop the count.

Of course you never let the brakes off completely on the descent. Between the velocity and the potholes, you could break your neck. Gale *did* break a leg once, making a brilliant run. She went into a skid at the curve, and instead of recovering, she just kept going right into the concrete abutment on the far side. The crossbar of her bike snapped her leg. Somebody called her grandmother and Lois knew where to find Neil. They put off telling Mindy for as long as possible, knowing she'd come down on Gale. Which she did. *What are you taking your little sister out on those hills for?*

When Gale's cast hardened, Buddie got out her orange marker and drew a cyclone with an upside down Scottie dog and two spinning popcorn trees.

THE LIGHT CHANGED. Gale opened her hands and the brakes released with a light click. She pumped to get up speed, let gravity take her, aligning her feet on the pedals, one forward, one back, picking a course exactly at the lip of the pavement. She held the handlebars loose and steady, her fingers hovering over the brakes. She burst through the air, the road a blur under her, the tires in a high sing. At the bottom, traffic bunched at a set of lights. Gale knew she should brake but she didn't. Her stomach felt hollow and loose. She closed her eyes, felt the perfect fall of the bike, opened her eyes, and squeezed her fingers. The bike slowly bucked to a stop. She set down a toe and straightened up.

A raven hopped up and down on the hood of a parked car beside her, shoulders hunched, wings half spread, relishing the timpani of its claws on the metal. Gale laughed. "You tell 'em, Raven."

GALE AND HELEN sat together in Helen's office. It was the last week of school. Gale's uniform was a shambles, circles of sweat spreading from the armpits of her blouse, socks lagging around her ankles. Summer break couldn't come soon enough.

Mindy was still away. Neil and Dan had worked out between them that Gale could go home for August, which was in five weeks. The thought of hanging out with Buddie took Gale's breath away.

"What'll it be like seeing your little sister?" Helen asked.

Gale tried for a casual tone. "It's been two years. A lot can change between being eight and being ten. She might be a jerk by now."

"You mean, forgotten you?"

"Not that. Just ... Mom's gone now, but if she's been around the past couple of years while I've been up here, what's that done to Buddie?"

"Without you there. Do you think she'll show up?"

"You never know. After jail, she might come back. Buddie's hoping she'll just stay away, leave her and Neil alone."

"What are the chances?"

Gale took her time. "It depends. She likes to fight. Last time I saw Neil he looked wore out. She might have hooked up with somebody else."

"If she came home, would she send for you? Like before, the way she relied on you."

Gale flinched. "Why would she? She's the one who sent me up here. But that's what everybody's afraid of." Gale shifted in her chair, out of patience. "Sandy and my dad are just freaking out about this trip. They're the ones who said yes — they're paying for it — but they're freaking out anyway. I'll be in the same *province*, so she could abduct me at any moment."

"They give her a lot of weight, eh?"

"Oh yeah."

"How do you deal with that?"

Gale had no answer. She threw Helen a bone. "Just keep up the breathing exercises," she said. "If I lose my cool and they don't let me go ... that'd do me." The time between school ending and getting on the plane in August was going to take every bit of nerve she had. Her whole life, her mother could smell every good thing that had ever come Gale's way and had gotten in the way of it.

Helen was on another track, pursuing Dan and Sandy. "Their worrying must feel like a no-confidence vote."

Gale frowned. "That's what I tell them. I'm like, 'I have a say in this too, you know,' but Sandy just goes into her social worky voice — 'It isn't about not trusting you, Gale' — whereas it's totally about not trusting me. Every speck of my life is about not trusting me. They watch me like a hawk." Her voice rose. "What other fifteen-year-old goes to her father's office after school instead of taking the bus home? Who else sits in front of the boob tube all weekend in her pajamas? I get the third degree if I go to the Qwik Mart. Forget the mall. Forget downtown. I know she searches my room. What is she looking for? Drugs? Condoms? If I can't go home this summer I'll fricking *die*."

Helen said, "Because Buddie is all you have."

"Correct."

Gale brooded. Living with Sandy and her dad wasn't like a family. It was like the shelter she'd been to in Cobalt, everybody keeping their eyes down when they passed in the hall like they didn't know one another.

"What do they want from me anyway?" she wailed. "They have all these stupid rules. Like whose turn is it to do certain jobs. Who cares? And Sandy has this thing about food. Certain foods that are just hers, Dad and I can't have any."

"Like what?"

"Yogurt, those little cups? Packages of red licorice she keeps in the fridge." She mimicked Sandy's voice. "'Gale, these are my special foods I keep for myself. Please don't touch them.' But I do. Plus I nab cigarettes from them all the time."

"You're kidding. They don't know you smoke?"

"They pretend they don't."

After a minute Helen said, "Do you blame them for your coming up here?"

Gale scowled. "Oh, so now I'm not supposed to be mad at them? Because they did me this big favour?"

"No. Only you're hot at them, and I don't hear much blame going to Neil or your mom."

Gale shook it off. "What do I care whose fault it is?"

It struck Helen how alone Gale was. "Do you ever talk to your dad and Sandy? Like how it came about, you moving up here?"

"*No!* I never talk to them."

"Why not? What would happen if you brought it up? With your dad for instance."

Gale shook her head. "I can't. He's not like that."

"How do you mean?"

"You've seen him. He gets a look on his face, like he just can't stand one more thing going wrong."

Helen pondered. "Did you ever think you might need to talk more than he needs to not get stirred up? Your dad isn't comfortable with certain conversations, so you don't have them. What strikes you about that? There are two people here, but only one of them gets represented."

Gale chewed her cuticles. She had zero interest in equal opportunity with her father. Helen never got this.

"Gale, having a mother who's dangerous, who you always have to watch out for, trains you. A kid will do whatever she has to for the person she's dependent on. She'll make herself invisible, take the blame, be the mother — whatever she has to do to stay safe. Do you know what I'm talking about?"

Gale continued torturing her fingers and didn't answer. Helen leaned back. She was on the verge of overcooking it. She reminded herself not to impersonate Virginia Satir, who she once saw on videotape doing an interview jackknifed over her knees. The therapist cannot be the most invested person in the room.

Making her tone less earnest, she continued, "We're wired pretty simply. What we do early on with one vital person, we generalize. You went silent with your mom to keep yourself safe, now you do it with everybody, whether you need to or not."

Gale took her fingers out of her mouth. "What's wrong with that?"

"Well, between you and your dad for instance, you don't talk to him, so nothing changes between you, nothing opens up."

"Fine with me."

"Come on Gale, what's the worst that could happen if you asked him a question or two?"

"You mean apart from me having zero interest in doing that?"

"Gale."

Gale sighed. "He'll get mad. He hates anything like that."

"And do what?"

"Nothing. Stomp around. Not speak."

"Forever?"

Gale rolled her eyes. "He'll be *mad*."

"So what? At least he'd have some idea what's on your mind.

He'd know you better, start to trust you, maybe trust himself around you more."

"I don't *care*," Gale howled. "I don't want anyone to know me or trust me or any of that shit. I *hate* everyone. If my father hates me, or anyone hates me, fine."

Gale looked wretched, her face blotched, her hair in her eyes. Helen thought of a photo she'd seen: a bear cub on a breakaway ice floe, prowling the edges, worried. She wanted to go over but she stayed where she was.

"You're angry, Gale. You have a right to be ... but you're not hateful. Even being a ball of anger doesn't make you hateful." She waited a minute. "This is a patch of time that really sucks, but it won't always be like this."

Gale looked at her, looked away. "If you say so."

16

THE LIFE DRAWING CLASS downtown was attended by fellows with grime in the cracks of their fingers year-round, a short range of conversation, and an un-nuanced view on most subjects. On Wednesday nights, they met in a room over the Talisman Café, a neglected space with the varnish long worn off the rolling parquet floors and the windows painted shut. Their subject was a nude model, never the same one for long. Participants stood in a circle, leaning into their easels, sketching away in silence with charcoal or chalk.

Most weeks, Helen joined them. She worked late and walked over, ordered a bowl of soup in the café downstairs. The odd time, Rita put off going home and joined her. Lately, before she went over, Helen had been paying attention to how she looked. Not a usual concern of hers, but tonight she had a date.

Deadpan, as though posing for a passport photo, she studied herself in the staff washroom mirror, gauging how someone, how Wes Robertson, might see her. Her brown hair was too fine, clinging to her skull, petering out mid-neck. Mostly she clipped it to one side or bound it in a ponytail. Tonight she let it hang. Dark grey eyes — rainy eyes her father called them — with a slight squint, as though fending off fine sand. She had an athlete's body, long, knobby arms and legs, broad shoulders, a spring in her walk like a cat.

People around town knew her, by sight at least. She was the counsellor in the office over Black's Gym. She lived on her own along the river north of town. She was the one whose sister died right in front of her on Llewellyn Glacier.

Everybody knew the story, even years later. In the supermarket, on the street, Helen would catch a glint of recognition, a curiosity in peoples' glances. It made her feel strange, made her lonely, this detail that set her apart. As if she weren't doing enough of that on her own.

What was good about the drawing group was the fellows didn't care who she was. They had come to draw, lose themselves for a couple of hours.

Under the lights in the staff washroom, she smoothed her hair, studied her solemn face.

Did she want a steady man? It didn't look like it. She and Juerg were working up to it when he left. Her neighbour Conor still spent the night once in a while. They'd settled some time ago they weren't going anywhere. For her it was strictly sex, her appetite voracious for eight minutes, flattened before she got her clothes back on. The only way she could get close, it seemed to her, was under cover of arousal, a few minutes of mayhem. The more gradual kind of intimacy was out of her range. A shared meal, a walk, an ordinary time with another person felt cordoned off.

So far.

WES ROBERTSON was already in the restaurant when Helen arrived, reading a newspaper at a table facing the door. With his head bowed, he could have been any other Whitehorse guy, untrimmed beard, black-and-red checked work jacket; but when he looked up, there was no one like him. Eyes green as ice, with an expression so ready, Helen had to look away.

It was she who'd made the move to meet for dinner, once she'd gotten up her nerve.

"How's it going, Helen?" Wes said, half rising to greet her.

Helen sat down and worked out of her jacket. On the walk over she'd thought of a topic. Yukon had been trying to talk the BC government into permitting a weir in the Atlin River to dam the lake and make hydro available to Yukon Energy. Both she and Wes had joined Friends of Atlin to try to impede them. This conservation endeavour was their other context besides drawing. "Did you see the letter from Wayne about Statute 39?" Helen asked. "Some obscure rule he found in the Park terms that says nothing can be done to disturb the Park without a permit, and permits are only granted to recreational, not commercial, projects."

"Yeah, I saw it," Wes said. "Hallelujah for the small print. Though it's YE, eh. How long will a measly park statute hold off a big company hungry for wattage?"

Helen studied the specials on the blackboard. Hamburger soup, or hot and sour; that'd be another name for cabbage.

"Wayne thinks the lake is safe for years. YE won't bother," she said.

The thing about Wes, she didn't know what he had going. He was all over the territory, repairing power lines, a job in high demand. For all Helen knew, he had a wife and five kids in Mayo, though ... something about him, she thought not.

SHE ORDERED the hot and sour and looked at Wes. "I liked what Gary had to say about what'll happen to the trout in the lake if the weir goes in. What an arcane detail. What was it? If they mess with the water levels in the lake, trout eggs will be left high and dry in spring and won't hatch? Crazy what is destroyed forever by something so innocent as how high the water rises and when."

"Arcane," said Wes, treating her to his eyes. A five-dollar word.

UPSTAIRS, she and Wes set up their easels side by side. The model that night was one Bert often hired, Elroy, a shambles of a man with a ruined body, its folds and creases showing hard use over every inch. Elroy could stand without a ripple of movement for twenty minutes. Wonderful to draw.

At nine thirty, Wes and Helen walked outside into the June night, the sun still dancing heel and toe above the escarpment.

"My truck's parked down the way if you'd care to drop in for a nightcap," Wes said.

"Sure." He'd read her mind.

Wes drove a pale blue Ford pickup, vintage, not the rig Helen expected. Wes certainly had the income for a truck more in line with Whitehorse, a sixty-grand, four-wheel drive, in glossy black or dark red.

The inside of the cab was as personal as a shoe, a Navajo blanket spread across the seat, giving off his smell, woodsmoke, solitude. Wes got in beside her and leaned across her to the glove compartment to extract a steel flask. "Just rum," he said, unscrewing the cap. "I could walk down to the Qwik Mart for cola if you like." Helen shook her head, tilted her chin, and took a sip, gasped.

What the hell. It was the smell of the truck, like a den for soft animals. Next time he passed the flask, she tightened the lid, dropped it to the floor, turned her face to him, and splayed her hand on his thigh. His forehead crinkled in surprise. He glanced through the windshield where people were still walking past, then ducked his head towards Helen and put his mouth on hers. Their teeth collided; he tasted of burned coffee, but Helen willed herself to keep still for once. She let her head drop back against the seat and relaxed her neck. She kept her hand where it was on his leg, not moving, not gripping. He laid his fingers on her neck very gently, deepened his kiss. Helen softened her mouth, bared her throat. Holding still grew unbearable. Tears came to her eyes. She gulped and straightened up. Wes drew back, something in his eyes she didn't want to see. She pulled away from him, fumbled for her bag, got a hold of the door handle, and cranked it open. The swing of the door almost dragged her out.

"Sorry," she muttered. "Bad idea." She stood on the pavement and gave the door a shove. Wes made a move to get out his side, but Helen caught his eye and shot up a stern forefinger. *No!*

She turned and took off down the road, no idea where she'd left her car.

17

NEIL WAS SHEARING sheep in Ville-Marie, Quebec. This would be an easy run, an hour's drive over the top of Lake Temiskaming. He'd be back in his own bed tonight. Sometimes when he was shearing along the St. Lawrence River, he'd be gone ten days or more. Buddie stayed with his folks for the time, which was fine, but still.

The Gauthiers, where he was shearing that day, had been customers for years. Claude wasn't into it as a business; he just kept a small herd, a dozen ewes and their lambs and a servicing ram, more as a hobby. He didn't care about breed; his own herd was all mixed up. Most of the Quebec fellows were into Suffolks, for the meat. Neil and Claude liked arguing the relative merits, Neil using his cracked French.

It was a cool, overcast day late in June, the steady rain they'd had the last few days holding off. Driving over, Neil hoped Claude remembered to keep the sheep in the stable. He couldn't shear if the wool was wet.

He turned in at Claude's tidy farm above the lake, undid the latch at the end of the drive, closed the gate behind him. Claude strode down the hill towards him, a stocky, slope-shouldered man, hazel eyes wide-spaced in a tanned face, his expression ready to laugh, like all the Francophones in Neil's acquaintance.

Claude helped him set up. They used the small shed, plenty of light through the open door. Two pregnant ewes retreated to the corner when Claude and Neil dragged in a slab of plywood for Neil to work on.

Neil sheared by hand, outdated now that electric shears had finally caught on. Power shears, with an over-plate vibrating across a sharpened comb, could shave an animal in less than twenty minutes. A man had a chance of making a living. Neil stuck with hand shearing and took longer, but not much longer. He put money into his sharpeners and kept a brilliant edge on his shears.

He clamped a harness to the rafter, a wool-lined sling on bungee cords that was a real back-saver. The sling held him across the chest under the armpits, suspending his upper body over the animal, easing his weight while he worked.

He and Claude had the usual wretched time getting the sheep out of the stable. Sheep have no defences, but they can brace their feet so they have to be bodily hauled on rigid legs.

On the platform in the shed, Neil got into his harness and started to work. He slipped his thumb in the animal's mouth behind the incisor teeth and put his other hand on the sheep's right hip. He bent the head sharply over the right shoulder, rolled the ewe onto her rump, leaned her back against his legs, and picked up his shears. He started with the chest, shearing down the sternum and ribs, over the flaccid belly into the crotch and around the rump, back up over the left thigh. With no leverage to struggle, the animal held still.

Force was not effective. Over time, Neil had learned to rely on technique to immobilize an animal. He swung the sheep away from his legs, lowered her, cleared the left leg and flank, worked up the spine. Claude watched Neil's easy motions as he rolled the lolling sheep this way and that, the creamy wool peeling away ahead of his hands, which were soon gleaming with lanolin. He rarely nicked an animal, his movements relaxed and sure. The wool fell away in a solid clump, rich yellow, moist with the ewe's heat. Neil raised the sheep, supported her while she found her feet, released her.

Sixteen minutes.

He'd left her a little sweater of fleece, white streaked with orange, to protect from sunburn and cold. Claude gathered up the mound of wool and loaded it into a long burlap bag hanging from a hoop in the yard. The freed sheep stamped, relieved herself, wobbled into the pasture to graze. Her lamb didn't recognize its mother and tottered uncertainly behind.

By three o'clock, Neil had finished. He went into the yard for a smoke, stretched his back. A good day's work. It didn't always go this well. More and more, it was the condition of the sheep that made it or broke it for him. Sheep were prone to parasites. A load of worms in the stomach devoured the blood, the life of an animal. Having to skirmish with a sick ewe or ram, the jaw swollen, the wool patchy, obvious anemia in the blood-drained eyelids, sickened him. At farms where he knew he'd be bending over listless, infected animals, he showed up surly, a heaviness in him. It was the sickness itself he hated, the way the life was sucked out of a creature little by little by something it couldn't just shit out of itself and be done with.

Gauthier was okay. His animals were healthy, steady on their feet. Neil had no quibble with him.

He and Claude walked to the house together, Claude chattering about his *filles*.

"Doz two bred ewes still waiting eh? Terrible for dem last week in de 'eat. I tink the one is going to 'ave triplets again."

Neil was distracted. His mouth tasted sour and his stomach was paining him. The doctor said it was an ulcer. He passed up Claude's offer of coffee, accepted a glass of water, made his excuses to leave.

IN THE TRUCK, homebound along the shallow, scudding lake, he chewed on a Tums and watched the sky. There was a high-pressure ridge in the west, clear air coming in an azure line. Buddie was on his mind. In another week, school would be out for the summer.

Turning it over, he and Buddie had done okay this year. Mindy was in stir most of the time; her being gone meant night and day.

He could never have made the break on his own. God knows he'd tried. He'd been looking for a way to end it for a long time. It got so he couldn't stand the sight of her. His guts would buckle, his hands sweat just being in the same room with her. He knew they'd get into it and he knew, sooner or later, he'd hit her. Once they got started, that's the way it always went. She took him there.

What he did to her degraded him. That seemed to be the point. He'd lose it and hit her, shame himself. When she went to jail this time, a big load went off him. It was like being excused from the war and sent on R and R. Even so, it had taken him a long time to settle down. The house felt spoiled. He felt like he had rot in him nobody could see. He went through the days punch-drunk.

Buddie was clingy, which she never was. She put a sleeping bag on his bed and that was where he'd find her when he turned in.

But they'd come around. Little by little he'd picked up, gotten around to some repairs, taken more notice of Buddie. A few weeks ago, he'd started playing ball again, signed up Buddie too. He put her in a kid's league and she wasn't half bad. Wild hitter. It looked like it might be a pretty good summer. And Gale would be home in a few weeks.

The wild card was Mindy. He didn't know if she'd be back, or even when she was due to get out. He'd gone to see her a couple of times early on, but she'd told him not to bother. The prospect of her showing up was something he couldn't think about. In general, he avoided thinking if he possibly could. It fouled up his stomach.

Mike over at the school had called a couple of times, once just last week. He and Mike had gone to school together. Mike was a good guy, liked kids. He never got bent out of shape when there was a rumble, just waded in, calm and easy, and sorted it out.

Mike told him Buddie had had a pretty good year, worked away fine in the classroom, but she'd had some problems in the yard. Neil assumed he meant fights but Mike said no, fights weren't a problem. "The kids don't bother Buddie," he said. "She fights so flat out, they just stay clear of her. It's more the daredevil stuff." They were sitting in Mike's office, two heavyweight chairs brought around to the front of his desk. "I don't know if you see it at home," Mike went on. "She takes risks. I don't know how else to put it. She does things that are dangerous. She climbed up on the screen in the baseball diamond a couple of weeks ago. You know the shape that thing's in. And she was on the school roof after that, a bunch of kids cheering her on. It's not as if she doesn't have friends, Neil, not like she has anything to prove. I had her into the office and talked to her after she climbed the screen. She just gave me that twitchy little grin of hers. I know you care about her, but there's something not right here. She's sending us a message."

Neil couldn't swallow any more trouble just then. A kind of nausea overtook him any time a problem came up, especially anything to do with Mindy. It was like his mind went to the edge of a drop.

Buddie was fine, he reasoned. Whatever was going on with her, she'd come around. She was a little wild, Mike was right about that, but she'd simmer down. As long as her mother stayed away.

THEN, a day in July, Neil was eating a sandwich, walking around his front room, Buddie at his folks' for the night. It was a low-sky day, cool rain starting to patter on the north windows. Neil looked out the front room and saw Mindy walking up the drive.

Somebody must have given her a lift to the end of the road.

She looked the way she always looked, jeans, running shoes, her old suede windbreaker, a sports bag slung over her shoulder.

Neil put down his sandwich as if it were too heavy to hold and stood in the window, his throat working. He felt like he was going to wet himself and concentrated on holding on. When she reached the yard, she saw him. Instead of coming to the door, she walked to the window and stood in front of him, watching him quake, her face in shadow as though she were looking at him from inside a cave. She closed her eyes, opened them and focused on him."Don't get excited, Neil. I'm not here for long."

SHE CAME INTO the house then, sat down in her slow way at the kitchen table, chucked her bag on the tabletop, pulled out her cigarette makings. Neil had quit during one of Buddie's campaigns. The smell of the smoke made his throat prickle but he didn't say anything.

"I haven't come back for you," Mindy drawled. "Or for Buddie. I'm headed for Toronto, maybe the States. Time to make my break into pro." He didn't know what she meant. "Women's boxing is coming on, if you've been following. I'm thirty-three. It's now or never." She paused, pacing herself. "I just need some time to work it out."

Neil saw that the subject was finished. He went outside. Might as well get started on cleaning out the cistern. The water level was down enough. He went to the barn to collect his shovel and the tools he'd need. His hands were shaking.

Mindy would work on him, he knew that much. The thing about her, she needed to show everybody they were rotten inside. She'd done it to him. It had taken a while, but she'd sniffed him out. The track to him got so broken in she could lope it in her sleep.

What about Buddie though? If Mindy was back, shouldn't a kid have a mother? This was the part he could never get straight. Better Mindy, than no mother at all? That didn't make sense.

Neil got the ladder into the cistern and took a bucket and shovel down with him. The hydraulic pump was broken. He'd have to use his hand pump.

If this was just a stopover like Mindy said — big "if" there — Buddie would survive. Buddie never fought her mother, not so far. Back when Gale was home, if Mindy got on her, Buddie folded right away. She'd squeeze her eyes shut, scream for him or Gale. Buddie would do like always; she'd duck.

Not that Mindy cared. She thought it was funny. She mostly ignored Buddie. It was Gale she went after.

Neil had the surface water pumped out, a few trips up and down the ladder. Then he started in on the sludge with his shovel.

The thing about Gale, she never broke. Mindy would goad her, keep on her — he couldn't watch it. Where did the kid get the spine? She'd drop her head, look like she'd stopped breathing, stand there. It drove Mindy nuts.

The damn thing though, Gale was her girl. As long as he'd been around, Mindy counted on Gale. Whatever needed doing — chores, Buddie, cover-ups, Gale would do it for her. Mindy treated her like a kid sister, somebody to lord it over, push around. His mother said it could go that way if you had a kid when you were still a kid yourself.

Neil kept digging, loading silt into the bucket, dragging it up the ladder, dumping it where he'd deal with it later. He could never think unless he was working.

After the business with the hospital, it got worse. Mindy was gunning for Gale — made up cockamamie motives, built cases out of nothing; he couldn't stand it. Somebody had to get Gale out. He still thought he'd been right about that.

He took a break, climbed the ladder and sat on the rim, fished for his cigarettes. The work had calmed him. His gloom moved off a bit.

If Mindy was just taking a breather like she claimed, they might make it. It wasn't like it was forever and it was summer. Buddie would be outside most of the time, or at her gran's. She'd tough it out.

The shit of it was Gale, due home in a few weeks. He hadn't reckoned on Mindy being here too.

THE FIRST OF AUGUST Neil took Buddie to Toronto to meet Gale's plane. Gale looked good. Still a shrimp — Buddie nearly as tall as her, which she crowed about — but Gale had put on some pounds. He took them for pizza near the airport, Buddie over the moon seeing her big sister. All the way home in the truck, she never stopped jabbering. He hadn't gotten a chance to tell Gale she'd be staying at his folks'. It was what he'd worked out when Mindy decreed she wouldn't have Gale in the house. He'd thought about arguing with her, but in the end he hadn't.

When they were close to home, he drove past his own driveway and the girls took note. They were stricken, that was obvious. He waited for Buddie to let fly — he knew she would — but she sat tight. He could feel her body hard as a post on the seat next to him. He didn't look over at Gale. Probably, he should have told her.

When he got to his folks', they came out to meet them in the driveway. He stopped the truck and Gale pulled her duffle out of the back without a word, her face shut tight. Buddie stared straight at the dashboard, not making a sound.

"I'll be bringing Buddie over," he called to Gale, but she was already marching up the drive.

When he and Buddie got home, Mindy was curled up in an armchair smoking and flipping through a magazine. She had the old rattler buzz going, Neil could sense it from the door and braced himself.

Mindy glanced up at Buddie. "I hope you had a nice car ride," she said. "That's the last time you need to see your big sister this summer."

Neil caught his breath. Mindy said, "Don't block me, Neil. I'll take Buddie and clear out. You won't know where I am. I won't have Buddie around that little cow."

Buddie gaped at her father and let out a shriek. "I'll run away."

Mindy resumed perusing her magazine. "Up to you."

At the end of the month, Gale returned to Whitehorse having seen her sister exactly twice.

18

THE FIRST WEEK wasn't too bad. Gale went through the house
at her gran's, running her hands over every surface, confirming
the banister, the flat of her bed, the hard cool of the sink counter.
She waded through the long grass behind the barn, leaving a
trail. She felt herself roused to life again, Whitehorse like lost
time, nothing to do with her.

But it didn't last. She was part way home, not home. Gale had
never stayed with her grandparents more than a night or two,
as a treat. What kind of treat, if it was all she had? She wanted
to see Buddie. She wanted to go home.

A WEEK INTO HER STAY, she and Lois were doing errands in town. When they were ready to go, Gale stalled at the truck door. "Gran, I'll walk back, okay. You go ahead."

"Gale, it's five miles."

Gale would die if she had to get into the truck. She pulled off a wan smile. "I just want to see the sights on my own. I won't be long."

Lois sighed and hoisted herself into the seat. "See you at home then. You come right along."

There was nowhere for her to go, of course. She didn't know anyone, never had. There was the Bread'n Milk, the liquor store, the Fraser Hotel boarded up, the museum with its ore specimens in glass cases, the silver patterned in the rock like ferns. That was it for hot spots. Regardless, watching the truck disappear was pure relief.

Without thinking about it, she headed for Neil's. She hadn't planned it, but it was obvious once she was moving it was what she meant to do. The farther she went, the stronger the pull.

Things *weren't* fine at home, the way Neil told her. When he and Buddie met her plane, Buddie had that giddy squeak in her voice, like she always had when Mindy was around. Same with Neil, that way of his like he was listening for something. If Neil and her mother were fighting, what did Buddie do? Did she know enough to clear out?

Crazy as it seemed, it was worse to be five miles away than to be in Whitehorse. At her gran's, a hum-like current ran through her all the time, knowing how close Buddie was.

Gale skirted along on the shoulder of the road, gravel flipping up into her running shoes, but she didn't stop to shake it out.

She thought about the farm constantly. When she woke up at her grandmother's, she thought how Buddie was waking up too and needing the tats worked out of her hair. Buddie had a way of grinding the back of her head on her pillow that made a major nest. Or she pictured Neil plunking down food for the dogs in his beat-up raincoat, and she wasn't there to help. Every detail of home played in her mind all day: the basswood table in the living room with the matchbook steadying the leg, the dips of wear in the porch stairs, the orange stain in the tub. She tracked the three of them, snuffling like a dog, sniffing every cranny, worrying in her mind.

When the farm came into view, the sun was low, turning the buildings black. She stood in the road taking in every silhouette, the house half eclipsed by the barn, the dog kennels a bunch of nubs at this distance. The elm trees had grown. She kept herself beyond the fence where the dogs couldn't scent her.

Why couldn't she walk up the drive and go into the house? How was it that her mother could say no and no one challenged her? If she were to march up the drive right now, go and find Buddie, for fifteen seconds it would be great. She'd give her sister the old finger-fan across the chin. Buddie would pull a fist. Then it would change. All the fun and kidding would drain out. Mindy would find a way.

Gale left the road and got under the old oaks lining the property, wound an arm around one of the posts Neil had driven in long ago. She watched the yard, hoping somebody would come out, though she wouldn't know who it was anyway at this distance. Finally, she told herself what was the point of standing there. She was pathetic. She swung away, jumped the ditch, and remounted the road, stuck her thumb out to catch a ride.

TOWARDS THE END OF HER STAY, they went to one of Buddie's ball games. Carl assured Gale it would be fine. "Your mother doesn't bother with Buddie's games, and Neil won't care if you come."

It was a perfect summer evening, the air soft the way it turned in August, the bugs all died off. Gale and Buddie's grandparents mounted the bleachers and Gale spotted her sister right away in the outfield. Buddie was using a mangled glove customized by one of the dogs, her cap set straight across her eyes. Since Gale last had a look at her, Buddie had grown so fast she'd lost track of her legs; she didn't know where she was in space. Time and again, she bolted for the ball and overran it. As soon as she spotted Gale in the stands, she locked onto her. Every time she made a play, she scanned for a signal from Gale, a thumbs-up or a shrug.

Neil was over near the umpire, sitting with his hands drooped between his knees. He lifted some fingers to Gale in a wan greeting.

Sitting there, all of them at the game, Gale felt pretty good. They were just a family in the stands watching Buddie give her all. When the game ended, Neil headed over for a word with his folks and Gale climbed down to intercept her sister. Buddie was streaking off the field; she looked flustered about something. Charging past Gale, she nearly collided with her, but kept right on going. And out of the blue, Gale was livid. She went after her sister, grabbed her by the shoulder so hard she knocked her down. "Buddie, frig, what's going on? You belted right past me."

Buddie gaped at Gale under the peak of her cap, rubbing her shoulder, her face flushed. Her eyes flicked away, checking where Neil was. Gale saw in her face that Buddie was afraid of her. Appalled, she stepped back. "It's okay, Bud. It's okay."

HER LAST DAYS passed in a funk, trailing around back roads in the truck with her grandmother, scavenging junk for the flea barn, paying visits to old coots who looked like they'd blow away if you opened a window. Most thrilling of all, Gale got to sit in at euchre the night one of Lois's cronies couldn't make it.

She felt strange. Strange enough she didn't tell Lois. She wasn't having breathing fits — that was one thing — but she was losing weight. Her jeans sagged around her hips. She ate everything on her plate, everything Lois put down in front of her, but food just blew through her.

She felt as if she wasn't there, as if she wasn't anywhere. Certain actions she did over and over, as if repetition could weigh her down, stop the spacey feeling. She mowed the lawn; the lawn had never been so mowed. Carl complained about the gas. She made beds for the barn cats, finding little hidey-holes for them, her motive obvious even to her. After dinner she stood beside her grandmother drying dishes, sliding every plate exactly where it belonged. Evenings, she badgered her grandfather for a game of dominoes or scrabble, lining up her chair just so.

The light-headedness persisted. She went down past the barn and sat out of sight in the long grass, her legs straight out in front of her. She wound the long, slippery blades around her hands, hanging on as if the world were on a tilt. In bed at night she spread out on her stomach, gripped the edge of the mattress, a girl on a wafer, spinning through space.

Her last evening, sitting on the brown sofa together, Lois put a hand on Gale's thigh. "It'll come out right, Gale, you'll see."

Gale thought, *What will?*

Very early next morning, Neil arrived to drive her to the

airport. Buddie wasn't in the truck, which didn't surprise Gale, but it stung.

Neil kept up a steady patter on the way. Bird talk, her grandfather would have called it. He couldn't seem to stop. The new harnesses he needed, the freezer of meat he lost when the power went out for three days. He talked as if it were the old days when they worked in the barn together, as if Gale had been right there with him all along instead of hung out to dry. Gale kept her face turned away, barely answering, watching the cut rock go by, the sky growing pale, the road building into more and more lanes.

If she had a father, Neil was it, not Dan in Whitehorse. But on that ride she hated him. She kept seeing his guilty, stupid wave at the ballpark the night they went to watch Buddie. When had Neil ever stuck up for her? When had he ever stood in the way of her mother? She slumped against the door on her side, Neil across from her, his profile sharp, his arms straight out on the wheel, a faint oily smell of sheep lanolin in the cab. Anger bloomed in her. It had always been like this. Never anything from Neil but watery apology.

When they were nearly at the airport, he finally tried for something that wasn't nothing. He glanced at her sideways, his voice low, "Gale, she isn't staying forever."

And fast as lightning, Gale shot back, "Oh yeah? And if she changes her mind, who's going to stop her?"

GALE'S RETURN FLIGHT was cancelled. At the last moment, a fuel leak warning lit up on the scanner and the Vancouver-bound passengers were ordered off the plane, back into the terminal. Dozens of passengers stormed the phone booths. Gale broke the twenty Neil given her on a stiff coffee and hunched in a moulded chair, her feet on her pack. It had been the worst summer of her life.

Eventually, word came on the PA that it would take until mid-afternoon to secure another plane. Frenzy broke out in the waiting room, passengers mobbed the gate, frantic to get a flight to a connecting city — Ottawa, Montreal — anywhere to keep moving. Gale couldn't have cared less. She figured to kill time she may as well leave the building for a smoke. Except where to go? Toronto terminal was snaked with ramps and expressways a mile deep. There was nowhere to go other than the parking lot, if she could find it.

Past the departures level, she located a bridge leading to the garage. She passed through the doors into a vast, murky space. The shadowy tiers of parked cars had a subterranean atmosphere, like a morgue for cars. Her own gloom built. The garage smelled metallic and wet, the concrete too distant from any natural light to dry. She lit a cigarette and prowled. Headlights swept up the ramps from time to time, tires crunched on the gritty cement. Gale backed furtively between two cars out of sight. Being tucked away felt oddly fugitive. She squatted to take a pee and then was too tired to resume her patrol. She edged deeper in, hunched down on her pack against the abutment.

Her limbs felt heavy, as if her blood was too thick for her heart to push around. A weight in her chest made it hard to breathe. She felt the beginning of a shutdown. She closed her eyes, breathed the way Helen had shown her. She pictured Helen in her chair, her legs drawn up under her, the way she sat. She imagined her own lungs clenched under her ribs. She drew air in, begging them to relax.

She knew what was happening. She was losing it now that

she'd left her grandparents. Away from them, from their house and the long yard, and the hot shade of the barn, the light in ribbons over the dusty furniture, and the smell of rust and linseed oil, she wasn't going to make it. Now that she had lost even the frail intercession her grandparents offered, she had nothing. She had no place anywhere. Certainly not where she was going, if they ever found a plane.

Her eyes filled. She dropped her head. She drew slow breaths, willing air into her lungs, reeling it in, thin as thread. Her lungs began to ease; her breath slowly deepened. She stayed crouched where she was, taking slow breaths, feeling the heaviness in her limbs.

She spied a ballpoint pen on the pavement in front of her, the casing flattened into shards where a car had rolled over it. She rocked forward on her heels and picked it up. She thought of her grandfather's hands hovering over the checkerboard in the lamplight, the black stain of bruises under his thin skin. She scraped the shattered plastic over the back of her own hand, lightly, then pressing down hard. Beads of blood welled, a line of ruby drops. The sight satisfied her, a kind of counterweight. She could do it again. Not on her hands though. Somewhere no one could see.

19

FALL IN THE YUKON lasts three days. It is the barest threshold before the winter storms roll in. Over three days summer throws a last fond look over her shoulder, sets the land aglow, and then vanishes, taking the light with her. It is nothing like the south where Helen grew up, where the hillsides slowly flush scarlet and gold, and daylight ebbs measure by measure. Autumn in the Yukon is rose, a thousand shades of rose. It is fireweed and highbush cranberry and wild strawberry. For three days.

After botching her date with Wes, Helen stayed away from the drawing group. She was ashamed: getting things going in the truck and then copping out. What was the look in his eye? Amusement? It better not have been kindness.

For weeks she could not face him, and then, finally, missed
the group. For one thing, there was Bert, their fearless leader,
who rented the space and scheduled the models. Helen missed
Bert's stained white beard and sparkly eyes, his way of padding
around in his slippers, looking over their shoulders while they
worked, making the occasional cryptic comment. *Ahhhh.* And
she missed standing in the room, totally absorbed, time falling
away for an hour or two.

As the weeks went by, it became less of a deal that she'd been
an idiot with Wes. Wes had a sense of humour after all.

With that in mind, Helen showed up at the drawing group
one evening, having taken care with her looks — jeans and a
linen shirt under her jacket, her good boots. It was already dusk
when she walked over, autumn galloping through town with
the first snow hard on its heels. Her stomach fluttered as she
climbed the stairs. Bert was there, helping the model of the night
with her props, murmuring reassurance. It was a woman Helen
hadn't seen before: young, plush, wrapped in an electric-blue
kimono like a prizefighter. Helen felt a dip of disappointment.
She favoured the hard-worn bodies, their history in the skin.

Several of the regulars were setting up, the working guys
with their trucks parked downstairs, plus a few matronly landscape painters in flamboyant neck scarves. Helen took the last
easel. When they'd done a round of gestures and were into the
five-minute poses, it was plain Wes wasn't coming. Helen concentrated on drawing. She could see Bert on the other side of the
circle, the corners of his mouth turned up, the model's pneumatic
flesh plainly delighting him. During the final long pose of the
evening, the model pensively supine, Bert left his drawing and
paced slowly behind them. "Keep it moving," he breathed.

A FEW WEEKS LATER, as Helen was passing the Chocolate Claim, Wes emerged. "Hey, Helen," he said, veering towards her. She blushed at the vitality coming off him.

"Have you given up your drawing career?" she asked. "I haven't seen you for a while."

"For now. I'm kind of busy."

Helen dredged in her mind for news on the Atlin Lake dam front. "I called Wayne the other night," she said. "He had a few more details about Yukon Energy's motives." Wes nodded, waiting. "He found out that all the power generated by damming the lake would go to Yukon mining. No other purpose. That means a five-year lifespan for a construction that would end up being permanent for Atlin."

Wes nodded, holding her eyes. When he didn't say anything, Helen said, "Care to go for coffee," at the very moment she noticed two takeouts in his hands. She added, flushing, "Euphemistically."

He gave her a good smile. "Sorry, meeting somebody."

How did she know he meant somebody he'd spent the night with? He turned away, then looked back and gave her a wink. "Could have been you."

HELEN DIDN'T HEAR from Gale when school resumed. Her spot on Helen's caseload was taken by a kid from Edmonton, Keith Balboa. His mother, Audette, called the intake worker. "Yeah, I'm phoning about my son. I've got him living here with me as of three weeks ago, and right off the bat he's kicked out of school for reasons that don't exactly stand up."

"Where was he before he came to live with you, Mrs. Balboa?" the intake worker asked.

"Audette. I never married Denis. You'd have to be strange.

Keith was with his father in Edmonton. Now he's with me."

"Unexpectedly?"

"Sure. Don't get me wrong, Keith and me get along fine. I would have brought him with me in the first place, only I'm not in any shape."

"You said you have a disability."

"Nerves. Constant pain. Every doctor I go to tells me something different."

Audette informed the intake worker she had witnessed countless fights between Keith and his father. Denis was a Hells Angels enforcer.

The worker consulted her notes. "Keith was *twelve* when these fist fights began?"

"With a short fuse," Audette answered. "He's had I don't know how many assault charges. The last place he was in was a combination jail and hospital. The psychiatrist they had there said Keith was either traumatized or depressed and had better live with me. In spite of me being on Assistance and in constant pain. The Children's Aid Society is in on it too, but they don't want to take Keith into care so close to his sixteenth birthday. Which is in eleven months. I don't call that coming right up."

But that wasn't the reason Audette called. "Like I say, the first day of school, he gets expelled. Being as Keith is barely fifteen, I think the school has an obligation to give him an education. Last I heard."

REFERRALS LIKE KEITH, involving multiple agencies, crashed the wait-list. Along with the suicide attempts.

Two days later, Keith and his mother came in and Helen met them in reception.

As soon as they saw her, they leapt to their feet, shook hands and exuberantly commenced making an ally of her. Helen recognized them immediately as indomitable travellers on life's outrageous highway — her favourite. Extroverted families were always the most fun to work with, the only danger being that since everyone enjoyed themselves so much, nothing changed.

The three of them settled down in the interview room; Helen looked them over. Keith was more stylish than Whitehorse kids. He was wearing low-slung black surfer shorts, an XL grey hoodie, high-top running shoes, unlaced. His bowling ball-shaped head was bound tightly in a bandana. He had a broad face, floating hazel eyes, and a boxer's squashed nose. He smiled when he talked, showing small, perfect teeth, like milk teeth.

Audette was about Keith's size, with dark grizzled hair, a square body, and trim, strong legs in pedal-pushers. Her T-shirt read, *No One Knows I'm Gay*.

"I didn't even throw the first punch," Keith said. "I never lifted my fists until dude hit me over the ear with a piece of pipe. I don't even know this kid. I've been here two weeks. First they just suspended the two of us. Then he gets a concussion and goes to the hospital, so they decide to expel me, which makes no sense to me. I heard about this kid. He's always getting concussions. He scrapes his knee and gets a concussion. His mother wants to charge me. I'm already on probation." Keith paused for breath, looking aggrieved. "I feel hated on by people at that school," he said. "They see my clothes and know I'm city and hate me just on that. I lost care for people like that a long time ago."

"Is that why you're here? To get back into school?"

"Yeah. They've got some hoops I have to jump first. Anger management."

Helen sighed. What was that phrase supposed to mean? Showing anger *was* managing it. What did they think these kids were doing other than displaying? "Okay, we can do that," she said. "Anything else besides the hoops? Anything you want for yourself?"

Keith gave his ready smile. A furrow dug in between his eyebrows, a little line of worry, the crack in his bravado. "There was this shrink in Edmonton before I came here. Dude named Bradley, the main doc I talked to. He had this real slow voice. Not slow like he was having trouble keeping up, just real relaxed." Keith reminisced for a minute. "He was cool. On another plane, you could say."

Helen nodded, calm in the presence of these two storytellers.

"People say I'm just like my father," Keith continued. "He trained me, the doc said. But I have all kinds of people inside me, some good, some bad. Mainly that's what him and me talked about." He smiled contentedly.

"How did talking help?"

Keith half closed his eyes. Audette interjected, "Keith likes to think he's a schizophrenic. *Three Faces of Eve* kind of thing. Did you see that one? I don't know about him being schizophrenic, but he needs to get back in school. I can't have him around the house all day. We're in a very small apartment. My boyfriend Norman drives truck and needs his sleep. Plus, I'm in a lot of pain. In my legs, all over. Some days I can't get out of bed. I'm not just thinking about myself. It's a hardship for a boy Keith's age to have nowhere to go all day. He's supposed to be in school."

This made sense to Helen. "Okay. I'll broker with the school and you can come see me for counselling, Keith."

"Twice a week is about right," Keith volunteered, but Helen shook her head. The time she'd spend negotiating with the school would be monumental.

"I'D LIKE TO HEAR about your dad," Helen said in one of their early meetings.

Keith sat with his knees spread, hands on his thighs, chest pushed. *Warrior's chest*, Helen thought to herself.

"He's an animal, man. He's like those wild pigs in Africa that run around on little short legs tearing everything up."

"Fist fights with your father is pretty rich," Helen said. "Not a good kind of rich."

Keith leaned down to adjust his socks. He was fastidious, almost fretful about his appearance, Helen noticed. He straightened and put his hands back on his thighs.

"You can't hide from my old man," he said. "When I was a little kid, there was nowhere he couldn't find me. Every place in the house was a bad place to be. Waiting for him was the worst. I started asking for it. You know, get the drop on him. And when I was out of the house, I'd act like him, start something. Like, to get it over with." He shrugged. "That's how I got Jim. He's like my father. Only worse."

"Jim?" Helen had the feeling Keith had run through this many times; it was a schtick. Where was the real boy?

"Jim's the strongest," Keith went on. "He guards the others. Doctor Bradley said I grew him as protection from my father."

Helen thought about the boy Keith presumably assaulted. "Who's in charge, you or Jim?"

A worry line hunched into Keith's forehead, possibly genuine. "Jim goes too far," he said.

"You don't have him in check."

"Yeah."

After a minute Helen said, "Where do you keep your heart?"

Keith beamed, tapped his chest. "Right here. Angela. She's three."

BETWEEN THE INTRANSIGENCE of the school board and an avalanche of referrals, it didn't occur to Helen to wonder about Gale. Her other steadies weighed in; she saw the girls from the Catholic high school shrieking and jostling on the street in the thin autumn daylight after school, but Gale was not among them.

20

HELEN HESITATED to call up somebody who'd dropped out of counselling. It felt slightly like grovelling, or asking for a rating. *Where are you? Wasn't I helping?* She preferred to leave the initiative to her clients. The middle of a crisis was when to see people; at those times they tended to be motivated, receptive to change. Once their anxiety lowered, her families generally dropped out, whether anything had changed or not. She made exceptions. She didn't leave the initiative to clients she was attached to. She couldn't help it; she had to know how things turned out. And for different reasons, she tracked the high-risks, the self-destructive ones, which amounted to half the teenagers on her list. Gale had her on the first count; for all she knew, the second as well.

After many tries, she reached Gale at home. She kept her voice neutral. "How'd the summer go?"

Gale made a *nnnh* sound.

"Want to come in and catch up?"

"Ah, when?"

"Soon. Anytime."

"I don't know." Helen heard the drag in her voice. "It's more strict now with my dad and Sandy."

"Like how?"

"Getting a ride," Gale said. "My dad says we have the appointments too late for him to pick me up."

"That can be solved. I could drop you at home when we're finished meeting. You're in the subdivision, aren't you? It's on my way."

Gale was clearly stalling. "I'll have to talk to them."

"Okay. I'll call you in a few days." No response. "I'll call you, Gale," Helen repeated. "It'd be good to check in."

THEN ONE DAY when it was dusk at four o'clock, Helen heard from Sandy. "Dan and I need to come in."

She was surprised. She and Sandy didn't keep in touch.

"It's Gale. Everything's changed since she came back. We need to talk."

"What does Gale think about you coming to see me?"

"We didn't consult her."

Helen hesitated. She could lose Gale if they met without her consent. "Can we make it a family meeting, Sandy, including Gale? She'll have to be part of whatever we decide anyway."

"There are things you should know that I can't talk about in front of her."

"Having her there makes us pick our words," Helen agreed. "But I'm worried it will alienate her if we leave her out."

Reluctantly, Sandy agreed. They settled on an early time. It occurred to Helen that Gale would have to miss the first hour of school. "That shouldn't be a problem," Sandy said dryly. "She doesn't go to school most days anyway."

Helen winced. Gale's grades were so strong and school was such a ticket. What had happened?

WHEN SHE GOT to the office next morning, Dan and Sandy were already there. Sandy's face looked creased and tired. It looked like Gale wasn't with them.

"She's coming," Dan told her. "She's just in the ... she's just down the hall."

"Go ahead," Helen said. "You know the room. I'll wait for her."

Gale came out of the bathroom in her school duffle coat with the hood back. She had shaved her hair into a one-inch brush like a maid-warrior, like Joan of Arc. She gave Helen an ironic look and walked past her.

"Didja miss me?"

Helen followed her down the hall, her stomach cinched. In the room, Gale bypassed her usual chair, as though erasing any history there. She chose a place where Helen had to turn to look at her. Helen thought, *We're starting over.*

She composed herself. It wasn't just the hair. Gale's face looked throttled, her eyes glassy and fixed. Was she stoned at eight o'clock in the morning?

Sandy took a breath, but Helen intercepted, addressing Gale. "I'm glad you came, Gale. Sandy phoned, but we didn't go into any detail. Can you fill me in?"

Gale jerked her chin at Sandy. "Ask her. She's the one who called the meeting."

"I mean as far as you're concerned," Helen said.

Gale averted her head, stonewalling.

"She's cutting," Sandy said. "I found blood on her sheets and bloody socks balled up in her closet. It has to be her feet, but she won't show me."

"Don't go into my room, okay," Gale tossed out. Sandy ignored her.

"What's going on, Dan?" Helen asked.

Dan looked uneasily at Sandy who shook her head, leaving it to him. "It was a rough summer," he said slowly. "Things didn't go well down south. Gale's mother was back at Neil's. She ... Mindy ... wouldn't let Gale see her sister." He glanced at Gale. "It was pretty hard on her." He stopped, pushed his fingers through his hair. "Since she came back she's doing things I never thought she'd do. Skipping school ... this."

"The cutting," Helen clarified. He nodded. "Are you worried she'll take it further?"

He winced. "I don't know what she could do. That's why we're here."

Sandy spoke with asperity. "Gale is hiding a lot from us. The school's been calling about her absences. We drive her every day, so we assume she walks in one door and out the other. I have no idea where she goes. There are a couple of girls she's made friends with, if you can call them friends. I know their fathers. One of them is on my caseload, the other should be. When we confront her, she ignores us. She doesn't even bother to lie. Grounding her does nothing. She stays in her room, doesn't eat. As soon as she's off her grounding, it starts up again." Sandy took a breath.

"She doesn't give a damn what we do. I've searched her room. That's how I found the socks, the bloody sheets. I think she's high-risk."

"For what?"

Sandy looked at her as if she were hard of hearing. Helen was the counsellor, for Christ's sake. "Suicide. Running. She could do anything," Sandy said irritably. "I want a psychiatrist to see her."

The churning in Gale's face had stopped. She looked barely present.

"Can you join this conversation, Gale?" Helen said. "What's going on?"

Gale ignored her. Helen made a decision. "Give me a few minutes alone with Gale, will you?" she said.

Sandy and Dan got up as if they were relieved and left without a word.

As soon as they were gone, Helen leaned in. "My girl. This is terrible. What *happened* this summer?"

Helen's tone of voice caught Gale off guard. She'd expected Helen to be stern. She stared at her, and it was as if she suddenly recognized her, remembered the drab safety of the office. She let out a gasp. "I saw Buddie twice, *twice* the whole summer. My mother was home and Neil was useless. He acted like he can't even *think*." Helen saw her guard collapse; she began to cry. She swiped her cheeks with her hands. "Something's going on. I know there is. Buddie isn't phoning anymore and when I call there, every time I get Mindy and she hangs up on me." Gale began to pant.

Helen said, "Can I come over there?"

Gale dropped her head, lifted her arms straight up. Helen went to sit next to her, drew Gale to her awkwardly over the

arms of the chair. As soon as she had her, relief swept over
her, as if she'd caught the girl just about to go over a waterfall.
Gale sobbed into Helen's collarbone. Helen filled in the words.
"Gale, Gale, my poor girl. So looking forward to going home and
seeing Buddie. So worried for her with your mother there."

Gale shoved into Helen's neck and moaned. "What can I do?
I can't do anything."

She started to wail, grief and dismay rolling over the wall, a
levy bursting. Sound streamed out of her, wrenching her whole
body. Helen was stunned by the force of it, this buried girl crying
from her core. The sound was so pure and unrestrained Helen's
own eyes filled. She held Gale, gave herself up to it.

The waves went on and on, rasping, aching inhalations,
sirening exhalations. The noise was numbing. Helen wondered
how her colleagues were making out beyond the door. She willed
whoever was out there to cope and not disturb them. She thought
balefully about the way the room was set up. There ought to be
bolsters and cushions, thick rugs on the floor, room to thrash.
Instead, it looked like the office in a credit union.

Little by little Gale wore out and started working her way
back, the howls collapsing into sobs and gradually spacing out.
Her head was still dead weight on Helen's collarbone. Finally
she shoved herself up, sat slumped and dazed in her chair. She
groped in the pocket of her duffle for a Kleenex, found only her
beret and swabbed it over her face.

"Hoo boy," she said.

Helen kept her hand on Gale's back. Gale stared into space,
breathing. She looked like she was doing her lung-watching
exercise.

"The thing is," she said, "I have to be with Buddie."

163

Her eyes filled again and she shook her head. Helen gently patted her. If only she could stay like this, she thought, with her hand on Gale, she might ward off whatever harm Gale was headed for.

HELEN ASKED GALE to show her feet. She wanted this intimacy. If she could draw Gale to her, wouldn't that make it harder for Gale to harm herself?

Gale had cried from so deep, she offered no resistance. She cocked her ankle across her knee and pulled off her sock. Helen knelt in front of her and examined her foot.

There was an old cut over the anklebone where a big vein passed into her calf. It looked healed. There was dried blood on the gauze Gale had taped to the sole of her foot and Helen moved the gauze aside. The cuts were puffed and vivid but not infected.

"It must hurt to walk," Helen said. "What are you using to cut yourself?"

"My compass point. From my geometry set."

"What are you thinking when you cut?"

"Nothing — I'm not trying to kill myself. I just do it ... when I have to."

"To stop feeling terrible?"

"Yeah. It's like a relief."

The room was very quiet. Helen tapped the bandages on the right foot lightly. "Can I see this one?"

Gale's right foot had no ankle cuts. The sole was bandaged the same way as the left. One cut was a deep and shiny red. The incisions were methodical, painful. It was clear why Gale chose her feet. She could give herself a jolt of pain whenever she liked, without anyone knowing.

Helen passed her hand over the stubble of Gale's hair, replaced the sock and stood up. She dragged a chair over to face her. "It's chancy what you're doing, Gale. I don't know what they're making compasses out of these days, but there's a risk of a blood infection, or lockjaw. You could land in hospital very sick, a bunch of strangers knowing what you've been doing."

"I don't care about that."

Helen laid her fingers on Gale's knees, trying to leave prints on her, put the memory of care into her for later when Gale was alone.

21

GALE REFUSED to talk to Sandy and her father, but Helen was obliged to. They had been waiting all that time, listening to Gale howl. She left Gale and went looking for Rita, who was in her cubby, stabbing a pencil through her hair while she talked on the phone. Rita lifted an eyebrow.

"What's that all over your sweater?"

"Can you watch Gale for half an hour? I need to talk to her parents, and I can't get her to sit with us. I don't want to leave her by herself."

Rita shook her head. "I've got Mary Levy waiting for me. Oh, hang on; Mary brought Savannah with her. Is Gale up to entertaining an eight-year-old? We could set them up together in the playroom. Judy can keep an eye out through the glass."

Helen thought of Buddie. "That should work."

Gale followed Rita to the playroom like a sleepwalker. Savannah, clad in a bright yellow raincoat, was already engrossed in dressing a battered baby doll. She promptly incorporated Gale into her play.

Helen found Dan and Sandy in reception looking unnerved. In the interview room, they took their seats apprehensively. Helen felt scattered. Somehow she had to guide Dan and Sandy down the course she and Gale had just navigated and land them in the same place. She had only the frailest hold on Gale. Now she had to turn her over to Dan and Sandy, who had an even looser grip on her. She hadn't dared bargain with Gale not to cut herself because, if she *did* cut, she might quit Helen rather than face breaking her word.

"That must have been a tough wait," she said.

Sandy blew out her breath. "Are you going to arrange a psychiatric consult?"

Helen nodded. "If you like. We can talk to the psychiatric team in Vancouver by video link. What are you hoping to get from them?"

Sandy looked at Helen as if she were an idiot. "I want to know if she's suicidal, if she needs to be in a hospital. This is serious, by the way."

Helen sighed. Parents always wanted to haul in the docs, and doctors didn't know everything. Gale wouldn't even get a face-to-face interview. She'd talk to a head in a monitor, a consultant in a big city who probably didn't even work with adolescents. Most psychiatrists avoided them; too much behaviour, the diagnoses too unreliable. Gale probably wouldn't object to the video link, she was a kid, but how useful was the information?

"Hear me out, will you," she said. "You want Gale safe and you think a psychiatric consult will do it, but in my experience, we'll go through a process and the ball will land right back with us."

"But they can assess risk," Sandy objected.

"So can you. What's your opinion? You live with her."

"Oh no you don't," Sandy said. "I'm not an expert."

"Is an assessment what we need?" Helen persisted. "We already know the trouble. Gale feels stranded up here. She's her sister's protector and she isn't there to do it. In the deepest sense, she's out of place." Sandy began to protest but Helen kept going. "She has the two of you but, frankly, you got her too late to have much impact. If Gale wants to cut herself or skip school, what can you really do? Getting a label for what's wrong, even a stint in hospital, won't stop her."

That was not what Sandy and Dan wanted to hear.

"So what are we supposed to do?" Sandy said. "Sit on our hands?"

"Win her over," Helen said. "Change her mind about harming herself."

Sandy and Dan looked doubtful.

"Say you take her to the hospital," Helen said. "I assume that's what you have in mind. They might admit her, I don't know. They'll probably think she's a risk, but at the moment it's more mutilation than suicide. They might send her home, tell you to seek counselling. Or ... say they do admit her. Then she's safe for a couple of days, but, as you know, they have no psych unit over there. The minute Gale convinces them she's not actively suicidal, they're bound to release her. So she comes home and where are the three of you? Is she grateful you took charge, or have you lost even more ground because you forced her?"

"A few days in hospital would give her time to think," Sandy said.

Helen doubted it. No one she knew had ever had an epiphany in a hospital. "It's tempting to hope," she said.

They sat without talking. Helen looked past them out the window. She was tired. She'd like to go home and hang out with Chief Joseph. It was a good day to have a look at the river. A heavy tremor ran through the floor from the gym below, a muffled *Shit*.

She sighed. "Here's my bias. I think, in this crisis, you don't go the hospital or the video link route unless Gale wants it. You don't force anything. Instead, you concentrate on building the relationship. You give Gale a lot of care and respect. They track this stuff you know: the people who fund counselling agencies want to know if counselling works, or what works. They call people up months later and ask what helped. Some people say they were glad to get a diagnosis. They find it a relief to know they have an attention disorder or whatever. But mainly what people remember about therapy is whether the counsellor appeared to be listening. Whether she cared."

"The relationship, you mean," Sandy said.

"Yes. That's what people respond to." Helen turned her hands up, supplicating. "If in the end what gets Gale through is who cares about her, aren't we back to the two of you? You've known her a long time. You know all the people who matter to her, everything important that's happened to her. Don't you think that carries weight? Whitehorse may never be home, maybe it's too late for that, but if being here with you was an okay time, wouldn't that count?"

"She'll drive a truck over us," Sandy said glumly.

"Parents always worry they'll lose if they don't take charge," Helen said. "You don't have to give up anything. Just don't pull rank. Assume she's reasonable. Keep asking the next question. If Gale has a dumb idea, it'll topple by itself in the course of discussion."

Sandy drew a long breath, fixed her gaze on Helen. "I don't know what I'm doing here again. We've been through this before you know. I don't know if you remember; you haven't mentioned it. I brought my daughter Edie, years ago. You said at the time to stop acting like a cop. I had no idea what you were talking about. I still don't."

Helen was thinking about Gale and ignored her. "Okay, but can we do one thing? Number one for Gale is whether Buddie is safe. Can we check that out?"

WHEN HELEN BROUGHT GALE back into the room, Dan kept his eyes on the floor and Sandy hawk-eyed Gale, checking for storm damage. It occurred to Helen, Sandy was the one to bet on.

She ignored the chance to invite Gale to bring Sandy and Dan up to speed, and asked, "How can we find out how Buddie is doing?"

Sandy answered readily, "I can phone Neil. If Mindy answers, I'll let it go and call Neil's folks. They'll know."

Helen noticed Gale's shoulders drop a quarter of an inch.

"And where are we on the psychiatric referral?"

"No!" Gale burst out. "No shrinks, no hospitals."

Dan and Sandy looked chagrined.

"Gale, you scared the pants off your dad and Sandy," Helen said. "They need some reassurance."

Gale considered. "I'll come to counselling."

When she made no other concessions, Sandy pressed: "And will you go to school? And the cutting. I have to know that'll stop."

Gale didn't respond.

Out of left field, Dan cleared his throat. "What about Adult Ed, as far as school goes," he offered. "It's how I finished when I couldn't take it at high school anymore. They've got a storefront on 2nd Ave. I've seen them standing outside at breaks." He shrugged. Helen prayed he wouldn't take it back. He glanced at Gale. "Maybe you could get your credits there."

Gale looked intrigued. She had seen them too, half a dozen misfits standing on the sidewalk smoking. Anything was better than high school.

"I'll check it out at the guidance office," she said.

WHEN THEY HAD GONE, Helen donned her windbreaker and went out. She had an hour before her next appointment. It wasn't food she was after, it was weather. There was a storm on the way.

Everybody in the office had antidotes. After a tough session, Rita headed straight for the supply of Swiss chocolate she kept in her desk. For Helen, it was weather.

She walked along 4th Street past the handsome Tourism and Culture Centre with its sign on the front door: *Please, no overnight camping in the parking lot.* In the park, where the river curved past, the grass was yellow and spent, the picnic tables already stacked for the winter. There was nowhere to sit, so Helen hunched on the curb and watched the sky tear by.

It had been a long session. She couldn't gauge how it had gone.

Something she'd learned over the years: knowing what helped wasn't possible. What made a difference to people, what sense they made of a conversation in the therapy room was so personal, so unaccountable, that "being helpful" was best abandoned as a goal. Helen had trained herself to this thinking. The therapist's job, her only job, was to cause a disturbance, to open the log-jam that had brought people to her in the first place. After that, she must let them get on with things.

There was an elegance to this Helen liked.

It was the point of view of one of her teachers, an American psychiatrist with a reputation for groundbreaking work with psychotic families. Helen recalled during one of his lectures somebody asking how he knew he was helping his patients. He said he never thought about it; he wasn't doing it for them.

He was being provocative. This man would stick with people for years, follow them into any kind of hell. He was giving his students a tip. He was saying, fixers don't last. People won't oblige you by getting well. They will, or they won't. If you're in it for the outcome, you better find another line of work. He told them something else; Helen thought of it now. Every session stands alone. Every meeting may be your only chance; your people might not come back. In that case, give it all you've got. Be audacious.

Then go home.

In this light, how had she done with the Connellys?

She and Gale were back in business, she felt sure. She saw the two of them in her mind's eye, swimmers bobbing along, side by side in the fast current.

She was less sure about Sandy and Dan. Could they draw Gale in? Did they want to? Dan had barely looked at Gale when they all got back together, even when he had the brainwave about Adult Ed. There was a way he ducked Gale, afraid to see the mother in the daughter. Mindy's tire marks were still all over him.

Sandy seemed more up for it. She wasn't afraid of Gale. She had that lost daughter to make up for. It had taken Helen a while to twig to the previous round of counselling when Sandy brought her own daughter. Helen remembered now how it had played. Sandy had been intransigent, had tried to strong-arm the long-ago daughter into obeying her. You can't do that with adolescents. Even if they're bonded to you, you have to negotiate. Sandy had no authority with her girl, and none with Gale now.

For Gale, all the heavy hitters were back in Cobalt.

Had Helen given it her all, as her mentor advised? Had she caused a disturbance in how the Connellys behaved?

She had spooled a nice idea to Dan and Sandy about the relationship being the thing that counted. Truly, she believed Dan and Sandy were Gale's best shot. The trouble was, even as she'd been appealing to them, her words sounded make-believe to her ear. She was fooling them; she didn't believe they were up to it. There were too many drawbacks: Dan's fear of engaging with Gale, Sandy's lack of finesse, Gale's intransigence about being in Whitehorse at all. Helen's words to Sandy and Dan had been in the theoretical realm, without bearing on the actual people in the room. Interviews like that had a whiff of hokum.

Helen sat on the curb, the sky galloping by. Miniature tornados spun grit off the pavement. The light had the sallowness of coming snow.

Something else occurred to her: she hadn't booked a future session. Gale would come, but Helen hadn't prevailed on Dan and Sandy to set a date as well. She'd let them get away.

22

PREDICTABLY, Helen's efforts to help Keith Balboa were getting nowhere. When she finally reached Stan McNair, the school superintendent, he blandly suggested Keith move to Prince George, to one of the newly legislated programmes for expelled under-sixteen-year-olds.

"Or send him to Alberta," Stan said. "He's from there, isn't he? I hear they've just opened a shop in Edmonton. Send him back."

Helen had known Stan for years. In a place the size of White-horse, everyone knew everyone, and rank counted for nothing. The public sector was a flat hierarchy based on mutual bullying. She sighed. "That won't work, Stan. The boy has to stay here. Think of something else."

"Well, I don't know. He's a head case, isn't he? Six months in Chedoke? I heard he flipped a desk over when Charlie expelled him. Shouldn't he be in a facility?"

"Two-year wait-lists. Keith will be in jail by then."

"What about home tutoring?"

"How many hours would he get?"

Stan considered. "Four a week."

"C'mon Stan," Helen said. "He's fifteen years old. He's still ours. We have to come up with something."

Stan moved to his standard pre-emption: he told Helen to write a letter to the Ministry of Education, c.c. Probation, and Children's Mental Health. "Maybe one of them can think of something."

Helen tried her last-ditch idea. "Stan, what about this? What if Thom and Phil at Adult Ed take him? He's underage but if he keeps coming to me every week, and his PO ups his hours, if we have all the safeguards, would you back it?"

"Jesus, Helen, he's *expelled*," Stan said. "He's got a violence problem. What are Thom and Phil going to do with him?"

"They have a different set-up. Non-confrontational," Helen said. "You read my letter. This kid has really predictable triggers: crowds and aggressive men. It's a small group at Adult Ed, and Thom and Phil are like everybody's grannie. Keith has a chance there."

Stan didn't answer.

"Stan, we have to. We used the Safe Schools Act to expel him when the Act isn't even operational. There's no net to catch him. We can't do that."

Stan sighed. "Write a letter, Helen. Make your case."

Negotiations dragged on into November. Keith languished in

the apartment, coming to his appointments faithfully, his resilience seeping away before Helen's eyes. He continued to dress carefully, but the bones in his face showed, the baby fat had ebbed away. He looked older, unhealthy. In the basement where they lived, Keith and his mother's boyfriend gnawed on each other. Audette thought Keith should be grateful to Norman for the income he brought in, but Keith didn't see any of it. He told Helen the fridge was always empty, Norman treated him like dirt, didn't give him a cent. Nothing for Audette either, come to that. Keith thought his mother was soft in the head to put up with it.

"She's strong but weak, if you know what I mean," he said. "As far as picking men, that's her dim spot, man. She has the worst taste I've ever seen."

When he wasn't decrying his life, Keith and Helen investigated the various characters residing in him. Helen never got the impression Keith had a thought disorder, or that he was dissociating into one or another of his personalities. It seemed to her he constructed these characters as a way to understand himself, and feel more interesting than he generally felt. His personalities and his affection for them gave them a colourful way to work together. They drew on his characters like actors in a play, calling on them to step up and move the plot along. But this was makeshift and Helen knew it. Without a real stage outside Keith's imagination, the interesting players were just television.

He was so fluent Helen could enter his thinking, catch how his experience worked on him. Little by little, she constructed his psychological life, a boy growing up outside his father's care. His father only claimed the older brother.

In this he reminded Helen of Gale. No good-enough adult ever chose either of them. No one said, *I pick you.*

THE LETTERS HELEN WROTE trying to get Keith out of his basement circulated sluggishly. One day she walked the three blocks over to the Adult Education Centre. It was mid-November, dusk by three o'clock. The hills around town were full of snow, the streets cold and bony, waiting for cover.

Adult Ed was housed in a dingy storefront crammed with Herculean metal desks from another era, a loo in back, and a closet-sized coffee room. Helen was looking for Phil or Thom, one or the other of two rumpled instructors who presided over the programme with an enervated tolerance. They'd been running it for years, their own little dome of sanity in a heartless world. Anyone over the age of sixteen who wanted to pick up high-school credits and didn't scare people could enrol.

When Helen let herself in, the place smelled of pencils from the days when it was an office supply store. As she'd hoped, Phil Lewin was still there, sitting in back on an old sofa, working up the energy to go home. He wagged some fingers at Helen when she tapped on his doorframe.

"Hey Hélène, how's it going?"

She liked it when people used her proper name. She moved a pile of grimy science magazines off a chair and sat down, stretched her legs. Phil had on his usual gold acrylic sweater and baggy corduroys. His hair was a grizzled brush cut, steel-frame glasses heavy on his nose, cheeks corrugated by acne scars. His big shoulders folded over a hollow chest. The "masochist's stoop," Rita called it.

Phil played a great saxophone.

On a scarred table were the remains of a package of store-bought cookies and a pot of ink-coloured tea. Phil got up and poured decorously as if the tea were fresh and piping. Helen added a cube of sugar, which she found intact at the bottom of her mug when she was finished. They chatted one-sidedly about music, a subject that never failed to animate Phil. Helen told him her troubles with Keith, and without much pondering, Phil said, "Try him here. Off the record. If it works, we'll do the paperwork."

Twenty minutes later, Helen was back on the street, Keith set to come in Friday. Helen figured they were like any business that way — the margins were still where the deals went down.

CONFIDENTIALITY prevented Helen from saying to either Keith or Gale, "There's an interesting person you're going to meet at school." Social work was stern in this regard, and Helen abided by the rules. Counselling was such a mug's game, she was glad for a few guidelines. It was Keith who made the link.

He came in after his third day at Adult Ed, antic with relief to have somewhere to go during the day. He prowled the room, bouncing on his toes, cracking his knuckles. His agitation was so infectious, Helen had to stand up too and lean against the wall.

Keith showed his tiny teeth, jabbed a finger at her. "I know someone who *knows* you, man," he said. "I forget her name. She comes here. Small girl, kind of butch."

Helen wondered what sort of mix Keith and Gale would be. She doubted they'd be attracted to each other. They were the same age, but Keith was too extroverted, too showy to appeal to Gale. Which brought her to who Keith might be attracted to now that he was at large. When he had blown off steam awhile, she waded in. "Keith, can we talk about the wide, wide world of sex?" He stopped prowling and lifted his eyebrows. "You're out of the apartment now, starting to circulate. I was wondering, are girls ... your cup of tea?"

She had never gotten the knack of asking kids about sex. Rita could do it; she came across interested but neutral. It was the centre of the known universe for kids Keith's age; Helen had no choice but to cover the ground, but it never came easily.

Questions about abuse were in a different realm. Querying sexual abuse was like asking if you happened to be in the path of the headless horseman when he rode through.

Keith blinked, deciphering for a minute before he caught Helen's drift. "Definitely," he said, the vertical crease in his brow digging in. "More the short term than the long. Girls like me, you know, but they're funny. They put weight on me. They want to know when am I coming over, what am I doing. Which is not my thing. I tell them, I'm here for a good time, not a long time."

"Really? You declare yourself like that?"

"It's the truth, man. I have to speak it. They say, 'Oh, that's cool, me too,' but they don't mean it." Keith pulled his toque over his ears, grinned his worried grin. "Every femme wants to be the one who cracks the nut."

"Are you saying you haven't gone with any one girl? There hasn't been anybody special?"

"Yeah. That looks to me like a major project. If I had a more regular life, maybe. Mostly the last two years I've been in custody. Or charges pending. It takes a toll."

"So, are you a virgin then?"

Keith squinted as if the air were full of smoke.

"There's a word I haven't heard in a while."

23

WEEKDAYS, through the failing daylight while the sun made its wan journey over the airstrip above town, Gale took a ride downtown with her father to Adult Ed. The guidance office had taken one look at her absentee rate since September and signed the transfer.

It was a thousand times better than high school. The two fellows who ran it were so relaxed, they were practically asleep. No hassle whatsoever. The other dropouts besides Gale were mostly adults in various stages of caving in, but there were one or two Gale's age. Notably a hefty eighteen-year-old named Linda, who wore studded leather armbands and looping dog chains. After a couple of weeks of ignoring Gale, Linda in an offhand way began bumming smokes from her at break.

In her after-school meetings with Helen, Gale wore jeans and sweatshirts, liberated now from her school uniform. Nothing at home had changed, she reported. "For a few days after that time here, we went around like we didn't know what to do, nobody saying anything. Now it's back to normal."

"Which is?"

Gale shrugged. "Dad bitching about how much his Explorer costs him, Sandy out every night with the dogs at obedience school."

"You sound kind of let down."

"No I don't."

To herself, Gale had to admit it wasn't quite true nothing had changed. She'd say things were more real. Now that Dan and Sandy knew about her cutting, a wall was down, some bit of fakery had ended. Gale told Helen her hermit-browner act was over.

"What's your disguise now?" Helen asked.

"I'm between disguises," Gale said dryly. "Lying low."

"And the cutting?"

"Giving it a rest."

Gale was full of anecdotes about school and Linda, who she hung out with sometimes. Sandy and Dan had relaxed on that front now that Gale was attending school regularly and — to their knowledge — not cutting. Helen was gratified. Maybe they'd heard what Helen said about building their ties.

"What do you and Linda talk about?" she asked.

Gale looked evasive, as she did with most questions. "We don't talk that much. Mostly who she decked on the weekend."

The excursions into memory were a thing of the past. Since her return from her awful summer, Gale had put a "Do not disturb" sign on the door. "Nothing comes up," she told Helen when asked. The subject of her mother was out of bounds as well.

"What's the point," Gale said coldly. "You don't know her. She's not here. You couldn't change her if she were."

"Gale, I'm not talking about *her*," Helen said. "I'm talking about *you*. You can change how she affects you."

Gale regarded her. "Why would I?"

As far as Gale was concerned, the good thing about these meetings was that Helen *didn't* know her mother, had never seen her, and never would. The office, along with Helen's cluelessness, formed a kind of safety zone. Gale could be a normal kid for an hour, shoot the breeze about school, whatever.

Helen was tempted to ask Gale why she bothered coming, since they didn't talk about anything of import, but she didn't risk it.

She picked up that Gale had withdrawn. The question was why? After the meltdown in her office, she had expected Gale's trust to rise, but if anything, it was the reverse.

Maybe that was okay. Gale was changing; she had peers now, she was more at home in the new school. And, while more evasive with Helen, she also seemed more at ease with her. Or maybe she just didn't care as much. Helen noted Gale took less care with her words, used terms Helen would not use — disapproved of, actually — calling Linda's friends "chicks" or "hos," taking a derisive tone.

GALE SETTLED ON HER LOOK. She kept her hair in a brush, mashed, usually, on the side she slept on, and she abandoned head-to-toe black, went more industrial. Cargo pants dragging off her hips, army boots — not the yuppie ones, the real Army surplus item, twelve bucks — with a boiled wool turtleneck, Coast Guard issue. For winter, she found a torn sheepskin jacket, vintage sixties Greenwich Village, made in China.

"I think I'll go for a tat next," she told Helen.

"What?"

"A tattoo. Might as well."

Her conformity to the tribe was so innocent, so long overdue, Helen took it for granted Dan and Sandy were taking it in stride. She didn't know for sure because they didn't call her. Neither Sandy nor Dan had been in touch since the meeting when Gale was cutting. Nor had Helen pursued them, for whatever motive.

The drawback was, Dan and Sandy's distance isolated Gale. To her list of resentments Gale added that they didn't come to counselling. "Don't get me wrong," she said, slumped in her chair. "It's okay coming here. But am I the only one with a problem?"

She told Helen she had started stepping out at night. Dan and Sandy turned in after the ten o'clock news, at which point Gale adjusted the volume on her television, slid out of her room, and left by the side door through the garage. She went across town to Linda's.

"How do you get there?" Helen asked with alarm. "It's at least five kilometres."

"My bike. It's a nice coast downtown. Wicked climb on the way back, but that's cool."

Gale's route included the famous Two Mile Hill at the north end of town. Helen pictured her labouring up the grade in the freezing dark. "Gale, crikey," she said. "You ride your bike up that hill in the middle of the night? Impaired drivers heading home?"

"My bike's got reflectors."

"Yeah, but on your person?"

"Oh certainly," Gale said, amused. "I wear one of those orange bibs with the X's like the guys in sewers."

"What are you and Linda doing on these late-night forays?"

Gale frowned. Something in Helen's tone she didn't care for.

"Okay, but what?" Helen persisted.

Gale shrugged. "Different stuff. Pit parties. We get a bonfire going. Couple of weeks ago we cut up shopping carts to make barbecue grills. Except all we had was bologna." She added breezily, "Plenty of Smirnoff and Sprite though."

"You're into alcohol now?"

"I'm getting a taste for it. It beats puking on Percocets. Or giving up my underwear on ecstasy." Gale narrowed her eyes. "These meetings are private, right? You aren't allowed to pass on what I say?"

Helen said sternly, "Unless you scare the hell out of me. Which you're starting to."

These friends Gale referred to were mainly Linda's crowd, Helen found out. Linda was a Whitehorse girl, with the same friends since grade school. Most of them didn't go to school; they were out on their own in shaky arrangements that constantly broke down. Linda was one of the better off ones, living with her employed mother in a house with a furnace and taps that worked. Gale described a house a relative of Linda's mother used to rent out, until it got trashed. Now it was empty, waiting for repairs. A bunch of them went there to smoke dope, be out of sight.

"How do you get along with Linda's friends?"

Gale gave her usual shrug. "They're alright, a couple of them. There's one real pill, Destiny, who gets on my nerves. *Major* sucking up to Linda."

"Is Linda the star?"

"I guess. Don't ask me why. She isn't cute. She's Indian. She's got arms like tires. Destiny hangs off her like a little charm. She's *always* around." Gale pulled her knees up on the chair and hugged them.

"Linda likes Destiny more than you?"

Gale rolled her head. "I have no idea. She said on the phone last weekend her mother had some stuff for her to do, she had to stay in. I thought I'd go over and help out, but Linda told me her mom said no visitors. After Sandy and Dad crashed, I went downtown anyway. Saturday night, right? Nobody was on the corner so I ended up riding over to Linda's. When I got there, I heard music thumping, lights on upstairs. I knocked and Linda sticks her head out the window and Destiny is right there beside her. I asked Linda what's up. She said her mom went out after all." Gale ran her thumb over what was left of her fingertips. "They didn't ask me in so I split."

"Gale, don't do that."

Gale frowned. "What?"

"Don't lay yourself out for people like that." Gale sharpened her eyes at Helen. "Sorry. I just don't like the picture of you standing out there."

"You're starting to act weird, Helen," Gale said. "Don't tell me what to do, okay."

A silence followed, which Gale finally broke. "Keith says hi."

"Oh yeah," Helen said, relieved. "What do you think of him?"

"He's different, different from me, anyway. Sucks up to everybody, bops around, jabs his fingers like a rapper."

"Do you two hang out?"

"Not really. He doesn't go with Linda's crowd. Us chicks don't mind him, but the guys shut him out completely. Sometimes me and him go up to the dam after school, till I have to meet my dad. He's had a pretty crappy life — same as me." She chewed her cuticles. "I'm thinking of moving out."

This was not news. So far, when Gale mused about moving out, Helen let it go, assuming the threat would pass. This time she said, "I guess I don't follow you, Gale. You've had more gripes about Sandy and your dad lately — I noticed that — but in other ways things have picked up, haven't they? You've got a new look and an adventurous social life. You're fine at school." She paused. "Are you cutting?"

"No."

"Would it be okay if I looked?"

"Do you think I'd lie to you?"

"If you had to."

Gale sighed and pulled off her socks, flexed her feet towards Helen. There were fine white lines on her soles and over her ankle bones. No fresh cuts. Helen sat back. "Why now, Gale? Why make a move now? You're safe where you are. What's so bad about Sandy and your dad?"

Gale was pulling her socks back on and snorted. "Try living with them."

"Sure, but you could talk to them. Maybe they don't know what's up with you."

"We tried talking, remember," Gale said.

"We *met*. That's not the same as talking."

Gale shook her head.

"You can't think of anything to do but leave?"

"Not right at the moment."

"Where would you go?"

"Any ideas?"

"Oh no you don't. I'm not your accomplice. I think moving out is a lousy idea."

"I don't know then. Maybe Linda's. I wouldn't be the first to crash there." Gale cocked her head. "I heard you can go on welfare if you're sixteen and stay in school. I'm sixteen in February."

Helen would rather Gale didn't know about this provision. If Gale moved out, her tie with Sandy and her dad was so fragile, she'd probably cut them loose altogether. She'd be high and dry, nobody knowing whether she was getting enough sleep, enough to eat . . . anything at all. "There's money for students who can't live at home," Helen said reluctantly. "You need a letter from a social worker stating there is irreconcilable conflict at home. You also need a trustee, a credible adult who vouches for you. And you have to attend school every day, no skips. There are serious hoops, Gale, and the allowance is paltry. It'd be Kraft Dinner every night."

Irrelevant to Gale.

"What's going on at home?" Helen said. "What's bugging you?"

"*Them*," Gale burst out. "They bug me. They're so fricking dead." Gale wrung her sleeves, squirmed in her clothes. "It's like they're scared of me, like the next thing I do is going to be *dire* and they better watch out. Especially Sandy." She shook her head, vehement. "No way they want me there." She took a breath. "I'm just biding my time. Waiting to fly."

"To Cobalt."

"Yeah. That's where I belong. That house, Buddie, that's my spot.

Helen sighed. "Okay, Gale. You worry about your sister. But think it through. What are you going to do once you get there and you're assured Buddie is okay? Isn't home just another bad scene, like here only worse? Watching out for your mother. Wouldn't you just be trading one bad deal for another?"

Gale didn't respond. Helen leaned in. "Listen. The girl with the vicious mother, the girl stuck in Whitehorse, they're temporary. They're scenes that aren't going to last. You're almost sixteen. You can start putting together your own plan very soon. Why not bide your time in a place where you're okay while you figure out what you want, what your real gig is."

Eventually Gale said, "Those are just words, man." She sounded like Keith.

Helen straightened. "Ideas, actually. Ideas run everything." She tapped her head. "You could get an idea who you are from something else, nothing to do with the vicious mother or the girl stuck in Whitehorse. Those are just situations you found yourself in when it was someone else's call."

If Gale couldn't see a future for herself in Whitehorse, she would leave. She would take any kind of risk and clear out. Helen knew that much. She lowered her voice. "Isn't it possible you are not just your mother's daughter in one hell, or your father's daughter in a different hell? Isn't it possible you're someone else?"

Gale breathed. "Who?"

"You tell me."

Gale's eyes shimmered. For a second something caught her mind. Then a cloud rolled in. "Sure."

THE NEXT WEEK, Gale didn't come to her appointment. She didn't phone; she just didn't come. Helen called her house and got the machine. She left a message, *Did we mix up our dates?* A week passed and still she didn't hear. She was uneasy about it.

Something had come undone. She waited until the weekend and called Gale from her phone at home. Gale picked up, mumbled recognition.

"Did you get my message? We missed an appointment last week. How are you?"

"Alright."

"Do you want to set another date?"

"I don't know." Gale's voice was dull.

"What's up, Gale?"

"Mmm . . . they don't want me to come to see you anymore."

"How come?" Gale didn't answer. "What did they say was their reason?"

"It came up about me moving out," Gale said. "I mentioned about the letter you were going to write, about how we don't get along, and they freaked."

Helen was stunned. "Gale, we talked about this, remember? I didn't tell you I'd write a letter. I'm *against* you moving out. You can't have missed that."

No response from Gale. Helen groped for a reason Gale would misrepresent her to Sandy and Dan. "Did you think you'd have a better case if they thought I was backing you?"

Gale sniffed.

Helen was at a loss. "Gale, why are you going along with this? Why didn't you take it back when it backfired? They *can't* see me as the enemy. This has to be fixed." She stopped to think. "What if I call them, explain you misunderstood me. What you did isn't so terrible. It shows things have to change is all."

"No," Gale said, and Helen understood from her tone she would not bring Sandy and Dan in. More than that, she was going to do a bolt for Cobalt. Helen had another insight. "You know, at your age you're free to come to counselling with or without your parents' consent. Since you didn't show up, can I take it that's your choice? Is it you who wants to stop?"

Gale took a long time to reply. "They're really mad."

As if that would matter to Gale. When had she cared a fig what Sandy and her father thought? Helen couldn't go to Dan and Sandy and tell them Gale lied to them, not without Gale's permission. Deliberately or not, Gale had cut her loose.

Helen looked at the thin wire running out of her house along the miles to the phone line in Gale's house. She and Gale sat silently, as they had sat silently so many times in Helen's office. Helen didn't see a way to save this.

"We've worked together a long time, Gale," she said at last. "I'd be sorry to break it off without saying goodbye. It would be good to tally up the gains you've made, where you want to go from here, to have a proper goodbye. Can you manage that?"

"Yeah, I guess."

They went through the motions of setting a date. Helen mustered every positive remark she could think of in case she never saw Gale again.

On the day of the appointment, Gale didn't show.

WHEN HELEN was in trouble in the years after Jo died, she had a recurring dream. It went on for months, the details gradually filling in, the dream gaining features but never coming sharp. It enveloped her without revealing itself. Eventually she stopped having the dream.

In it, Helen is blind, or lacks sight, though she has her other senses. She feels her skin, her limbs moving, rhythmic and effortful, weighed down by what might be heavy clothing. She feels the surface of wherever she is walking, flat as a road, crusty, slightly yielding. There is damp cold on her face, like falling snow or ice fog. For a long time, this is all the dream is, the sensation of moving and breathing in black cold.

Little by little, her sight improves. Daybreak is coming, or the fog is receding. She apprehends that she's walking on a frozen lake, a dense rise of trees passing slowly on either side, black on black, hills converging far ahead of her. She is heading towards the point where all the lines converge.

One of the last times she had the dream, she realizes she isn't alone. She has a companion. She feels the air stirring around her head, the beat of wings, opening and closing, powerful and close. She divines that it is a night bird, an owl or a raptor of some kind, flying down-lake with her. Its presence is neither menacing nor guiding; a bird of prey, a companion without sympathy.

24

THE EMPTY HOUSE Linda's gang used was on a street of woebegone bungalows, the neighbours mostly renters who didn't care who came and went. The kids sneaked in to perform any number of forbidden acts. None of the renters stuck around long. The hydro and water were turned off. It was crude shelter, especially in winter.

A Saturday afternoon in December, Keith and Gale went around back to the dilapidated porch. Gale jiggled aside a loose pane of glass in the door and wound her arm in to release the lock. Inside was stone cold and stank of kerosene. Heading for the front of the house, they passed a room and noted two mounds, faintly wheezing in a tangle of sleeping bags on the floor.

Otherwise, they had the place to themselves. They settled down in the grey light of a smeared window. A low sky hovered over the yard, threatening snow. Keith lit a joint and worked it to the corner of his mouth so his hands were free. He drew a deck of cards out of an inside pocket, kept his gloves on to shuffle, the finger pads worn through. Gale had on her sheepskin jacket and army pants. She re-wound her scarf around her head turban-style. She could see her breath.

Keith dealt languorously, drawing on the joint without removing it from his lips, a trick he saw on afternoon television. Gale, as usual, refrained. Her light use of drugs and unavailability for sex set her apart in Linda's crowd. Early on she made an impression and was tolerated for that reason. It was a time when a bunch of them were standing around. As Gale approached, one of the tough girls rolled her shoulders, blocking Gale's way. Without a second's hesitation, Gale spun the girl around, rapped her cheekbone with her fist and knocked her down. The punch was so deft, so quick the girl stayed where she was, big-eyed on the ground.

Since then, Gale floated in Linda's crowd unchallenged. Keith was shunned absolutely, being a southern city boy. Their loner status tended to pair them.

Keith lifted a hip and reached into his pocket. Some of the kids played for smokes or weed. Keith and Gale played for spare change, stud poker usually. Keith glanced at the window.

"Once we get this load of snow, we're gonna have to teleport in here," he said. "There'll be tracks all over."

Gale nodded, looking at her hand. Her mind wasn't on the game. She was dismally cold. The sleeping bags she'd smuggled in were in use in the other room — probably beyond use. Keith had fired up the kerosene lamps to catch a bit of heat, but kerosene gave her headaches.

It was good he showed up today. She was going nuts at home. It amazed her Sandy let her go out, but then again, Keith was Keith. Gale had seen him charm harder cases than Sandy with that pudgy baby-face of his. Not much threat there.

Gale barely looked at her cards. She needed to talk. Her lungs ached wanting to talk, as if she'd been underwater too long. From Keith's tales of the road, it seemed like he wouldn't be one to judge. She was having trouble getting started though. Keith was the talker. After a few hands, she lay her cards face up on the floor, blowing the hand. Keith lifted his eyebrows.

"Keith, you know I have a shitstorm of a mother, right," she said.

He frowned. Shitstorm must be one of Gale's Ontario terms. "You mean fucked up?"

"Yeah. All kinds of shit happened when I was home, right?... but there's this one thing."

Gale was more than her usual tense. Keith held off any jocular remarks.

"It isn't even one thing," Gale went on. "It's one thing that turns into everything. Whatever anything is about, it's really about this." Gale sat with her back straight, her hands clenched in her lap, a pantomime of strain. She closed her eyes. "Would you turn the other way now," she said. "Because if you look at me, I can't keep going."

Keith spun a quarter turn, occupied himself rolling a regular cigarette, lit it, inhaled, passed it to Gale. Her hands were trembling. She smoked for a while, blinking. For all the billion times she'd thought about this, she'd never tried it out on another person. Keith was the first. She took a breath.

"My mother had this friend," she said. "She started out as Neil's friend, but my mother got to like her too. Minor miracle right there. Her name was Hester. Mindy called her Heck. Hester had a kid, a little baby Colin, with this thing wrong with him ever since he was born — his spine outside his body or something. He was supposed to die, but he didn't die right away. Probably Hester being so careful. She used to carry him around in this special carrier, like a lunch bucket, to keep the pressure off his spine."

Gale and Keith passed the cigarette back and forth. Gale fixed on the shadow Keith cast on the wall behind him. "Hester brought Colin over one time," she continued. "This was a long time ago; I was like, six. I was eating a peanut butter sandwich and I went over to see Colin in his carrier. Hester and my mom were in the other room. Next thing I know, Colin is making these tiny gagging noises and his face is turning blue. I had *no* clue what was going on. Hester comes roaring into the room, picks up Colin, rolls him over her arm, and sticks her finger in his mouth. He's still wailing this tiny cry, like he's so tired he can hardly do it. I started bawling too, I'm so freaked out. Then my mother comes tearing into the room and says I tried to kill him. She said I pushed part of my sandwich down his throat and tried to choke him."

Keith looked at her. "Did you?"

"No, man, no," Gale said. "How could I?"

"Did he die?"

"Not then. A few months later, maybe a year. Hester said it wasn't my fault. She told Mindy to climb down off of me, I was only a kid. But Mindy wouldn't let go. She'd bring it up over and over, like it was the one thing everyone had to bear in mind about me. Every time she was mad at me, or wanted to get Neil or anybody on her side, she'd remind them about me choking Colin."

Keith shook his head. "She's one twisted lady, your mother."

"It used to freak me out when she said it," Gale said. "I'd just shake and bawl. It was like the worst thing she could say." Gale drew a long breath. "The thing is, I don't remember. I can't remember anything about putting bread in Colin's mouth. I've wracked my brain. I can see myself standing in front of him and I can see Hester barrelling into the room, and in between is a blank. Mindy told me so many times what I did, it's like ... I must have." She looked at Keith. "You know, like if you hear a thing over and over, it ends up true. It has to be. Whatever really happened gets so hammered down it doesn't matter anymore."

Keith shook his head. It was time to get out of there. He'd just as soon not run into any of Linda's pals. He gave Gale a wink. "Let's go."

He blew out the lamp and rolled onto his feet. Gale followed him. They gave the bedroom a glance as they passed. One of the heaps had flung out a skinny arm.

Gale's bike was on the next street. Keith didn't own a bike. She unlocked it and Keith got on the seat behind and Gale shoved off standing up. After the freezing house, the exertion of pedalling gave them a boost. When they got downtown they stopped outside Shoppers and high-fived each other. Gale's scarf had come unwound and her ears were white. She looked small.

"Are you still seeing that counsellor?" Keith asked.

"Helen."

"Did you tell her about Colin and them?"

Gale shook her head. "Naw. I don't tell her stuff like that."

25

IN DECEMBER the dark engulfed them. The planet tipped away from the sun, and humans in those northern latitudes dug into their shelters and handholds to keep from falling off the earth. Helen tried to bear in mind what she knew about Inuit culture, prior to the advent of artificial light, going into their songs and stories in this season, enduring the darkness, even embracing it.

At her office, the grudging daylight cast a despair of its own. Like clockwork, referrals doubled in December, as people braced themselves for Christmas.

Helen's job right now was like television soap operas. She was embattled with the Children's Aid Society over the inexplicable release to their father's care of three children she was seeing in counselling. The father's sister lived with them and had been charged with sexually abusing these children. The CAS reasoned that, in spite of this, the father was a better option than the mother, who changed domiciles continually and was currently living with a convicted rapist.

How was either parent an option, Helen wanted to know. Why didn't Children's Aid refuse access to both of them? The worker in the case told Helen she had no authority until the court made a custody ruling. Every adult in these children's lives was failing them, either by violation or betrayal, Helen's agency included. They were all sliding down the chute together, the kids, their wretched parents, the so-called health professionals, and the courts.

To add to it, Eve's father was still stalling on visits with his daughter. Eve's foster family brought her to Whitehorse once a month to see Helen. Over French fries at a lunch counter, Eve told Helen dismally, "If I could do it over, I'd keep it to myself. I'd tell any kid, if you see your old man coming, just make a run for it. That way you'll still have a home."

Gale had still not called.

Rita's life was no easier. She had worked for months with one of the schools to persuade exhausted teachers to hang in with a kindergarten child who soiled herself daily no matter what. Whatever diaper contrivance they tried, the child removed so that she could shit freely wherever she chose. Whatever incentive or punishment they applied failed. Finally, with the help of a teacher's aid, two volunteers, the child's aunt, and dozens of meetings, the situation began slowly to resolve, only to have the child's parent show up in her life again and move her to another school.

"If I didn't have two boys to put through college, I'd quit this crazy scene," Rita fumed.

It was a weeknight and a winter storm was brewing. Rita lived forty-five minutes the other direction from Helen, but Helen wanted company and couldn't get too worked up about fuel consumption or winter hazards. If you wanted a social life in the Territory, you had to drive for it. It was stay home and drink, or get in the vehicle.

"Go on ahead," Rita told her. "I have to pick Simon up from skiing. I'll meet you at my place."

Rita and Dave bought property out at Marsh Lake when the waterfront was being developed. They built a tidy house with nice details, but their yard was overrun with a clutter of snowmobiles and trail bikes, a camper with two flat tires, half a dozen canoes and kayaks on a teetering rack, a woodshed, a steel garage, and Dave's Dodge Ram. Helen took the last seven feet of available space.

She made her way to the porch door by the light of the back floodlight, choosing a route around humps of dog turd glistening with fresh snow. When she let herself in, Dave was sitting in front of the TV tuned to the weather channel, still in his work clothes, a fine layer of plaster dust over his shoulders and thin, curly hair. Dave built houses for a living and was so fit and muscular he made Helen's stomach go watery. At one time she thought she'd have to stop coming around, but she'd gotten a hold of herself.

She shook off her boots into the heap by the door and piled her coat on the sofa. "What's that good smell?"

Dave looked up and grinned. "Chef Philippe," he said, jerking his thumb upstairs. Helen stood beside him watching the forecast for a minute, relocated to the kitchen where Dave's ten-year-old was working on dinner.

Philip was Helen's godson. He had Rita's wayward dark hair and serious, pointed face and his father's attenuated, angular body. He stood at the sink earnestly filling the big kettle with water. Two jars of tomato sauce sputtered in a saucepan. He was wearing his hockey skates, equipped with guards, so he'd be tall enough to reach the stove. He had a beach towel wrapped around his waist as an apron.

Helen sniffed deeply. "Hi, Philip, my best boy. What are you making that smells so good? Can I have a hug?"

Philip clumped over and Helen hugged him hard and they got on with dinner. Helen had brought salad makings, including everyone's favourite Caesar dressing.

CHIEF WAS HAVING a sleepover at Conor's, and Helen was glad to have her own night out, navigate chaos at Dave and Rita's for a while, though the ruckus would soon wear her out. She liked the way Dave and Rita treated their boys. It was butter on her nerves to be around them after the wreck some of her parents were making of things.

Helen was over one time when Philip was about six. Simon and Dave were away on some errand; Rita was playing a game of catch with Philip in the yard while Helen yanked weeds. Philip's throw went awry, and the sponge ball hit Helen square on the back of the head. It startled her and she let out a *yeow*.

Rita looked over at her son. "Philip, my love, apologize to Helen. You didn't hurt her but you gave her a start." Philip looked solemn. He stared at the ground and didn't move. Rita said, "It's no big deal, my son. Just a mistake, easily fixed by saying sorry."

Philip didn't budge. He appeared frozen. Helen could see Rita's effort was to help her boy save face, but he had to get this point.

"Son, this is going to happen again and again. Mistakes happen to everybody. You can fix it. Do you want to take a break? You can be by yourself for a minute while you sort it out." Rita excused him, not to punish him, but as a relief from the embarrassment he was imposing on himself, this proud little boy. Philip walked away towards the house and stood with his back to his mother and Helen for several minutes. When he returned, he came up to Helen, two bright spots in his cheeks, and addressed her foot.

"Accuse me, Helen."

RITA AND SIMON arrived safely. They had driven in behind a snowplow that was making the run to Jakes Corners. "It took forever," Rita said, shaking snow out of her hair. "But way easier on the nerves staying behind the plow."

Since the storm was in full swing and Chief was safely battened down at Conor's, it was settled that Helen would spend the night. When the dishes were done, Two Shoes needed a walk. Rita and Helen bundled up and went out into a slanting curtain of snow. Fatso the cat followed gingerly as far as the end of the driveway, then turned back. Their headlamps made two blurred cones of seething snow. Two Shoes led, barely visible at the end of the lamps' reach. Conversation was impossible. They pushed into the wind, cocooned in their parkas, the driveways they passed along the road filling up with snow.

They turned off the road when they recognized the bush trail. In the thick pines, the wind settled down and the snow seemed calmer. They made their way, staggering into old boot prints hidden under fresh snow. At the turnaround, they squatted in a snowbank to rest. Two Shoes, ahead on the trail, smelled a partridge burrowed in the drifts and began vigorously excavating. Rita and Helen snuggled deeper into the bank and turned off their lamps. Snow hushed around them in the dark.

Helen took the opportunity to tell Rita that Gale had quit.

Rita's voice came back in the dark. "Why didn't you call her folks and straighten it out?"

"Gale had lied to them. I couldn't expose her."

She felt Rita turn towards her. "Why not? You guys talk, don't you?"

Helen had not forgotten Rita's point of view on this. If Gale had been hers, Rita would not have seen her alone. She would have insisted Sandy or Dan come with her every time.

"I told you," Helen answered testily, "they never signed up. I don't have anything going with them."

"Huh. That's funny coming from you," Rita said. "You're the one who told *me* not to see kids on their own; it drives a wedge between the kids and the parents. How come you ran it that way?"

Helen thought to blame Dan and Sandy, to make some excuse about them being disinclined to join Gale's therapy, but stopped herself. "I didn't trust them," she said into the dark. "I didn't think they could help."

"Oh, so you thought *you'd* do it. In your hour a week. And who'd do right by Gale the rest of the time?"

Helen flushed. It was obvious now.

Rita braced and heaved herself out of the snowbank. "My rear end's getting cold," she said. She whistled for Two Shoes and brushed off the seat of her parka. "You've got an Achilles hoof there, Cotillard," she said down at Helen. "A kid like Gale needs everything going for her, all hands on deck. Not just you, playing cozy-cozy. I don't have to tell you." She flicked on her lamp and started back down the trail, Two Shoes shouldering ahead of her to get in the lead. Helen hoisted herself up and plodded after them.

They returned with the wind behind them, snow rollicking past their hoods, spinning in their lamps. Helen slit her eyes, let the wind shove her. When they were under the light at her door, Rita turned and pushed back her hood.

"Hélène," she said, her pronunciation a sign of affection, "never mind about not including the parents. Call it an error in judgment. What's the difference in the long run? We're not that crucial." The snow spun around her face in the light. She stood, considering Helen. "This is more about you and Jo, eh. You must have figured that out. You've got this idea you should have been able to save her ..." Helen began to protest, but Rita went on: "I know, it was long ago, but it happens, Hélène ... these ghosts get into our work."

"What's that got to do with Gale?" Helen responded, though she knew.

Rita eased her tone. "We all have our blind spots. Look how I hand the custody battles over to you. I can't work with those parents. I just want to slap them." She waited, gauging Helen. "Maybe you got into a blind spot with Gale; she's the kid sister you have to save, just you and her, out on the ice. Maybe something you were asking Gale to solve for you, without meaning to." The fur around Rita's hood shimmered with snow. "Am I talking Greek?"

"No," Helen said. "Probably not."

26

JO WOULD BE TWENTY-NINE if she had lived. Helen always knew Jo's age, quick as she knew her own. Nobody else came to her mind like that. Not her father, nor the boys, nor her mother, gone now as well. Jo was Helen's shadow. Who was the Disney character who had a shadow sewn to her feet? Tinker Bell? Peter Pan? Jo was her familiar like that.

Helen sketched her in, the probable details at twenty, twenty-five. Would she have work she loved by then? A family? It became harder to imagine as more time passed. Nineteen didn't predict twenty-nine very well. At twenty-nine, what would Jo's life have been? Maybe her health crashed. Not likely, but it was possible.

Maybe she still hadn't met anyone. Maybe she had, at a party and moved to Cape Town and never came back.

No, Jo would never not come back.

Helen hoped she didn't die a virgin. Why pick that of all things? How splendid was it for anybody at first? Just that she hoped Jo covered as many milestones as she could in nineteen years.

There had been a guy. After Nic. He might have been Jo's first. Helen met him over Christmas at home. This memory had worn thin as silver. She had rubbed it over and over in her mind. It was the Christmas everybody was there, and the family still whole, no idea what was about to go down.

Helen always went home at Christmas, impelled by the shallow light in the Yukon more than holiday spirit. Solstice was the time to leave the North if you had anywhere to go. Get out of the dark. When the lakes had not yet frozen and the heavy water rolled and steamed, the sky hunched on the black surface, refusing to lift, the sun a cold moth.

In Jo's day, when it was time to head home for the holidays, Helen had a routine. She left the car in long-term parking and flew to Vancouver, where she'd stay over a few days with her school friend, Khairoon. Helen, Khairoon, and their friend Vince had trained together, roomed together in Vancouver. Khairoon had grown up in Jaipur and cold was still a horror to her. After graduation, she'd stayed on in Vancouver, the only Canadian city she could imagine living in. Vince was a Toronto boy. He'd gone back east and gotten a job in a big centre with lots of opportunity, lots of ongoing training. Over the years, his letters to Helen exhorted her to quit wasting her time in the hinterland and come south where the action was. "We see it all here, Helly."

Khairoon was more philosophical. *If it's what you have, it's for you.*

During her stopover, Helen and Khairoon shopped in Chinatown, trucks for the boys, lacquered bowls for Jo and Luze Mery. They took the ferry to the Gulf Islands, Helen inhaling the smell of the sea until she was dizzy, relishing the soaked air on her face.

For the flight east, Helen always cadged a window seat. She pressed her face to the Plexiglas as the plane moved out over the wrinkled ocean and lifted over the mountains. Along the mountain ridges, black razed lines looked like private scribblings written under sugar snow. The weather was clear that year, the year of the boyfriend. Helen watched the tiny shadow of the plane on the mountaintops, their ancient history sliding slowly past, the mountains pushed up by colliding continents, snow heaping in the valleys and blowing across the stone faces. She spotted Okanagan Lake, a long beaten-tin dish, the road above it a wire glinting in the sun. The broad valley floors were traced with roads, like veins running through charcoal heaves of land; grizzled trees, cloud stretched in scraps. There was a band of atmosphere at the earth's curve, a white fog with airless blue above it. She floated in her droning capsule over unperturbed silence. It always seemed to Helen at thirty thousand feet, human enterprise was in its rightful place, incidental and brief.

Then the Rockies subsided and they passed over the Great Plains with its fossilized dinosaurs and ferns, the creamy oil paint of the prairie, the snow whirled and puckered, fine geometrical seams of farms cut by roads straight as cheese wire. There might have been a winter storm in Winnipeg that year, sky and land all one muffled grey, the city ghostlike, no more than thin black scratches in the snow.

Then the last glacial pools in the hollow of the Shield, Lake Superior cracking through the clouds, an edge of land ragged and disappearing, scrags of ice trailing out from shore. And finally in purple dusk, the splay of Toronto's lights came up, improbable, a galaxy glittering on a shore.

JO'S NINETEENTH CHRISTMAS, Helen's mother and father were at the airport to meet her. They always came, always both of them, whatever time of night or day the plane landed. This was a family ritual imposed by her mother, and whatever Helen's father thought, he came along. Helen spotted them outside the baggage room while she waited for her suitcase, the only people facing each other rather than the arrivals door, a tall couple in good clothes. When Helen came through the door, they turned to her, her mother wrapping her in a voluptuous fur embrace. Her father's eyes, charcoal like Helen's, crinkled over Luze's shoulder.

"Darling girl, can you eat? We're going to dinner."

Helen's parents were glamorous. The specialized work they did imparted a gravitas, an air of emergency. HIV was a cause as well as a lethal illness, and they were two of its soldiers. Walking with them to the parking lot, Helen was conscious of her parka and overkill snow boots.

At dinner, her parents filled her in on the AIDS front. Luze had been away at a conference. Georges informed her that some of his patients were now surviving HIV — not cured, but outlasting the disease.

"Darling, that is a question of resources," Luze interrupted. "Since no such progress exists in Africa."

Leaning on the upholstered chair back, Helen eased into the

207

family vernacular, like walking into water; her parents' absorption in their work and Helen's place their lives as their renegade, temporarily on leave in the North. She felt herself come under their protection, a child again in a certain way.

When they got home, Luze turned on the porch light for Jo, who had a swim meet in the city and was expected, unless the weather turned bad. Georges' brother and his wife were also due, making the drive from Vermont. Every Christmas, Chris locked the door of his small press and Mimi laid down her carving tools for a few precious days away.

Helen went to bed in her old room under the slanted ceiling, slept deep, and in the grey of morning, found Jo's heavy arm slung over her neck. She shifted it and snuggled into Jo's chlorine-scented back. "Scratch," Jo mumbled.

It was Christmas Eve. The aroma of Luze's plum salsa wafted up the stairs, and her murmured imprecations to the boys to keep their voices down. Chris and Mimi must have come in late.

"Good you're here," Jo said, shifting onto her back and squaring the eiderdown over them. "There's somebody I want you to meet."

Helen caught the undercurrent of excitement in her voice.

"Oh-oh. Is it love?"

"Could be," Jo crooned. "It's the guy I told you about, in second year at Mac. He's been out to the house a couple of times. Luze and Dad have met him."

Helen felt a flutter under her ribs. A big love affair could derail Jo's visits north. Inevitable of course — a more demanding school load, or a boyfriend; one or the other.

She drew a breath. "I can hardly wait."

THE HOUSE AT CHRISTMAS was beautiful. When Luze was pregnant with the twins, she and Georges bought a farm on an old apple orchard forty minutes from the city, a gabled brick house with honey-coloured pine floors, a huge kitchen wood stove, and a glass vestibule Luze converted into a greenhouse. Anyone entering the house ran a gamut of hibiscus and rosemary and, in spring, the acrid smell of tomato plants. At Christmas, there was eucalyptus and juniper set with tiny candles in tin holders. That year, more candles lined the walk outside, a faint fall of snow wetting the glass shield around them.

By four o'clock the bird was in the oven, the long basswood table in the dining room set for eleven. Luze's Mexican plates were laid out on hemp mats, heavy wine and water goblets balanced on the edges. A centrepiece of dogwood branches the boys had cut from a nearby creek glinted with Jo's felt and glitter ornaments.

Helen's father was sequestered in his studio with Rafael and Jonathan, boning up for a recital later. Jo hid out upstairs wrapping the last of her gifts. Her guest hadn't arrived yet.

Chris and Mimi were in the kitchen, working on the vegetables and opening wine. Helen joined them. Her uncle was curly-haired and built like a bear, as unlike Georges as two brothers could be. Chris published a small newspaper in the States that was bitingly critical of Washington. By mid-afternoon he was already several sheets to the wind. His embrace nearly toppled Helen.

Miriam was vivid like Luze, in a different way. She made furniture, a few pieces a year, the detail fine and elegant. Last year, she'd given Helen a cherrywood bowl, as glossy and slippery as glass. She had her sleeves pushed up over her elbows and was dexterously scooping pepper squash, her blunt hands quick and sure. Luze had been up since five, engaged in meticulous, exhausting preparations. Helen could see the generous, talkative presence of Chris and Mimi eased her labour.

Jo finally descended in a white angora sweater and embraced everyone, shedding fine hairs all over them.

"Taste the sauce, Hélène. Guess Luze's secret ingredient."

"Port?"

"She *told* you."

Jo's young man arrived, in a black turtleneck, with a dozen blood red roses for Luze. His name was Salvador. Helen didn't catch his last name. He had feline good looks and French Intellectual horn rims so large they looked like a diving mask. Helen had psyched herself to like him, but immediately didn't. He stepped up to their questions about his studies, unselfconscious and eager to participate, but he did not follow Jo's every move the way Helen would have liked him to. He was tracking his own moves, an inbound man, whereas the ones Helen favoured were the outbound ones, like Jo, the ones bending over backwards to make everybody feel better.

When the goose came out of the oven, Helen's father and the boys were summoned. Just as they sat down, Georges took a call in the other room. "Georges, *NO!*" Helen's mother importuned. Chris, now quite drunk, was pressed to carve in his place, which he did with a cavalier offhandedness while engaging Jo's boyfriend about arms stockpiles. Helen glanced at her mother to see how she was taking this lack of decorum, but Luze kept a serene eye on the vegetables moving around the table.

The meal was discursive and noisy, everyone slightly larger than life in the way of families when they're crowded in a room together. Helen's father rejoined them and kept up a fervent exposition on politics with Chris and Mimi, the little boys, oblivious, peppering each other with silly jokes. Jo was subdued, her eyes on Salvador, who made alert observations whenever the opportunity presented. Watching Jo, it occurred to Helen this young man and Jo were already lovers. How they could be when Jo was still living at home, she didn't know, but she was certain it was true. She could see it in Jo's face.

The thought distracted her. How must it be making love to this selfish boy? Did their mother know? And — ruefully — why hadn't Jo told her? She was certainly aware that Helen had had her share of lovers, she would be safe to confide in — and yet Jo had not. Perhaps she was feeling a tremor in their relationship, a change coming down the way, she didn't quite know what to do about.

Helen had forgotten the starter she'd worked on all morning. She had left the coquilles St. Jacques languishing in the pantry, and it was Luze who remembered. Appalled, Luze insisted they all put on their coats and tramp around, swollen with dinner, in the wizened orchard, after which they trooped in and had the coquilles with pear and endive salad.

Over dessert, Luze described to Chris and Miriam an exhibit of Blake's drawings she had seen at the AGO in Toronto a couple of years before. "Hélène and I couldn't tear ourselves away," she said warmly. Except that Helen recalled it was Jo, not her, who had gone with their mother. Jo had written to Helen about seeing it. The error went by Jo. She was whispering to Salvador, but the transposition pleased Helen. She'd been gone from home so long, she was glad to be represented even mistakenly.

Later, coming out of the bathroom upstairs, Chris lumbered

into her. "Wicked scallops, you bugger," he said chummily. "What do you think of frogman?"

"He doesn't fool me for a second," Helen said. "He's a shitheel."

"My sentiments exactly."

"And don't you say anything."

At the recital, Rafi, doing nicely on his violin, was overwhelmed by Jon's zany banjo accompaniment; everyone applauded anyway.

When Salvador had driven away and order restored to the kitchen, Jo and Helen went outdoors to extinguish the candles, snow wafting into Jo's Birkenstocks. She put a hand on Helen's arm. "Well, what did you think of him?"

Helen bent to rescue a drowned wick. "Ah ... intelligent, sweetheart, that's for sure," she said, straightening up. "And pretty confident. Not the easiest gathering in the world, and he seemed quite up for it."

Jo sighed happily. "I know."

That was three months before Jo backed up on the glacier and died.

Helen didn't know if anyone told the boy.

27

AN OFFICIAL at the Education Ministry happened to notice there was a fifteen-and-a-half-year-old enrolled in the Adult Education Programme and saw fit to forbid Keith's attendance there.

Phil and Thom, along with Helen and Keith's probation officer, all wrote letters decrying Keith's exclusion, noting his unsuitability for a regular high school, his articulate, courteous presence in the Adult Ed environment, and the likelihood of his returning to anti-social behaviour if tossed out on the street. They got no reply.

Phil canvassed widely for a mentor — a person with a trade, to whom Keith could apprentice himself — without success.

Keith was back in the basement with his mother and Norman.

His spirits continued to slide. Audette accompanied him to meetings with Helen, though less often than she used to. Her habitual spunk was showing strain. Helen asked how she was holding up. "Laugh or go nuts," Audette said. "Take your pick."

Audette and Keith griped at each other. Keith was aggravated by his mother's inertia with her boyfriend; Audette was worn out by Keith's surliness with Norman. She couldn't leave the two of them alone together. She looked shifty and caught. She was down to the choice poverty forced on mothers. Without resources, who was she going to save, herself or her boy?

Their meetings with Helen were tense. Something had to give and Helen couldn't make it happen.

When Keith and Helen were by themselves, Keith visited his metaphorical parts of self. Helen was aware that they distracted and soothed him, but without a real life, without engagement in the world, these personalities were only an evasion.

"Listen to this, man," Keith told her. "The other day I couldn't take it anymore. The place stank, junk everywhere. I went upstairs and snagged a couple of garbage bags, threw everything out: clothes, pizza boxes, Styrofoam shit from tools Norman buys himself. I shoved the bags under the stairs. Then the people upstairs left the door open and their dog got in, one of those Great Danes or whatever, with the tight skin and huge effing claws, and found the bags. When I woke up, the whole place was a mess again, only worse. You know what I did?" Keith bugged his eyes at Helen. "I cried. I fricking cried. I do not cry. My old man took a tire iron to my bike, I faced him down. All the lousy, shit-scared stuff I've been through, I do not cry. Now I'm bawling over garbage."

THE SCHOOL BOARD was a wall. Stan told Helen the Ministry hadn't made a decision. She shook her head. Who were these people? A bunch of guys who curled together. Keith and his mother never reproached her, but she knew she wasn't helping them. She couldn't even get the fundamentals covered, the physical and social domains. Keith had to have food and his own bed. The psychological inquiry she and Keith were conducting was important; Helen didn't discount it. Keith's personalities made a brave and poignant troupe, commissioned as they were to raise him up, save his life. But he had to have a context where he could try himself.

Then, on a freezing day in February, Keith arrived at his appointment, high-stepping. He was wearing what looked like hockey shorts, his bare legs blue with cold. He'd "found" a phone card on the street and used it to call his friend Nathan Big Canoe in Edmonton.

This was the first Helen had heard of Nathan Big Canoe.

"An *on* dude," Keith beamed. "Any time it got heavy with the old man, I'd go hang with Nate, share his crib for a few days. No problem with his folks. Very cool people."

Helen played along. "Good to hear you've got a pal. What did Nathan say?"

"Any time I want to come back, I've got a spot. Man says they got one of those Safe School outfits, like you've been trying to find for me? An easy ride from Nate's. Says his folks don't need bread or anything from me. Though I'd get a job, do my share." Keith blushed. It occurred to him he had been able to wangle for himself what Helen couldn't. They smiled at each other, feeling the shift between them.

"It's back on your father's turf isn't it, Keith? Does he know Nathan or his family? Is there any chance you'll run into him?"

Keith gave his charming smile. "No way. I'm like their little dog. The old man would never mess with Nate and his family."

Helen nodded. Edmonton used to be anathema for Keith, a futile place, since his father lived there. Now he couldn't afford to see it that way.

"If this is on the level," Helen said. "If your mom is in agreement, I'll call the Safe Schools people in Edmonton, see what they can do for you."

"Excellent," Keith said. "I'm ready."

Helen eyed his bare legs. "In the meantime, let's take a ride over to Adult Ed. Phil and Thom have a lost and found box, if you recall. Maybe there's a pair of track pants you can see yourself in."

This was a pathetic offer, the booby prize, since the Territory had given Keith the back of its hand in every way that mattered.

Keith didn't seem to notice.

When they got there, school was still in process. Torpor reigned. Four students leaned into computer screens, one of whom must be Gale's friend Linda, a strapping girl in a logging shirt, black hair stacked on top of her head like a raven's nest. Three adults were grouped around a table having a hushed discussion. Thom Pegamagabo was in the back on the phone. Phil was playing chess with a hugely obese young man sweating heavily in a dress shirt. The room was breathtakingly overheated.

When they spotted Keith, the three at the table waved. Helen recognized two haggard-faced women in decorative earrings, regular aficionados of AA meetings and bingo downtown. She didn't know their male companion, sallow and frail-looking, his thin hair in a comb-over like a Roman emperor.

Gale was not present.

Helen pointed to the lost and found box and Phil gave them a help-yourself wave, intent on his game. Helen went back and rummaged in the cardboard carton among the lank windbreakers, pilled acrylic scarves, and nylon baseball caps. She located some jogging pants with the rear worn through, a pair of size 4 jeans with a broken zipper, one rubber boot. Nothing in Keith's range.

Thom hung up and Helen asked about Gale.

"No sign of her all week," he said. "I phone and get the machine."

When they left, Helen took Keith to the thrift store next to the Esso station, where they unearthed a pair of barely used, super-sized black denims. Then they went to Sun Woo's for Chinese. This would not have been kosher if Helen were still Keith's therapist, but that was no longer the case. Now she could buy him whatever she liked.

28

EVENTUALLY PHIL LEWIN went in person to call on Gale's father and Sandy. It was a Saturday morning, too early for anyone to be heading for the mall. Sandy answered the door, gripping the front of a pea-green bathrobe. The mist of a recent shower wafted out behind her. Phil reminded her who he was, and she stepped out to speak to him. She didn't smile.

"We haven't seen Gale for a couple of weeks, Mrs. Connelly," Phil said. "I just wanted to check if she's okay."

"I wouldn't know," Sandy said. "She's gone."

Phil comprehended Sandy didn't mean gone for the day. "She didn't mention she was leaving," he pursued. He noted Sandy's guardedness and added, "We like her, Mrs. Connelly. My calling on you isn't administrative. We'd like to know what happened, if you're willing to say."

The porch was glassed in, not uncomfortably cold in the March sun. Sandy indicated a couple of curlicued wrought-iron chairs at a glass table. "We can sit here. I'll be out in a minute."

She returned with a bulky cardigan over her robe and a pack of cigarettes. She dragged a chair out and sat down, lit a cigarette, exhaled heavily, and apologized. Phil took a seat and loosened his parka. Pale sunlight through the glass shed a frail warmth over them.

"Dan and I got up one morning two weeks ago and Gale was gone," Sandy said. "She left a note on her bed. *Sorry.* We notified the police." She spoke as if reciting. "You probably know, Gale suffers from depression. We were concerned what the note implied. The police haven't found anything, but I think we can rule out suicide." Sandy drew on her cigarette, set it in a heavy ashtray on felt tabs, pushed the ashtray away from her.

"Why is that?" Phil asked.

"We think Gale's with her sister. We phoned her stepfather when she went missing. Neil wasn't around, but we found out from his father that Buddie ran away and Neil went to Toronto looking for her. We think Buddie contacted Gale, or the other way round, and they met up some place."

Phil nodded slowly. "Are you likely to hear from her? Would she let you know where she is?"

"Not likely," Sandy said dryly. "Gale took money from her father before she left. All he had, as a matter of fact. I don't mean grocery money. That's another reason we're not thinking suicide. What she did took planning. Gale didn't leave on a whim. First she burned her bridges." Sandy gave Phil a level look. "I don't think she'll be in touch."

Phil absorbed this. "Quite a shock," he said. "It's a rough way to part." He ran his fingers over the tabletop for a minute. "I'm sorry, Mrs. Connelly. Gale's a good person, whatever it looks like now. She may land on her feet, make it good with you."

Sandy let this go. "It's not Mrs. Connelly, by the way. I kept my own name. Veraldi."

Phil scraped his chair back. "I'd like to let a couple of people know, if you don't mind. My colleague Thom and Helen Cotillard. They would want to know."

Sandy stubbed out her cigarette. "I have no say over who you tell."

HELEN CALLED DAN AND SANDY as soon as she heard. She had no idea what she'd say when they answered, but it wasn't possible not to phone.

They didn't pick up. Not early in the morning, not late in the evening. Why did they install a telephone if they couldn't bear to answer it?

A few days later, when Helen was picking up groceries at Extra Foods, she ran into Sandy. She was staring at soya sauce in one of the aisles, looking shapeless and sallow, the same as everyone in Whitehorse by mid-March. Helen rolled her cart up to Sandy's, tapping it to get her attention. They hadn't seen each other since the fall. "Hello Sandy. It's Helen."

"I know," Sandy said, without expression. "Even without the office."

"I've phoned you many times," Helen said. "I heard about Gale." Sandy made no acknowledgement. Helen said, "It's a lot to take in."

"Yup. She's gone. No thanks to you."

Helen took this rudeness as an invitation. "I'd be mad at me too, in your shoes," she said. "But how about we skip it? It's the end of the day, I'm tired, you're tired, Gale's gone. Why don't we go somewhere and have a drink."

Sandy sized up the offer. "The Capital," she said. "I can smoke there."

The last time Helen was in the Cap was several years ago. What she was doing there in the first place was lost to memory; someone from work must have lured her. She was drinking something she wasn't used to and had gotten silly. She ended up on the dance floor butting hips with a trucker from Tumbler Ridge, round after round of "Light My Fire" on the turntable. She might have taken the fellow home; she couldn't vouch for it.

That night, a Tuesday, the place was nearly empty. She and Sandy took a booth, waited for their eyes to adjust, shed their coats, and ordered a couple of drafts.

Two solo men at the bar stared despondently at the sports channel on a TV pitched above them. A sign beside the cash register said, *Be nice or leave. Thanks.*

Sandy tilted her head back against the seat and closed her eyes, a sign of truce, Helen thought.

"How's Dan?" she asked.

Sandy rolled her head up. "Dan's Dan. A vault. I hear him down the hall grinding his teeth in his sleep."

Helen nodded. "It's an unnerving sound. How about you? How're you doing?"

Sandy shrugged. "Burned again."

"Why take it that way?" Helen countered. She hated passive verbs, done-to verbs. "Did you expect Gale to be considerate?"

Sandy scowled. "Are you going to lecture me?"

"No," Helen said, blushing. "I just don't think it's about you."

"Robbing us is not about us?" Sandy said. "What planet are you living on? There's such a thing as being responsible, you know. What if Gale really is an ungrateful little shit? What if I could have helped her and didn't? What if you could have?"

Helen felt heat spread in her chest. Sandy's rudeness animated her. "Well that's what happened, isn't it," she said crisply. "You failed, I failed . . . Personally I'm used to it. Anyway, how do we know? We aren't in Gale's head. What if nobody failed her? What if this just wasn't her scene? Maybe she couldn't see herself here and had to try something else."

Sandy took a swallow of beer. "And cleaned her father out on her way to the bus station. You're whitewashing, Helen. I'm not even talking about taking off. I'm talking about wrecking everything she had here."

"She was in a box, Sandy," Helen argued. "I have to believe that. We don't have the whole story."

"We have enough of the story," Sandy said, unimpressed. "What she did stands, no matter what kind of bind she was in. We're all in binds. And don't tell me she's better off wherever she and her little sister are. The streets of Toronto? Give me a break. She'd have been far better off here."

This, of course, was exactly what Helen thought. "For the record, I told her that."

A tall couple in expensive skiwear came in, looked chagrined, and left. One of the men at the bar barked a laugh, which turned into a prolonged coughing fit. The bartender came out from behind the counter and thumped him on the back.

Sandy and Helen brooded. For Helen, what stuck was not

that Gale took off. She'd seen that coming. Every kid went home, no matter if home was barren or crazy or dangerous. There was no future for a kid unless it started from someplace known to her, some place with her scent on it.

What she couldn't get used to was all those chatty meetings the two of them had had about barbecues and capers, when all the time Gale was working out a way to pull off this reckless, heartbreaking manoeuvre. The way Gale never gave a hint to Helen how much trouble she was in.

What stuck was how Helen had been useless to her.

She watched Sandy morosely smoking. "What about your own girl?"

Sandy pulled her cigarette pack close to her, making a small rampart. "Edie's in Prince George," she said curtly. "She keeps in touch with my mother."

"Oh yes," Helen recalled. "Your mother was the other parent."

"My mother was the *only* parent. My job was chopping vegetables, doing the washing up."

"It didn't look like that to me," Helen said. "You had your oar in. You and your mother were in some kind of contest."

"You had a word for it."

"Polarized."

"Whatever," Sandy said. "She let Edie get away with murder. Anything she wanted."

"And you opposed her. The war was really you and your mother, huh?"

"So you said at the time." Sandy hooked two fingers in her turtleneck, ventilated her neck. "I hated those meetings," she said.

"How come?"

"The way you kept harping on her father. Whereas Edie never thought about him. And you always wanted to talk about my mother and me. Totally beside the point."

"What was the point?"

"That Edie wanted too much freedom," Sandy said, exasperated. "You missed that, apparently."

Helen couldn't resist. "How come you brought Gale to me, since I did such a bang-up job with your own girl?"

Sandy flicked her eyes at Helen. "You're the only show in town. It's you or Rita, and Rita and I go back. She isn't an option."

They looked at the tabletop in silence. Helen remembered her name. "What's it like with you and Ramona these days?"

Sandy drained her glass. "She's an old woman now, and I've spent my whole life hating her."

"Edie must be furious that you don't come looking for her."

"You mean, why doesn't Edie come looking for *me*. She's grown up now. She can move around."

"Yeah, and you're still her mother. Or do you think she doesn't need one?"

Helen didn't expect an answer. She glanced at her empty glass. "I could use another. How about you?"

She excused herself and went down some hazardous stairs to the bathroom. The door to the women's had a wooden decal of a cowgirl twirling a lasso. When she returned, their drafts were on the table. She slipped into the booth. Sandy was staring at the tabletop.

"How did you find out Gale met up with her sister?" Helen asked.

"From her grandfather. Neil's father. If anyone knows, he does."

"Have you got a phone number?" Helen said. "I'd like to call him."

Sandy looked uneasy.

"What?" Helen said. "I need to track her, Sandy." Until that moment, Helen hadn't known she needed to find out what happened to Gale, whatever it took.

Sandy sat back, drew a long breath. Her voice was slow. "If you find Gale and you're wanting to get her back here, you should know Dan and I can't have any part of it."

"Not up for another round?"

"She *stole* from us, for Christ's sake," Sandy flared. "She tracked down where Dan kept his cash — which even *I* didn't know — and took every cent."

"Almost a grand, wasn't it?" Helen said. "I mean ..."

"You're really something," Sandy seethed. "What do they teach you in social work school? Blindfold lessons? It was more than a grand. Her father is one of those guys that's his own bank. Gale took *everything*. She should be charged if she ever shows up. You don't just wave a thing like that off." She let out a sigh. "Except that her father hasn't got the stomach for it. Dan says, 'Think of it as her college education. In that case we got off easy.'" Sandy drew a long breath. "Even without the stealing, I'm not going through that again."

"Living with Gale?"

Sandy's face aged. For an instant Helen saw the mother whose daughter ran away and never came back.

She said heavily, "Gale's a hard girl. She's quiet, toes the line — until last fall she did — but she has a way of letting you know you're ... nothing." Sandy closed her eyes, swallowed, drew on her cigarette. "I can't do that again."

Helen signalled for the bill. She cleared her throat. "Find Edie, alright," she said. "Your mother isn't the mother she needs." They shrugged into their jackets and went out into the dark.

29

IN THE OFFICE MONDAY, Helen dug out the scrap of paper Sandy gave her with Carl and Lois Stoltenhoff's phone number on it. She settled into her desk and dialed. A man barked hello on the second ring.

"Mr. Stoltenhoff? It's Helen Cotillard. We don't know each other. I'm calling from Whitehorse. I work at a counselling agency here and I know Gale. She used to come to me for counselling."

"What's that?" He sounded irritated.

"Helen Cotillard. In Whitehorse," Helen shouted in case he was deaf. "I'm trying to find out where Gale is. I'm not chasing her down or anything. We aren't an agency with any authority. Could you talk to me for a minute or two?"

"Who did you say you were?"

"Gale's counsellor when she lived here. Helen. You can call her father if you need to check."

Carl grunted. "I never heard about her seeing a counsellor."

Helen made her voice as disarming as possible. "Well, I knew her for about a year. We got on alright. I was trying to help her settle in. Being up here wasn't easy for her."

"Well no, it's not her home. We told Neil shipping her off wasn't right. Gale'd been through too much. There'd be no getting used to a new place."

"Can you tell me anything about that? I'd be glad to talk to somebody who's in her family."

"How did you get this phone number?"

"Sandy gave it to me. She thought you and your wife might know where Gale is."

"We might, but Gale wouldn't want us passing it around."

"Mr. Stoltenhoff, do you know what happened to her? That's what I'm trying to find out. The last I heard, her sister ran away. Dan and Sandy think the girls might have arranged to meet somewhere in Toronto."

"Well, they're behind the times," Carl said. "Buddie was back home in one day. Neil had her back here pronto. Knew right where to look for her. Toronto airport. It's the only place Buddie's ever been. Found her sitting in arrivals, waiting for Gale."

Helen sent up thanks and double thanks that Carl was a talker. "Good lord. And did Gale arrive? Did she get off a plane?"

"Neil didn't wait around to see. He nabbed the little girl and brought her home. Buddie was pretty glad to see him too. I'd like to know what sort of person would sell a ten-year-old a bus ticket."

"And the wonder of Neil finding her in an airport that size," Helen said.

"Like I told you, he knew where to look. Only thing worrying him was whether she'd pull it off. There's a lot of loopholes where her plan could've gone wrong. But she done it."

"And no sign of Gale?"

"Nope."

Helen rubbed dust off the base of her lamp. "Mr. Stoltenhoff, can you tell me anything else? Like, why Buddie took off in the first place? Did she and Gale have a plan?"

"Hold on a minute. I need to sit." The phone clunked and Helen heard the sound of a chair scraping, a grunt, the jostle of the phone. "They mighta had a plan, or not," Carl resumed. "With her mother back in the house, Buddie'd have a reason to scat anytime. The principal over at the school told us the day she took off there was a fight. Happened in morning recess in the woods back of school property. The children like to go there when they're up to something they shouldn't be. One of the grade five fellers came running out of the woods, hands over his face, blood all over the front of him, bellowing that Buddie broke his nose. This boy is a prize bully. Nobody would have objected if Buddie did pop him. Mike had to go look for her. She wasn't coming out. He found her in the woods crouched in the snow, rubbing a snowball over her knuckles. She didn't say anything about it. Mike took her back and sat her in a chair outside his office, give her a chance to think it over. When he went out to check on her, she'd taken off. Took the Red Cross collection while she was at it."

Helen waited. "Then what?"

"Well, she'd have to be pretty good at hiding. No more than half an hour till her father was at the school. But they couldn't find her. They didn't think of trying the bus station till later. Man in Liskeard at the depot remembered her. He couldn't recall where she'd bought a ticket to. Neil figured it had to be Toronto."

"Why would she run? Would she be afraid to face her folks after the fight?"

"Not likely. Fighting's how they settle things themselves. Buddie always found it peculiar, hearing this 'walk away' style of doing things. She thinks when you have a grievance with somebody you just hit them with a rock."

"How's she doing now that she's back home?"

Carl's voice took an edge. "I'll tell you something. It's a helluva lot better now it's just her and her dad. Mindy's gone. She's been gone since Neil went down to the city to fetch Buddie."

"Mindy cleared out?"

"Neil *drove* her off. That boy has been in some kind of daydream since that woman came along. I could tell you some things, but it's water under the bridge. Mindy is a piece of work. She puts a grip on you like a python, squeezes the life right out of you. To my thinking, it was Buddie taking off, nearly losing her like that, made Neil give himself a shake. He was over at the house here before he went down to get Buddie and told us he was going home first to settle with Mindy. Couldn't have her around anymore. How she knew he meant it when he didn't mean it all the other times, I'll never know, but she got it figured and cleared out. Had the last word though."

"What was that?"

Carl exhaled heavily. "His best dog, Ivan, is what. Neil had Ivan nine years. His lead dog, small, but the best dog you ever saw, smart as a person. That animal could work with any of them, any dog you teamed him with. Mindy hung Ivan up on a coat hook before she left. Hung him up right inside the door where he'd be the first thing Neil saw. Lucky Neil came in ahead of the little girl, pushed her right back out again till he could take Ivan down." Carl Stoltenhoff stopped. "That man cried like he'd break."

It took Helen a minute to speak. So this was the mother Gale had to deal with.

Carl said, "Anybody there?"

"Would Gale come home now that Mindy's gone?"

"She'd have to know, wouldn't she."

"She hasn't called?"

"Nope."

"Mr. Stoltenhoff," Helen said. Her voice was shaking. "It's a lot to ask, but Gale disappeared from here and I can't stop thinking about her. Could you phone me if you hear from her, if you find out anything? Just leave a message. I'll call you back."

Carl didn't answer right away. "What was your name again?"

THE TWENTY-FOUR-HOUR GROCERY in Whitehorse sold everything: soft drinks, pepperoni, farm eggs, shoelaces. Driving by one day on her way to the highway, Helen spotted Keith coming out of the store, peeling the wrapper off an ice cream bar. They'd said their goodbyes; she hadn't seen Keith since Gale disappeared. She hadn't known he was still in town. On an impulse, she made a U-turn and swerved to a stop beside him. Keith jumped, startled.

Helen leaned across the seat, yanked up the handle on the passenger door. "Keith. Got a minute?"

Keith bent warily and looked in, gave his worried smile.

"Helen, how's it going?" He glanced around and climbed in.

"Eat your ice cream, Keith," Helen said. "I just want to talk for a minute. Is right here okay?" She reached to turn off the ignition.

"A different locale maybe," Keith said.

Helen drove to the Schwatka Dam at the edge of town, parked in the empty lot. There'd been so little snow that year it looked like the plow hadn't been in once. The car engine ticked, cooling down. The late sun through the windshield made a square across their laps. They wedged their backs against the car doors to face each other.

"What about Edmonton?" Helen said. "I'm surprised to see you. Is the plan still on?"

"Any day now."

Helen waited for their old rapport, but Keith seemed edgy, working his ice cream stick from one side of his mouth to the other, fidgeting. Helen plowed in. "Keith, I'm trying to find Gale. She left without saying where she was going. It looks as though she might have been headed for Toronto, but nobody knows if she got there or if she's safe." Keith floated his eyes towards Helen. "I don't want to put you on the spot," she said, "but remember at the Centre, Phil and Thom saying if your friend is up to something that isn't right, or puts them in danger, you have to speak up. You can't stand by. Keeping quiet isn't always the mark of a friend." She looked hard at him. "I mean it, Keith. I'm pretty sure Gale's in trouble. Whatever you know about it, you better say."

Keith looked away. "I know that 'good friend/bad friend' rap. They use it in jail."

"Where is Gale?"

He nodded. "Toronto, like you say. She likely made it."

"To meet Buddie? To find her sister?"

"I don't know about that. She mighta hooked up with Buddie."

"But wasn't that the whole idea? Why leave, otherwise?"

Keith frowned. "You know about the money, don't you? You take a chunk like that, you need a *large* place to go to."

Helen hadn't particularly thought about how much money it was. "A chunk like what?"

Keith shrugged.

"You mean more than a thousand?" Helen tried to remember what Sandy had said. "Crikey, Keith, *five?*" Keith still didn't respond. "Ten? Fifteen?"

Keith sighed. "That'd be the range."

Helen caught her breath. *Shit*, Gale. "I can't see it, Keith. I don't get it."

Keith looked at her, weighing. "Her mother, man," he said. "Gale nabbed the cash for Mindy."

"*What?* What are you talking about?" Helen's voice was loud. "Mindy has nothing to *do* with Gale. She banished Gale, don't you know that?" And even as she pushed against the probability, even as she warded it off, a new picture slid and clicked into place.

"Mindy was there all along," Keith said. "She started calling up. Gale figured she wanted something, but she didn't know what. Mindy didn't say, just chatted her up, shot the breeze, mother to daughter. Gale kept waiting for her to put the touch on her, but it's her mother right? She must've hoped it was for real."

Helen's head was spinning. "How would Mindy call her? Have you ever tried phoning their place? Dan and Sandy never pick up. They screen everything."

Keith sighed. "Cell phones, Helen. Ever heard of them?"

"But what about Buddie? I thought this was about Buddie."

"Yeah," said Keith, "that was the draw for Gale. Hold back a cut for her and Buddie, make their getaway."

Helen had to get out of the car. Keith followed her, leaned against the car door, and folded his arms. Helen paced back and forth in the narrow parking lot. She could have wept. She had been down the wrong road completely. Gale in trouble, so much trouble, but not where Helen was looking. All those weeks, Gale rattling on about Linda and school, and Helen thinking, are we ever going to get down to it? Couldn't she have asked, just once, *Gale, is there something else?*

Keith cleared his throat. "Mindy claimed Gale's old man owed her for all the time Mindy took care of Gale while he was having fun up in Whitehorse. Mindy said he was into her for thousands. Gale knew it was bullshit but ..." He shrugged. "Maybe she just couldn't hold out." Keith gave the smile he gave when things were outrageous. "Mindy and my old man should have met up. Gale and I used to talk about it. In our lighter moments."

Helen narrowed her eyes. "Are you the one who told her how to steal ten grand — or whatever it was?"

"Hey, not me," Keith said, offended. "It was Mindy. I didn't even know when it was going to happen. Gale never said goodbye or anything. She did it alone, man. A solo act."

Helen's eyes brimmed. A theft like that and nobody to tell. Send the money, get on a plane. That took nerve. No wonder Gale called Buddie. Somebody waiting for her at the other end. Helen dropped her head.

Keith came over, gave her a light jab on the shoulder. "She liked you, man."

"Oh for Christ's sake," Helen said. She went around to her

side of the car, got in, and slammed the door. Keith climbed in and they drove back downtown. When she let him off, she'd gone numb. "Do you think you would have gotten around to telling one of us, Thom or Phil or me?"

Keith looked down the street. "I kinda wondered why I'm still here."

30

GALE WAITED FOR BUDDIE in the Toronto airport for two days. On the phone, she had told her to stand at the gate for flights arriving from Vancouver. Buddie knew the gate. Air Canada only had the one, and Buddie had been there half a dozen times with Neil.

Arrivals level felt like a dungeon, purposefully depressing. Meet your person and get out. To break the monotony, Gale roamed around upstairs in departures where there was more going on. At night when the terminal quieted down, Gale stretched out across three seats against a wall downstairs where the lights weren't as ferocious. There was the roar of the fans circulating stale air, sleep wasn't an option, but at least no one bothered her.

She had no money. She'd meant to hang onto some, she and Buddie would need money, but in the end she made a clean break. It'd be so like Mindy to begrudge anything Gale took for herself, to *know* Gale had tried to pull a fast one. She allowed herself the purchase of a plane ticket and put the rest in a book with the centre cut out, like in the movies, and parcelled it to Mindy from the post office in Whitehorse.

It felt like she'd set down a boulder the size of a house. She walked out of the post office and told the clear, cold air, "We're done now, you and me."

She would find a job and take care of Buddie on her own.

Meanwhile, what had happened to Buddie? Ten years old, it could be anything. Gale racked her brain. Was it possible she'd never left Cobalt? Or maybe everybody at home knew what Gale had done, and the cops were just waiting for her to turn up. Maybe Buddie stayed away as a warning.

Finally Gale couldn't take the fretting. She had her cell phone, she had to know. On her forays to the upper level, she'd noticed one of the servers in a food kiosk, a steady-looking girl, not stuck-up. Gale noted the way she took orders, went about her job, no fuss.

Gale waited until the girl was on a break and approached her. "Would you make a call for me?" she said, extending her phone. "Something I'm trying to find out without letting on it's me." The girl looked her over and took the phone from her. Gale tried not to rush her words. "Tell whoever answers you're Rusty's mom. Ask if Rusty went home on the school bus with Buddie today, as if Rusty's late and you're looking for her." Gale had thought how to word it. If whoever answered said Buddie didn't go to school that day, Gale would know something had happened: Buddie was lost, something bad. Her heart banged in her chest.

The girl listened to the ring. She put her hand over the mouthpiece. "It's a kid."

Gale's mind went blank. That had to be Buddie. There was no other kid who'd answer. Which meant Buddie never left. "Hang up," Gale said, at a loss.

The girl handed the phone back. Gale's mind was spinning. It must be Mindy was still home, the Wicked Witch of the East, waiting for the money and sussing out, as she always did, that Gale and Buddie were up to something. She must have Buddie chained to the floor.

The girl cocked her head. "I've seen you around. You living at the airport now?" Gale stared at her. "If you need somewheres for a couple of nights, you can come home with me. Long as you don't mind a blow-up mattress on the floor."

Gale pictured another night on the bench downstairs. Not much point now. "How do you know I'm not a psycho?"

The girl gave her a mild look. "You're not a psycho."

Rhonda had a couple of hours until her shift ended. Gale put her backpack against an air vent, lay down, and immediately fell asleep. Rhonda woke her when she was ready to leave. They caught a bus outside, transferred to another one, gradually entered a wasteland of identical townhouses. They deboarded, walked a block until Rhonda picked a house. She opened the door, climbed steps into a room with skylights, and introduced Gale to her mother and two sisters. None of them bore any resemblance to the other, so much so that Gale wondered if the other two young women were airport refugees like her, if even the mother might be. Rhonda's household could be the lost and found of stranded girls.

If it was, she had come to the right place. Over the next few days, Gale worked out the arrangement. The mother figure was an invalid. Gale never learned her name; she was just called Ma. She was the size of a wren and lived propped on pillows in a gigantic bed in the centre of the living room. Life in the household swirled around the bed, all the routines down to a science. Lorraine, the biggest girl, stayed home, kept house, tended the mother, heated meals in the microwave when the other two returned from jobs outside. Supper was taken as a picnic on the bed. In the evenings, they watched a movie together, whatever Rhonda or Lana brought home. The routine was so unvarying and frictionless Gale imagined they'd been perfecting it for eons. She didn't wonder very hard. From the first evening, their company soothed her, like living in a poppy field, a parallel world.

That first night, Rhonda showed her the room where she could sleep. It was hardly more than a closet, piled floor to ceiling with old books and magazines, *National Geographics*, nature books, whole bargain bins of print, as well as stacks of every conceivable household item: picnic ware, novelty lamps, juice pitchers, tea trays, flower vases, afghans, towels and linen, the cull of countless garage sales.

Rhonda nodded at the stockpile. "It's Ma's thing. When she's better, she's going into the flea market business."

"What's wrong with her?"

"I don't know the name. You can ask home care when she comes. Some days her muscles don't work. Some days they do."

"Garage sale days?"

"And meeting nights. We're Jehovah's Witnesses."

Gale could hardly have fallen out of the sky into a safer net. At first Rhonda's sisters plied her with questions about the

Yukon — how cold did it get? was there still gold? — as if she were a new channel on TV, but when it was plain Gale wasn't a talker, they let her be.

The duration of her stay was never raised. The four of them just budged over and made room for her, one more sister on the bus.

Gale's first few days, she barely left the mattress. It was as if she'd been drugged. Ever since calling home, she couldn't seem to wake up. She slept and slept, woke and conked out again. In her interludes of consciousness, she perused the nature magazines stacked around her, absorbing photographs of cheetahs and rain forests as if they were phenomena she'd never heard of. In the evenings, she joined the group on the bed watching movies, animation being the group favourite, along with anything starring Eddie Murphy.

After three weeks, Lana found her a job cleaning rooms in the same hotel she worked in. Gale wore a checkered smock, with a plastic ID clipped to the front, and spent her time swabbing bathtubs and stripping beds, the days passing in a kind of fog.

She couldn't go home with her mother there. Mindy would love having her busted for robbing her father. And Whitehorse was burned. She couldn't see what her choices were. All the time in Whitehorse, those three years nearly, she had longed for home. Home was her place, what she was all about, her and Buddie outmanoeuvring their mother. Now she couldn't get there, and she had no idea what was happening to Buddie. She couldn't get a grip on what to do. When she let herself think, the pain in her chest brought tears.

One day she walked into the bathroom of one of the rooms she was cleaning at the hotel and found a face cloth soaked in blood on the floor. She didn't worry about how it got there. She had given up trying to fathom what went on in those rooms, the evidence people left for some stranger to deal with. The starkness of the bright blood on the spotless tile struck her eye. The hotel supplied towels and face cloths of such unearthly white, the bathrooms scoured and bleached to such a blinding gleam, the blood soaking the cloth was stunning. Gale stared at it. She thought of her own blood, which she hadn't seen in some time, and the pain in her chest.

Gale went back to the bedroom and locked the door to the hall. No one was likely to come along: this was her floor and the room had been vacated. In the bathroom she unwrapped the complimentary razor and released the blade from its plastic holder. She sat on the rim of the tub, took off her running shoes and socks. She braced a foot across her knee, took a breath, stroked firmly down from mid-arch across her heel. Blood welled and while she stared, dripped slowly onto the floor. She leaned forward and ran toilet paper off the spool, folded it into a packet, and clapped in against the brimming cut. She replaced her socks and shoes, gasped when her heel took her weight, fetched the mop, and swabbed the floor. Tidy. She scanned the room for anything left amiss and went out into the hall.

The next day or the one after that, she would do the other foot.

Gale understood, in a way she hadn't before when she had tried to explain to Helen, cutting brought her back to herself. It made her real. Nothing else in Whitehorse had, and nothing did here in the mindless job and the microwave dinners at Rhonda's. Somehow the act of cutting, the swift, hard stroke, and the pain of it made her real.

THE REST OF THE TIME she drifted. At Rhonda's she found no remnant of her old life. She thought less and less about White-horse, about Linda and Keith, even about riding her bike. As much as possible, she veered away from thoughts of Buddie and home.

The drudgery of her job suited her. The long corridors with their opposing doors, room after room of identical rumpled beds, foggy bathrooms, the smell of drip coffee and deodorant, a mumbled good morning or good afternoon to any guests she encountered, took nothing out of her. At the end of the day, she rode the bus home with an army of drooping Caribbean mothers. Somebody at Rhonda's — sometimes it was her — brought home pizza or Colonel Sanders. Gale paid her share, and understood that by some alchemy or mercy she could stay as long as she liked.

The odd day off, if Rhonda was working, Gale went out to the airport with her, sat reading a paperback or a boxing magazine while Rhonda did her shift. The airport lulled her, the same as being at Rhonda's, the people in the lineups, parents shepherding their children, travellers in nowhere-land like she was. During Rhonda's breaks, the two of them played virtual badminton at one of the kiosks, competing placidly the way she and Buddie used to do. Gale shadowed Rhonda, though they hardly spoke. Rhonda carried, and Gale weighed almost nothing.

In the end, she stayed four months.

31

THE TAKHINI HOT SPRINGS was under renovation. Builders had tacked an open-air enclosure onto the cafeteria, Plexiglas walls that blocked the wind and gave a view of the pool. Now that it was spring, visitors could sit outside. Rita was watching Simon and Philip blast away at each other with water guns, while she and Helen shared a Cobb salad.

Helen's mind was far away. She spread a puddle of condensation from her club soda over the tabletop, ignoring her meal. She'd been disoriented for days, a sensation like coming out of a dark movie house onto a bright street and not quite being able to get her bearings, or remember where she was. Rita asked her what was up, but Helen couldn't say. She knew though. It was finding her mother's letters. They were in a packet wrapped in ribbon in Jo's lower bunk in Helen's house. She used the bunk as a catch-all for file receipts, case notes, articles she meant to read, and there they were: letters dated from her first year at McGill twenty-odd years ago. She had untied the ribbon and had begun to sort through. To her surprise, they were nearly all from her mother. Had Luze written so often? Helen had dragged a low chair from the bathroom and sat with her knees against the bunk, the letters on her lap. There were dozens, each one mailed in a three-by-six envelope, identically addressed, the ink at the tops of the capitals slightly faded. That old Remington electric her mother had used. Each letter was exactly a page in length.

Dear scholar: my darling, I've read your letter over and over. "A touch homesick," you say. I know you. This means you feel terrible. I know this feeling. When I came to Canada, around the time Columbus made his voyage, I didn't think I would survive. Everything in me said fly, fly. I found a trick. See if it will do for you. I told myself, I'll stay one more week. If I can't bear it, I can leave. I'm free to go home. All I had to do every week was last until Saturday. I kept it up a long time, I think my whole first year.

By then I knew I was in the right place.

I ache for you, darling. But I think your choice of McGill might prove brilliant. See what you think. Bear it a little longer. You'll know what to do.

Sunday
Darlingest college kid,
You were much missed at breakfast today. Your uncle is visiting, so the grapefruit comes out even, but the table comes out lonesome. We adore you, that's all.

Wednesday
You say you'll make a visit home a weekend soon. I am tied up with a
conference in Virginia the weekend of the 5th. If that's the weekend
you're coming, I will simply set fire to the building and come home.

THIS WAS NOT THE MOTHER Helen had conjured. She was shaken by the charm of the writer, her care dealing with a homesick daughter. What was she to make of it? Helen's memory must have played tricks on her. Letters were evidence, veritable documents from a certain time and place. They were not susceptible to the reconfiguring of memory. They showed the truth.

How could Helen have had it so wrong?

She had sat a long time, not wanting to disturb the feeling in the room, the sense, palpable, of her mother comforting her.

Luze had not been careless of her daughter, as Helen had supposed. The intent in her letters was plain to see: to entertain, to encourage and buoy up a beloved daughter far from home for the first time.

RITA WATCHED HER BOYS and Helen mused. Finding the letters had shifted her perspective. Helen felt it to her core. At last she spoke: "You remember the mother who thought she was going to murder her sons if they didn't quit fighting? I inherited them in that last bunch we got."

Rita nodded absent-mindedly. She had three new cases herself and couldn't recall which ones went to her and which to Helen.

"I met them last week," Helen said. "The boys are cute as puppies, raising hell with everything they've got. I think they're trying to keep their mother too busy to off herself."

Rita frowned at a piece of tempeh on her plate and scraped it onto Helen's.

"Our second meeting was today. Just the mother," Helen went on. "I meant to read the riot act, tell her she's scaring her kids." She pictured the woman, feisty, too thin. "Except she showed up on crutches, a brand new cast on her foot. I asked her why she didn't phone, cancel the meeting; her foot must hurt like hell. She told me she did it yesterday, mowing the lawn. She was furious at Josh, her younger one, and shoved the mower as hard as she could up a rise, and it rolled back down on her and sheared off two toes. She *laughed* telling me, as if cutting off body parts happened every day. My plan for our conversation went out the window. Think how out of it she must be to barely notice she's cut off two toes. How completely past it she'd have to be." Helen put her fork down, folded her hands. "She's just a hurt kid herself. We never got around to the boys, to anything about doing a better job. We just talked about her, the ride she's been on all her life. I don't know if I'll even see the boys."

Helen sat still for a moment. "I always pick the kids. They're the draw for me. You know that." A glance at Rita. "Not this time. I don't blame Bonnie. It's just not that big a deal how she's managing her boys at this moment. She can fix that later."

ALSO NEW ON HELEN'S LIST was a girl whose father had been killed when he stopped to help a stranger change a flat. A truck came howling down the highway, and the driver didn't see him crouched beside the road until too late.

The girl was paralyzed with loss, and the mother, buried under her own grief, couldn't respond.

The mother brought her in, an intelligent, thoughtful girl whom Helen, at another time, would have loved to work with. But it was the mother she invited back.

Rita lifted an eyebrow, catching on. "Are you out of the little sister business?"

Helen's smile was rueful. "Maybe just taking a break."

It seemed to her she had more to learn from mothers right now. In a way she didn't understand, her allegiance had shifted.

ON A WINDY DAY, she ran into Keith's mother on the street. Audette's windbreaker was flying open and she'd dyed her hair bright orange. Helen steered her into a doorway out of the wind, glad to see her. "What do you hear from Keith?"

Audette ran a hand through her hair, smoothed her jacket. Helen was reminded of Keith, his habit of adjusting his clothing before answering. "Well, he called a couple of times," Audette said in her drawl, "but he must've got Norm and Norm wouldn't accept the charges." She shifted her parcels to the other arm. "I phoned up Nathan there. He says Keith crashes at his place the odd time, but Nate doesn't think he ever hooked up with that school you told him about. He's just doing the rounds." She gave Helen a short nod. "That's good enough for me. He's not in jail and I haven't heard about any broken bones."

"How about you? You're looking good."

Audette nodded again. "Me and Norman are quits. I'm a lesbian now. It's easier than Norm."

HELEN STILL PHONED COBALT. "It's me again, Mr. Stoltenhof. Any word?"

"Got a postcard a while ago," Carl said with his usual gruffness.

"It's on the fridge door, picture of the CN Tower and a lake. The back says, *Say hi to Buddie.*"

Helen was getting used to the idea that Gale might be alright, that somehow she might have landed on her feet, wherever she was. So many kids Helen worked with came and went, and she never heard what happened. Maybe she should trust Carl's rough optimism. Everyone seemed to have a better handle on Gale than hers. What she comprehended now was she didn't catch on to the mother Gale had; she'd missed by a mile Mindy's power over Gale, the reach she had. Not until Carl told her the story about Neil's dog.

She'd been too busy spinning in her own story, the parallels between her and Gale, two girls having risky adventures with their little sisters.

Gale came in on her blind side. Helen never really saw her.

EARLY IN MAY there was a freak snowstorm and spring ground to a halt. The wind shook the chimney of Helen's house and gusted over the deck, heaping grainy drifts like breakers against the house. She was snowbound all day. The following morning came a glorious calm. The sun glittered on the storm's work, ravens yelped in the woods, resuming their courting.

Helen cast an eye around her house and shovelled her way to the car, Chief Joseph plowing dauntlessly ahead.

Three hours later she was in Atlin — Chief visiting at Gwen's, Helen drinking rosehip tea with denizens of the Pine Tree Café. The room was a haze of cigarette smoke, survivors of the storm deploring the labour it had taken to dig out. Outside, silver water sluiced off the eaves. Atlin Mountain looked cut out of the sky with a knife, the air an incandescent blue. Gwen was busy staffing the library that afternoon. Helen would ski, instead of taking a walk with her. She hadn't been out to Surprise Lake in ages.

She parked at the bridge where the road ended. Chief clambered over a snowbank and high-stepped in circles waiting for Helen to clamp on her skis. Her hands trembled with anticipation. She loved Surprise, its huge boomerang shape, curving east. Except for the odd prospector with a claim on one or another of the creeks, no one came there anymore. She set off, sinking in the fresh snow.

On the lake, she was in a ball of light, an immense globe of sky and mountains and ice. There was a slight sough, the sound of volumes of air gently moving. She steered towards the north side, her skis catching in breakable crust, following the shoreline with its gallery of driftwood, the willows rouged up for spring, lodgepole pine glistening.

Chief loped ahead, his stride matching Helen's, always just off her ski tips.

In the strong sun, she stripped to her undershirt, the layers she'd donned this morning now bulging in her pack. She headed for her old campsite across from Ruby Mountain, feeling the air on her bare arms, the first exposed skin of the year, the earth wobbling towards the sun at last.

Of all the mountains she was acquainted with, Ruby was her oldest familiar. She had camped across from Ruby many times. Its mass was printed deep inside her; its great lumbering base, the belt of spruce trees wavering upwards, faltering into cracks and crannies, finally giving out, giving way to the broad, gleaming dome that arched over the lake.

She used to come in deep winter, in the season before Jo

was due. She'd come in February, when daylight was returning, but the arc of the sun was still low, dusk proceeding on and on behind the mountains, the sky a pearl, slowly flushing dusk-rose, pale green, cerulean blue. She'd drag her sleigh the four kilometres from the bridge, set up in the little pines the beetles had killed off. Viewed from camp across the frozen lake, Ruby seemed to float. At night, when the stars swarmed and there was no moon, Helen came down to the shore and stood in the open. Across the ice, she'd watch the mountain's face, figured and luminous in the dark, its features formed in code, its character, like all mountains, changeable, unknowable.

Now she crossed the lake and skied below Ruby, the metronome whisk of her poles and skis the only sound. There were wolf tracks tracing a straight line in the scabby shoreline snow, each hind foot stepping into the print of the front. After an hour, she stamped up onto land, hungry for lunch. Hunting for shelter, she spotted a spruce with dry ground beneath, snapped off her skis, and crawled under its branches. Lunch was brie, rye crisps, a hard pear. The sweat chilled on her chest and she freed a sweater from her pack. A squirrel gibbered on a branch above her. Chief tossed back his head and leapt towards it, snapping and jumping while the squirrel taunted. At last he gave it up, lay down, and chewed snow.

Helen caught herself happy. This was her element, this huge space thrumming with life. A bolt of joy shot through her.

32

GALE STILL HAD Rhonda phone home every so often. Spot checks, hoping for a clue about Buddie. It was useless, since she never found out anything, but she couldn't give it up.

Rhonda got good at disguises: bogus prizes, surveys. It was always Neil who answered, never Buddie, and never Mindy, who ignored the phone anyway. These homeward lobs with nothing gained bummed her out for days.

She sent the odd postcard to Neil's folks, so they'd know she was alive, and so Buddie would know. Otherwise, she severed her lines. No one knew where she was, no one knew her. It was like being in a coma, what she imagined a coma to be. Being aware in a foggy way, but not responding. Except when she cut.

When she cut she exploded into herself. Then one day at Rhonda's she sat up on the mattress and it was over. No more coma, no more fog. She now had a clear lens. All of a sudden, there was no reason not to call Buddie.

Neil answered. "Shit, Gale."

"Um, how's Buddie? Is Mindy still around?"

"No. Hell. She left a long time ago."

"She did? Where is she?"

"I don't know where she is, Gale. She's gone. Gone since you've been gone." He paused while Gale took this in. "The folks got your card. You still in Toronto?"

"Yeah. I've been staying with some people. I'm okay."

Silence on the line; then Neil spoke in a hurry. "Look Gale, I don't know why you're calling, but far as I'm concerned, we got a little girl here who'd be glad to see you."

Gale felt dizzy, as though she'd gotten up too fast. She said, "I guess you heard what happened back there. There must be a warrant out."

"Your dad let it pass," Neil told her. "There's no warrant I know of."

No Mindy, no warrant. What was she doing in Toronto?

Neil said, "Why don't you come home and tell us."

HER LAST DAY, Gale went out to the airport and hung around until Rhonda's shift finished. The two of them went into the Arctic-Inuvik gift shop on departures level, and Gale bought five pairs of fleece-lined moccasins, a pair for Rhonda, Ma, Lorraine, Lana, and Buddie. She had to guess at Buddie's size. Her stomach did a flip when she thought about Buddie being nearly eleven years old. She probably had feet like boats.

They had a little goodbye that night on the king-size, with a movie and Sara Lee cherry cheesecake. Gale handed around the slippers and everyone put them on. Before she left for work in the morning, Rhonda came to her door. She leaned on the door frame and Gale rolled over and opened her eyes. Rhonda was her usual calm self.

"Have a good one."

AT HOME, she expected everything to be the same, but nothing was. Her granddad had cancer. He'd been getting some radiation and no longer fit his clothes. His head was bald and powdery-looking, and he slept a lot. Her gram had put on weight, her brown eyes cloudy. She told Gale it was cataracts; she'd have them fixed when granddad was better. Neil had a scooped-out look to him, like he'd had a fright. Buddie had grown tall and wary. She didn't meet Gale's bus, and she wouldn't look at her when Gale got to the house.

Gale assumed she herself was the reason everybody seemed low, because she had stolen from her father and that proved she was Mindy's daughter fair and square. But the longer she was home, the more she saw she had it wrong. What happened in Whitehorse wasn't that big a deal for anybody. Though no one said so in words, Neil and her grandparents let it be known that they didn't see Gale as entirely at fault. Since Mindy put her up to it, stealing from her father wasn't exactly a free choice. Call it a crime with extenuating circumstances.

What had befallen everybody was more like battle fatigue. Neil kept looking over his shoulder, as if Mindy might walk up the drive any time. He kept his guard up with Gale too, as if he weren't sure of her, whether she was going to stay, or what was her plan. Gale longed to tell him she had no plan. She was home for good. She longed to tell everyone. She was to blame for the shape her family was in, whether they saw it that way or not. If she'd never left, her grandfather wouldn't have gotten sick, Buddie and Neil wouldn't be spooked. None of it would have played the same way if she'd been there.

And another part of her knew it wouldn't have mattered. If she'd been home, she'd have been just as helpless as the rest of them.

GALE MOVED BACK to the loft she and Buddie shared. At least that hadn't changed. Her same bumblebee sheets were on the bed under the multicolour quilt her grandmother had found somewhere. Her clothes from grade nine were still hanging in the cupboard next to Buddie's. On Buddie's side of the room, time had passed. Buddie had taken down her Ninja Turtles poster and hung up Kurt Cobain, sucking pensively on a cigarette.

Buddie was slow to come around. Gale told herself her sister had always been weird; when Buddie got a grudge, she kept it. Gale would have to wait her out. Week after week, Buddie didn't speak to her, averted her head when Gale came in the room, sulked like a four-year-old. It would have been amusing except Gale could see Buddie meant it. Gale had truly failed her and Buddie didn't know what to do.

One morning Gale rolled over at first light, wakened by the dogs. There must be a fox in the yard. Across the room, Buddie's bed was empty. Buddie wasn't a kid who woke early. Getting her to wake any time took perseverance. Gale got up quickly and pulled a second XL T-shirt over the one she'd slept in, yanked on jeans and moccasins, and climbed down the ladder. She did a quick search of the house, though she could feel Buddie wasn't there. No sign of her in the yard or barn either, and no sign of her bike. Gale stood in the drive gazing straight-shot to the road. She let her mind roam the highway north and south. She had an image of her sister furiously pedalling her bike by the light of the moon, now a ghost orb across from the rising sun.

Gale went back to the house and called for Neil, heard him huff awake and the bedsprings creak. "It's okay," she called. "Just me. Buddie's gone for a spin. Can I take the truck and get her?" There was silence for a few seconds, then further groaning from the springs. Neil stood in the doorway, shaking his head like a horse. "What?"

"Her bike's gone. I've got an idea where she is. Probably your folks."

Neil frowned. "Is it day yet?"

"Nearly."

He sighed. "Lemme get dressed."

"Can I do it, Neil? I think it should be me."

Neil took her in. He crossed his arms over the hollow of his stomach. Gale thought he was going to say no, he'd just go fetch Buddie himself, but he sighed again. "Watch out for cops."

Gale took the keys off the peg, went out, and climbed into the truck. She hadn't gotten around to getting her licence, but she'd been running Neil's truck since she was twelve.

She covered the nine miles to Neil's folks', four to town, five past, without seeing a soul. The sky flushed deep red, rain coming. She turned in at Lois's Crooked Broom sign and stopped the truck well back of the house. She glanced at the windows. The upstairs curtains were still drawn. Since her grandfather had gotten sick, he wasn't an early riser anymore. Gale started towards the flea barn and spotted Buddie's bike in the long grass outside the door. She let herself in, helped herself to a butterscotch candy from the jar beside the cash register, made her way through the clutter of furniture and crockery to the back. None of the lamps was lit, but she had half-light coming through the skylights Carl had installed. Buddie was scrunched in the corner of an old bed, a ship's cradle with a pine frame and tick mattress. She had a couple of barn kittens with her, one curled on her ankles and the other bundled in her sweater. She stared at Gale with eyes dark as slate and said nothing. Gale climbed onto the bed, lay on her back beside Buddie, folded her arms under her head, and gazed at the ceiling. Buddie didn't speak. Gale could feel the tension in her and glanced over. Buddie's jaw was set like it would break. "Mom was gone," Buddie finally spoke through her teeth. "How come you didn't come home?"

What could Gale say? What answer would make sense to Buddie? *I didn't know she was gone?* True but insubstantial.

I had done stuff that needed time to settle.

Once in Whitehorse, Gale got caught in a whiteout. She was half a block from her father's house, but it could have been Mongolia for all she could see. Snow whirled around her head like a shroud. She had no bearing point. There was nothing to do but stand still and wait until it passed. Could Buddie follow that?

She made a stab at it and lay still while the tension slowly went out of Buddie. Then she rolled over and pinned her sister under her, laid an arm gently across Buddie's throat. "If we're on speaking terms, how 'bout we go see if they're up yet? You could probably use some breakfast."

33

GALE WAS GETTING READY to take the dogs for a run. There was an inch of fresh powder on the hard pack, perfect going. This wasn't the first time Neil had let run her own team, but so far they'd stuck to bush trails, Gale following him. Today they would head out on the lake where there was more scope, more handling required. Neil said it was time to try her in open space, terrain where the dogs, famously, didn't listen and did what they liked.

Gale decided to go with four: two leaders, two wheel dogs. As soon as the dogs spotted her and Neil pulling out the sleighs that morning, they'd gone berserk, leaping and back flipping, barking insanely at the end of their chains, setting up a racket that in former days unnerved her completely. And that was no good.

With sled dogs, you had to get all your thinking done in advance. Once the dogs were harnessed, there was no time to remember your Thermos of coffee on the kitchen counter. You had to *go*.

She anchored the sled to a tree and laid out her lines, not looking at Neil who was bound to be much further along. She attached the gang line, trudged harness in hand into the chaos of howling dogs, and selected her favourite, Buba, a Siberian with his wits about him. Buba knew the harness and helped Gale get his legs into it, staggered with her to his place at the head of the sleigh. She snapped on the tug and neck lines, tethered Buba to the lead, and headed back into the dogs with another harness.

When she got the last dog, Buttercup, clipped in, her four dogs were set to go, a moiling mass of jumping and colliding fur, barking deliriously. Neil was at the head of the trail, waiting to undo his anchor. Gale floundered to the back of the sled, yanked her hat down over her ears, freed the rope. She leapt onto the runners as the dogs rocketed forward, Buba in pursuit of Neil's team. The sleigh sailed over the snow down to the lake, the dogs bumping and jostling where the trail narrowed through the tag alders, nearly capsizing the sleigh. Gale pitched her weight to get them through the bush, and the lake spread before them. At the sight, the dogs stopped barking and threw their whole beings into propulsion. They bounded straight across the ice, Gale crying out to Buba to veer, to circle the shore as Neil was doing. Would the dogs heed her? She was too thrilled to care. The wind streamed into her face, the runners zinging, the dogs' thick breath rolling over their lolling tongues, their lips pulled back with exertion and joy. She saw Neil dashing along the far shore, his head turned towards her. Buba started to arc towards him.

She knew Neil was testing her; that was their deal. Neil paid her what he used to pay Matt to help with the farm and the dogs, as long as she took her high-school credits. What she learned about driving the dogs, how far she went with that, was up to her. While they were hanging up the gear in the barn the other night, he'd said, "What d'you think about picking four for a run on the lake Saturday?"

"Run my own show, you mean?" Gale piped.

He'd nodded. "You've got intention. That's what it takes."

It ended in a schmozzle. Buba refused to trail Neil's team no matter what Gale did, and charged to the far side of the lake where the creek ran out, where even in the dead of winter, there was never a proper freeze. First the dogs broke through, then the front of the sled tilted in. Gale braked with all her strength, but it wasn't enough to keep the whole assembly from dumping into the icy muck. She was mid-calf, cursing and scrambling to untangle the dogs when Neil arrived, tethered his own team, and strode in to help her. Neil grabbed Buba's neck line and hauled him up onto solid ice. The other dogs clambered behind and Gale righted the sleigh. Neil jerked his chin at her. "All in the life of a true musher, Tadpole."

THE WAY THINGS were on the farm with Buddie and Neil— the dogs slamming into her legs when she went out to them, taking a run over to check on her grandparents every few days, Buddie talking her head off like she used to—felt like a little circle of light around her, slowly filling out. That's how Gale saw it. She'd even joined the boxing club that had started up in town.

She hoped it would keep going like that, and that in a while things would take shape. Like figuring out what to do next. She could see stuff being possible that wasn't possible before.

But there were shadows at the edges she tried not to notice, a kind of storm warning. Her time in Whitehorse, that was one shadow. Whitehorse was like a grey doorway she walked past sometimes, not looking in.

The other shadow was her mother, darker, more ominous than Whitehorse, a threat crouched just beyond the present little glow around Gale. Her great dread, pretty much her only dread, was that someday Mindy would call on her. Why that might be, what she might want from Gale, Gale didn't know. If that happened, if she were summoned, what would she do?

ONE EVENING when she was fishing for tobacco papers in the pocket of her shirt, she found a balled-up scrap with a phone number on it. She stared at it uncomprehending for a minute and then remembered. Her grandfather had given it to her. He said some counsellor in Whitehorse was trying to find her. Whoever she was had phoned quite a few times, he said.

How could Gale tell Helen her mother had kept in touch all that time? She'd never told anyone, except Keith at the end. She couldn't. Helen, any of them, would think she was crazy taking calls from her mother and doing what she was told. They'd know what a puss Gale was. It was too messed up to tell anyone.

Mindy had called her at school, called whenever she liked, sometimes the middle of the night. Sometimes she'd be drunk, sometimes she'd phone every hour, and then Gale wouldn't hear from her for weeks. Some of the calls made her sick. Mindy would ask if Gale was getting it on with guys yet, did she know how to make them hard. At times Gale wouldn't pick up or she'd snap the phone shut when Mindy went on in a certain vein. It was never Gale who called. She had no desire to. She was just waiting for Mindy to tell her what she wanted.

And eventually she did.

At first Gale told her mother she was too scared to steal from Dan, and her mother called her a lame fuck and hung up and then phoned back, and they went through it again until Gale got it straight her mother would never let up. Then it began to seem like stealing the money had its points. Once her father was cleaned out, what use would Mindy have for either Dan or Gale? Mindy would move on. Gale would be free of both of them. She just had to settle her mind this was the only way.

"How do I do it?" she finally asked.

"There's two things to know about your father." Gale could hear the gloating in Mindy's voice. "First, he's a freak about his vehicles. His truck is his skin, the only thing he trusts. Second, he has a thing about banks. He doesn't believe in them. His money isn't in one. Start with the truck."

Gale knew her mother thought it was a big score convincing Gale, manipulating her from afar; whereas, the way Gale saw it, she was the one who would come out ahead.

That was the hope.

When she was staying at Rhonda's, she thought a lot about whether stealing from her father, and stealing so cold, meant she was cut from the same cloth as her mother. The thought kind of sickened her. There was a difference though, and Gale clung to it. She had Buddie, and Mindy only had Mindy.

Gale smoothed Helen's phone number in her hand.

She couldn't see Helen taking in what had happened in those meetings, that Gale had essentially ducked her the whole time.

The thing was, Helen had never seemed to comprehend that Gale would do whatever she had to in order to get out of there. Helen was on another track: Gale would stay in Whitehorse, come to counselling, pass high school, and have a nice life.

That made it hard to talk to her.

For Gale, from the start, there was only one thing to discuss — how to get home.

Gale folded the scrap of paper and put it away.

34

TWO YEARS AFTER Gale vanished, Helen was in Toronto visiting her father. Georges had met her plane the previous night, true to his wife's practice of greeting an arriving child no matter the child's age or the inconvenience involved. To Helen he seemed about the same as he had at Christmas: the same brief hug, a kind, slightly absent man, a widower now for fourteen years. Helen doubted the quiet in him would change. It had taken the extravagance of her mother to rouse him and, without Luze, he had lapsed into his natural state. Helen worried about him driving a car. She took over on the drive home.

When they walked in, the vestibule smelled of spring, moist earth fogging the glass, tiny lettuces in pots, the rosemary they'd kept going for years rising like a candelabra. The gardener these days was Rafi. Jonathan was away doing a course, something to do with soil, heritage orchards. It seemed one of the boys always found a way to stay close. Lately, it was Rafi, who had his music studio right on the property. As far as Helen could tell, it suited him to live at home.

Neither of her brothers had a steady partner yet. Helen wondered about that, but these days, more young people seemed to hold out for work that meant something, or be broke and live at home, or wait for a partner worth the trouble.

In the kitchen when they got home, her father touched Rafi's shoulder and passed by him, intent on spending an hour before dark inspecting the orchard.

"Jon's trying to talk him into bringing back some of the old breeds," Rafi told her. "Idas and Empires and such, get some diversity happening, but he loves his Macs. Fewer every year. They'll go out together, I guess, Dad and the Macs."

Helen carried frisée lettuce and endive to the sink. Rafi was layering cod filets and sliced onion in a baking pan.

"How is he?"

"He's him," Rafi shrugged. "Unbowed. You saw how he was with Mom at the end, never out of the room. The day after, back at work." He grated Parmesan, dashed it over the fish. "One thing Jon and I have taken note, this cold-water swimming he's into. He keeps a bike at the office. Did I write you about it? Rides it down to the lake a couple of times a week. We're talking Lake Ontario and it's early May. He dons his neoprene suit and does two k."

"A wetsuit? Like kayakers?"

"Thinner than that, like a second skin. Ocean swimmers use

them." Rafi doused the fish with white wine. "He's got the courage of a firefighter, but I don't get it. Looks like self-flagellation to me. Mortification of the flesh. Because he's alive and his HIV patients aren't? Because Luze isn't?" Rafi slid the fish into the oven and dropped onto the nearest couch, a low-slung one they'd kept by the wood stove since they moved in.

At twenty-five, Rafi affected exhaustion, pretending he could barely exert himself to move from one room to the next. Preparing the fish had wrung him out. Helen filled two glasses with some of the wine and plunked down beside him.

In the quiet between them, she took in the house around her. A certain zing of excitement was gone. So many years later, their mother's absence clung. There had been no woman staying in the house since her death.

When Luze was dying, Helen had come home. As soon as Georges had gotten the oxygen tank installed in their bedroom, he phoned her. Tumours were pressing on her mother's windpipe. "Come now, Hélène," he said.

Helen walked into her mother's room straight from the airport, still wearing her coat. The room wheezed with the sound of the tank, the blinds were down, the pale walls dusky, her mother's head raised on pillows, nearly shrouding her. Helen pressed them down away from her mother's face.

Luze looked at her calmly, as though Helen had only been out of the room for minutes. "It's bad," she said.

When Jo died, Helen had gone home, but couldn't stay, her part in Jo's death incapacitating her. Her mother's face had been like a skull, the flesh fallen away overnight. Helen was a spectre in the house; she could hardly breathe, the sight of her parents' suffering unbearable. When they had buried Jo's ashes in the orchard and Helen was packing to leave, her mother came to her. "I cannot lose you both."

Even with that, Helen had gone back to the Yukon.

But to see it through with her mother was natural. There was nowhere else to be. During Luze's last days, Helen greeted friends and sent them away when her mother was tired. She set the flowers in vases placed where Luze could see them. It was April and it rained every day. She played a hundred games of Dungeons & Dragons with her brothers and made endless peanut butter and banana sandwiches. She sat with her mother while Luze dozed and was there with her the night she died, her father in the bed beside his wife, asleep at last. She heard the percolating rattle of her mother's breath and saw the tremor in her body, the effort to gather herself.

Go on, mumma, almost there, keep going.

She stayed a month, longer than she'd ever spent in the house. Eventually her father arranged for a housekeeper. The boys would be alright, he assured Helen. He gave her his blessing to make her own choice, and she went back to Whitehorse.

She wondered about that. Why did she leave after Luze died? She'd been old enough to mother two stricken little boys. She could have stayed on.

On this visit, she sat beside her brother on the kitchen sofa, the silence between them not quite second nature. She'd been out of the house at school when Jon and Rafi were born. Now they were young men and she hardly knew them. "How's it been for you, Raf?" she finally asked.

He knew she didn't mean the last week or two. He kept his eyes in front of him, let the edge show in his voice. "We could have used some help."

When Helen didn't bolt, he went on: "We didn't know you, you were away and all, but ... you're family." Helen nodded and said nothing. "We've been here all along, Jon and me. He got so quiet when Mom died, I think we were afraid to leave him alone."

Helen said, "It must seem like I turned my back on you."

Rafi huffed, "Well you did, didn't you? You knew the score. First Jo and then her. Dad the way he is. It hasn't been great, Helen."

Try being the one who took Jo out on the glacier, Helen thought, but she didn't voice it. If Rafi was going to forgive her, he'd have to accuse her first.

"What was it like?"

Rafi shook his head. "We were just so ... small with only three of us, Dad, Jon, and me. We had Mrs. Watson, who we only ever called Mrs. Watson, even though she was here every day after school until we were fifteen." He took a long breath. "Really great with the educational games, Mrs. Watson. To this day, whip a towel off a tray of stuff for five seconds and I can remember every item." His voice was so sad, Helen's eyes brimmed. She didn't touch him.

"Who was it hardest for?"

"Dad, hands down. It buried him."

After a while Helen said, "I wish I'd stayed, Rafi. Better for all of us if I'd stayed."

Rafi pushed out of the sofa to check his fish. "Yeah, well."

LUZE HAD A ROOM of her own on the third floor. She'd had the idea to take up weaving. She painted the floors white enamel, and acquired a loom and spools of fine wool in the colours she loved, plum and cerise and blue, which she set on the floor at the ready. She didn't get around to weaving, but she had a low brocade chaise in the room she liked to take naps on, especially after she got sick.

Helen couldn't sleep the night she and Rafi spoke. She took a flashlight and climbed the stairs to her mother's room which, in the family tradition of never changing anything, was as her mother had left it. She pulled a stool over and set it by the chaise. She would have liked to sit this way with her mother when Luze was ill.

Rather than dismaying her, the conversation with Rafi had stirred her. It suggested an alternative. The boys were grown, but were still indentured to their father, albeit willingly. Her father's mourning continued, and now he was growing frail. Surely she could help at last. In the middle of the night, her father and brothers asleep below her, it seemed abundantly clear she didn't need to crouch on the brink of the crevasse with her sister any longer. It was unlikely Jo had ever needed her to. Jo had probably been up and out of that crack in the glacier the moment it happened.

In that case, come home.

She could bring some life to the house, spend time with her father, get to know her brothers on whatever terms they set. She could have a life with more meaning.

Perhaps not forever, but for now.

And she had a way to do it. Vince, from her training days, had been begging her for months to consider a job swap. After years practising in the city, Vince told her was ready for a little "backcountry." The agency he worked for could countenance such furloughs, and Helen's was improvisational enough to go for anything. "A couple of years, Helen," he said. "I don't want to spend my life up there, but a gig in Whitehorse — anywhere up there — sounds right to me. And for you, the resources we've got here, the range ... refreshing, no?"

Helen let the idea fill her. She smiled in the dark. The big family counselling agency Vince worked for was in the west end of Toronto, forty minutes' drive from her parents' farm.

It would mean a big plane ride for the Chief.

TUESDAY THAT WEEK, she borrowed Rafi's vintage pickup and drove downtown to pry her father out of his office for lunch. Georges worked long hours through early spring, a season when his patients were at low ebb and tended to die.

His office was on the ninth floor of a soot-black, four-storey medical building, with a pharmacy on the ground level and ancient green marble on the walls in the lobby. It was a perfect reflection of him: no pretensions, verging on austere, a shoebox-size reception area with a threadbare Persian rug and a pile of obscure magazines. Helen had checked out his examining room on one of her visits. It was so narrow, her father and his patient had to turn sideways to navigate around each other. The floor-to-ceiling window gave the sensation of being on a ledge.

When she arrived at noon, he was busy with a patient. Cynthia, his receptionist, looked up and smiled. "Okay, my dear. Wait awhile."

The four chairs were occupied. One man, burrowed deep in his overcoat in the hot room, looked gravely ill, his long, bluish hands lying upturned in his lap like shot birds. His companion read, absent-mindedly jogging the sick man's foot on his own. A young man with a shaved head and huge earlobes sat across from them, a laptop computer open on his knees. In the fourth chair was a gaunt woman working tension out of her jaw, her eyes closed, her body slumped so her head caught the chair back.

Helen leaned against the wall and fished for her reading glasses. Good jazz was turned low on the radio, French CBC.

Georges Cotillard came out of his office, brisk and tidy in a grey flannel shirt, followed by his patient. He wiggled his eyebrows at Helen, took a chart from Cynthia, and peered over his glasses at the woman. "Maureen Villeneuve, hello."

The woman hoisted herself out of her chair and followed him into his examining room. Helen had the sensation of the air whooshing out of the room.

Her memory for names was very good. She had trained herself. It would hardly do for her clients if she forgot who they were.

"How old were you when your father left, Nadeen?"

"Seven, and my name isn't Nadeen."

Helen could run into a client she hadn't seen for months, and inquire about each of her children by name. She knew at once who Maureen Villeneuve was.

She was Gale's mother.

Helen went out into the hall and started pacing.

This was it then. Full circle. Gale's mother was her father's patient. Mindy came to him because she was sick with AIDS.

Did Mindy know where Gale was? Had she seen her? How could Helen find out? What story would Mindy accept if Helen approached her? She couldn't say she used to be Gale's therapist. She was still bound by that. Mindy would stonewall anyway.

Helen could pretend to be someone innocuous, Gale's teacher, but how would she account for knowing the difference in their names: Villeneuve and Connelly? No teacher would recall that kind of detail.

She wracked her brain for a plausible entry.

While she was pacing, Mindy came out of the office, struggling into a heavy windbreaker, dwarfed in it. Her face was sallow, blotted with sores, the whites of her eyes an oily yellow when she glanced at Helen. She passed Helen and stood at the elevator, pulling a toque over her ears, elbows hugged to her body. She stepped forward to the slide of the door and was gone. Helen stood gawping.

So this was the devil incarnate who made Gale's life a living hell, who terrorized a family, and strangled a dog for spite? This pathetic, baleful wraith.

GEORGES SOON FINISHED. His last two patients were meds follow-ups and took no time. He donned the ski jacket he wore to work. Cynthia slid the glass across her window to close up. When they were on the street, Helen said lightly, "That was Mindy Villeneuve leaving your office."

He looked surprised. "It was. How do you know her?"

Helen cleared her throat. "That gym I used over on the Danforth when I was in town visiting you and Mom? I'd see her there, working out. Boxing or something, wasn't it?"

Her father shuddered in the chilly air, whether from the temperature or from a distaste for his recent patient, Helen could not tell. She took his arm.

"That's over," he said. "She's quite ill." He stopped on the sidewalk to zipper his jacket, frowning. "She's been difficult to treat. Unresponsive. I was surprised to see her alone today. Her daughter usually brings her."

Helen closed her eyes. "A daughter? She doesn't look the type. I mean, I know it doesn't work that way. She just always seemed so ... on her own."

"Mmm," her father said. "The daughter's quite nice. She's not from here. Some mining town up north, I believe. She came down when Mindy couldn't manage anymore. She's very capable — to the great relief of the home care nurses. They found Mindy ... abrasive." Georges looked distracted momentarily. "In any case, it's nearly over."

They came to a shuttered patio with a doorway set in from the sidewalk. Her father extracted his arm and took Helen's.

"Here we are. They'll be able to look after us here.

35

IT WAS RAINING IN TORONTO, dusk, the wet streets glassy in the headlights of the cars. The shops still had their doors open, spring flowers and imported fruit spilling out into the path of people hurrying past, intent on home.

There was a cul-de-sac off the busy street with a beer store on the corner, the all-weather panhandlers standing outside like hotel doormen. At the back of the street was an old garage, a square, brick building with high windows and a painted green door. A flurry of last year's oak leaves sailed past on the rain like crumpled kid gloves. The door was inscribed with twelve-inch block letters. BOXING.

John Mackie went into the building and flicked on the fluorescents for the gym upstairs. Helen followed him up the steps. The lights showed a low square room, yellow with wear. The walls were closely covered with banners and posters, photographs in old frames, black men smouldering behind raised gloves: Joe Lewis, Evander Holyfield, Mike Tyson, Al Sparks, and Frankie Bullard — a hundred years of men pounding each other to pulp.

There were banners in satin and felt, tall as the room. *2004 Kansas City, Missouri, August 17 — 21, Ringside World Championship.*

She had found the address in the phone book, hunting for somewhere that trained young boxers. How many gyms could there be? She phoned John, proprietor and prime mover, and asked to sit in on a practice for a story she was writing. He agreed to this fabrication at once. Publicity was always good for the profession.

Helen was looking for Gale. To run into Mindy the other day the way she had must be a sign, the hidden door in the wall she'd groped along for months. Over lunch she'd wormed out of her father the detail that Mindy's daughter was a boxer and that cinched it; Gale had told her the one link she had with her mother was boxing. She must have kept it up, which meant she was training somewhere in town.

If Helen could find out where, she would see at last whether Gale had survived her mother's wickedness and her father's uselessness and Helen's own failure.

It was a long shot, but what other lead did she have? She couldn't hide in her father's office until Mindy's next visit when Gale might come with her. She didn't want to ambush Gale that way.

She rang up John, told her small lie, and here she was, playing her only card.

John was talkative and filled her in while he moved around the room, appraising the room as he did every night. He was a retired cop who wanted to do something for the neighbourhood after he retired. He'd settled on raising money for a training gym. The gym was his baby, it was written all over him.

"Boxers who came out of my gym compete all over North America," he told Helen proudly. "Amateur and pro, bantams, featherweights, lightweights. The full spectrum." He'd started it for kids and it was still kids, anyone up to twenty, girls too. He winked at Helen. "Girls set a nice tone, keep a light talk going while they work out. The guys just pound away."

John checked the thermostat. "Have to keep it cool in here. By eight o'clock, after a three-hour workout, you can wring out the air." He showed Helen where she could sit out of the way so she didn't distract anyone.

He told her boxers were all-round types, arguably in the best overall condition of any athlete. "Wait till you see these boys," he said, chuffed. "By the time they get here, most of them are already into their workout. They've been running, playing soccer, weightlifting. You watch."

He left her and continued his scan.

The gym was fully equipped: mats, training stairs, heavy bags, all hard-used and serviceable. Helen noted a regulation-size ring, taking up half the room, with a raised platform, canvas floor, yellow taped ropes, the whole shebang.

At five o'clock the guys started to arrive, downtown boys vaulting up the stairs in fluffed-out windbreakers and running shoes, boys in their prime, the strength pent up in their bodies, ready to spend. They came out of the change room in their sweats, thin boxing shoes, toques. They wrapped their hands and cautiously started to engage, lightly noticing each other, but mainly pacing themselves for a long evening.

Then the women arrived, less showy, more at ease than the men. Mackie rejoined Helen and pointed out a trim, smooth-haired woman strapping on gloves. "Heading for law school, that one. Top-notch fighter."

The warmup sounds started up, the whir of jump ropes, the tap of gloves on the bags. John moved around the room, available and relaxed. The room began to heat up. A lithe woman was skipping, her body straight and still, her feet dancing. She skipped for forty-five minutes, Helen ascertained, without breaking a sweat.

John sat with her again, proud to show off his boxers. "Later in the workout, you'll see them get into the ring to spar. Doesn't matter who they spar with. Weight and experience don't enter into it, see, because a practice spar is very controlled. They all wear padded leather helmets, you notice that? Open at the crown, covering exposed bone." He touched his own cheeks, forehead and jaw. "In amateur boxing, headgear is mandatory. In a pro fight, there is no padding." He glanced at Helen, making sure she took this in.

"Are the rules different for men and women?"

Mackie nodded, approving the question. "You'll see here the boxers train to a timer," he said, pointing. "The buzzer sounds every three minutes. A round is three minutes for men, two for women. Out in the pro world, how many rounds a fighter goes is up to the Boxing Commission. They set every fight. A man is allowed up to twelve rounds — down from a pulverizing fifteen. For women, the limit is ten. A fighter works his way up. Over a career, he'll be head injured for sure, all the big organs scarred. Worst is to be knocked out. Being knocked unconscious lowers a fighter's marketability." With irony he added, "The sport of kings."

John indicated a man doing resistance training in the mirror, a stocky figure in his mid-twenties. "Over there is Eddy Brown. Eddy went professional as a lightweight three years ago. He's working his way along, but his trainer isn't hopeful. Eddy lacks reach. He's never been knocked out, but he hasn't won a fight either. And that's where something else comes into play: it's tough to get a favourable decision if the match is out of your hometown." He cocked an eye at Helen. "One of the ways boxing is a tough business."

John had his eyes on Eddy. "Eddy does some coaching here, they all respect him. There's a little girl now he's bringing along. See her over there across the room? White girl, junior featherweight, a fighter with short arms, like Eddy, but a dynamo." John pointed to a line of bags along the wall where a girl was working out, compact, in grey sweats, dark hair in a plait. "You can't knock her down, she's pegged to the floor."

Helen watched Eddy call the girl into the ring to spar with him. She came at once, and Eddy talked to her briefly while he donned the paddle gloves. John excused himself and went over to start the timer. The girl walked up to Eddy, spread her feet and crouched, hugged her arms in. She punched into his gloves, bouncing, turning with him. Eddy talked to her: "One, two, three, four. Hands up!" The girl punched to his count. They were both soaking wet in a minute. They kept it up until the buzzer went, then Eddy bounced away. The girl dropped her hands and went to the ropes. After thirty seconds, the timer sounded again and she took her stance. She boxed Eddy, he kept his eyes on her. "Stop holding your breath! One, two, three, four." Her jersey was wet to mid-back, sticking to her shoulders. Small yelps popped out of her when she hit.

It was Gale.

"Breathe!" Eddy shouted. "See what's available."

They kept it up twenty minutes. "Take a walk," Eddy told her. Gale veered away, climbed out of the ring. She sat on the bench wiping sweat out of her eyes with a towel, shaking, trying to calm down. She was twenty-five feet from Helen, her back to her.

John came over and sat with her, nodding approval.

"Nice, Gale. Very nice."

Gale took another swipe with her towel, still getting her breath.

"I got some news for you," he said, pausing for effect. "We booked you a fight. You been asking and Ed thinks you're ready. He says you got savvy."

Helen, behind them, could just make out his words. "Four rounds. Montreal, November 22. The woman you're fighting is a left-hander. Eddy'll train you for her."

Gale started to nod, rocking from the waist. "Okay. Okay."

John had a serious look. "I know you have your mom to think of. Can you make arrangements, somebody to come in? You'll be gone two nights."

Gale kept rocking, took a slow breath. "Yeah, should be okay. I'll figure it out."

John patted her knee, stood up. "Go get 'er. Finish your workout. We'll talk later."

Eddy climbed back in the ring, crooked a finger at Gale.

Pressed in the helmet, her face was glowing. "Come up here, Tornado," Eddy said. "I'll show you how to box a sou'paw."

Helen gathered her raincoat. John came over to see her out. "She's a good kid," he said. "I hope she makes it."

OUTSIDE, the rain had stopped; the wind was gusting ahead of a cold front. Helen turned into the wind and walked towards the lit street, her hair lifting.

ACKNOWLEDGEMENTS

I am grateful to the Canada Council, Northern Artists, and to the Writers in Residence Programme at the Banff Centre for the Arts, especially Tessa McWatt and John Burnside.

Thanks to the Transatlantic Literary Agency for its persistence, Marc Potevin for tech help, and the people at NeWest Press for scrupulous editing and care.

Special long-haul thanks to Anne Mackenzie and Marni Jackson. And to Jack.

A NOTE ON THE TYPE

This book was typeset in Financier, designed by Kris Sowersby and released by Klim Type Foundry. The cover typeface is Abril, a serif designed by José Scaglione and Veronika Burian and released by TypeTogether.

JILL FRAYNE worked for many years as a family counsellor in Toronto and Central Ontario. Following a solo journey to Canada's West Coast and Yukon Territory, her GG-nominated travel memoir, *Starting Out in the Afternoon*, was published by Random House. Since then, her outdoor adventure articles have appeared in several Canadian publications: *The Walrus, Explore Magazine, Up Here*, and *Canadian Geographic*, to name a few. She divides her time between a maple woods in Central Ontario and the mountains around Atlin, BC. *Why I'm Here* is her first novel.